The Revenge of the Mutant Spiders from Mars

By Danny Baron

First Edition

There are two ways of telling this story. There's the way that involves a certain amount of style, class and wit, and then there's this way.

Contents

1. The Ministry of Uncool

They were watching Ice Station Zebra, it had been on the better part of twenty-one minutes and Patrick McGoohan had just showed up.

Even the seething post-lobotomy patients sewn into the wheelchairs at the back began drooling as they realised who the bad guy was going to be. Their eyes narrowed with annoyance at the cliché. They started headbanging to a silent thrash metal band and chanted out a rhythmic nonsense, the incisions under the bandages began to bleed, and still they lurched back and forth, until tears of blood began to drip, until the fluids were pulsing from their nostrils and mouths and ears, the scarlet streams forming a striking contrast to the blue 'BRAIN' tattooed across their foreheads to counter any inferiority they might feel in later life on account of their missing lobes.

It is only fair to mention that despite any negative press in the following pages, the Ministry of Uncool are the good guys. Remember that. It could be important.

The matron swivelled on one sharpened stainless steel spike that passed as a high heel. She glared under a plucked and painted eyebrow that had just started to sag with the passing of the years. As she frowned under it she resigned herself to a further approach to Doctor Hacksaw, the lobotomy surgeon, about another face-lift.

The matron glared between her thick-rimmed glasses - she'd always fancied herself as a bit of a Bluddy Wolly.

"Quiet!" she snapped, her lip-glossed sags quivering with vehemence, her bloodshot eyes narrowing in her anger, "Everyone knows it's the Russian!"

The straitjacketed lunatics, as they were lovingly known, ceased their violent remonstrance at the American Producers' stereotyped idea of a baddy. They murmured and drooled around their mouth clamps, went cross-eyed, then forgot all about it and returned to watching the ceiling fan. The fan was motionless, it hadn't worked since one of the inmates had slopped some shaving cream on his face and tried to use it as a razor. He had only done this because Ernie Jeez had stuffed the entire stockpile of razor blades up his most convenient (and elastic) artery, for reasons that are still being debated. His consultant originally claimed to have understood Ernie, but in hindsight has admitted that this remark may have overstated the situation, not to mention the relationship, just a tad, and he is now in hiding.

The matron pivoted back to the television set with a terrifying squeal and ran her hands down her starched uniform, over the grey stains of brain matter. Her fingers still trembled a little, perhaps at the dwindling fury, or perhaps at Rock Hudson. She had a thing about Rock Hudson.

"Matron?" squeaked an old man at the front, the assorted mentally challenged and cranially special people behind hissed as one.

"Ssshhh!"

The old man fidgeted, half glancing over his shoulder at the crowd of white-clad inmates behind him. His fingers toyed with each other nervously, then he cast his vacant blue eyes up at the matron, trying to keep his gaze from wandering over those sexy, flabby sags on her neck.

"He knows a lot about bullets," whispered one of the inmates to another, reflecting at how intelligent Mister McGoohan was. He was a bit of a hero there, for reasons I shouldn't need to go into. If you didn't have a pin-up of the great man then there was something wrong with you. Well, there was something wrong with you anyway, but if you didn't have the pin-up, the chances were someone was going to do you. Make it easy on yourself - just take the bloody poster.

"Er, matron?" the old man said, quieter this time.

The matron looked down at him, that burning inferno of disapproval upon her bloodless features. She winced with distaste at the mottled and almost hairless scalp of the individual who had addressed her.

"What is it, Whine?" she snapped, her yellow teeth flashing behind her lips as she did so. She lifted her hands to where her hips had been, until hysterical Doctor Hacksaw had carried out the first frantic face-lift.

"Er, er, er," the old man stammered, the toothless gums slurping and slopping, "What is...what is...a zeebra?"

"Zeebra, Whine?" the corner of her mouth quivered with pleasure, the faint hint of a dimple darkened under her cheek, "It's like a zebra, Whine, only the stripes go the other way." She loved it when she looked clever.

"Oh, thank you, matron," Whine bobbed and bowed, tearing his eyes away from that Goddess of Sag.

The television screen shimmered and flashed in the corner, under the wire kidney brace that had been adapted as an aerial. Around the cluster of seated patients were grey walls, grey walls illuminated only by the on-off-flicker-flash of the television. Behind the wheelchair-bound back row stood the door, beyond showed the stark yellow light of bare sixty watt bulbs, and a corridor, a sterile, uninteresting corridor, running back into an unguessable distance.

Just outside the doorway stood two broad orderlies, arms folded against white overalls, with little identification tags pinned to their lapels. Behind them a sign hung from the ceiling, pointing out a side corridor and the gym at the end where the orderlies spent their time toning up so they could beat up the inmates more effectively and attractively. From further away in the building came the tippety-tap of secretaries typing and the monotonous drone of someone talking. Hang on a minute, that's just me. So anyway, there were secretaries typing. Unless that's me as well.

Down that side corridor, out of earshot of the two orderlies discussing their genital hygiene, or lack thereof, on past the notice board advertising such attractions as the weekly 'hang yourself from the ceiling with fish hooks through your nipples' therapy session and the 'stick things down your trousers until you aren't mad any more' lecture, were closed double doors. Like evil twins - the gatekeepers of the mysterious continent - the Last Continent whose name is known only to The Ferryman.

Prince Morg of Peuss came unto the great River Stinx and did not think much of it. It's a river, Squire, and if you've seen one, you've seen them all. The Isle of the Dead was pretty much like that painting, which should come as no great surprise, so all in all he was pretty non-plussed. The ferryman emerged from the mists as he is wont to do, and grounded himself a little carelessly upon the still shore. Prince Morg had seen this on TV, so he just handed over the cash and climbed into the boat.

"Where to, Squire?" inquired the aforementioned ferryman, taking pole in hand and making ready to shove off.

"Over yonder," Morg replied stiffly. "And get your bloody hands off my pole."

"My mistake. So. Over yonder is it? Which one's that then?"

"Which one what?"

"Which 'Over yonder' might the gentleman be referring to?"

"The Isle upon the river."

"Oh, right. Like I've never heard that one before. It's all I bloody get that is. 'Follow that taxi' 'Take me to yonder Isle.' Bloody day-trippers. I dunno, you all pile out of some night club half pissed and expect me to get you home. You're having a laugh, mate. Now come on - where to?"

"Yonder Isle. And I haven't come from any club. I was mortally wounded in battle against the Infidels. Most honourably did I meet my end."

"Yeah, I used to do Yoga too."

"Take me to the Isle."

"Are you taking the piss?"

"How hard is it, my good man? How many islands can you see, for goodness sake?"

"You are taking the piss," the ferryman hissed, thrusting his skull out from its black hood, vacant eye sockets fixing the prince with their icy stare. "I can't see a bloody thing. Now cut the crap. Where to?"

So they were double doors, not only in so much as they were doors, but also in that they were doubly so. A handwritten sign taped to the left door announced what lay beyond as the patients' gym. The windows were frosted and reinforced, from beyond came the crash of the first recorded fatal accident resulting from a foot sauna. Much in the vein of Andy Warhol, it doesn't matter if what you did is a load of old bollocks, as long as you did it first. Not that the victim was contemplating the Art of the situation, much less whether he now qualified as a genius.

The doors were flappy doors - they flapped backwards and forwards, each time going less far, until they quivered and stopped in the middle. Some of the more enlightened inmates would spend hours watching them, while they formulated scientific theories on what made them do it. The doors, that is, I suppose, or maybe it's the inmates. Not that it matters.

The gym beyond them was a forbidding place, a large, cold, brightly lit space with all the cybernetic and hydraulic body-building, muscle-toning, Yogatron and firmamatic machinery that the various manufacturers (largely Scandinavian) could dream up while as high as the proverbials on all manner of illegal narcotics. Way up in the walls were rows of small windows, embedded with thick grey bars, behind which hung a starless night sky. The walls were littered with graffiti, written in blood, urine, excrement, and the tomato sauce from cans of baked beans.

"Stop playing with your food," was often heard, as was, "And stop playing with the tomato sauce from cans of baked beans."

Among the machines, down in front of the leg gyrator, which spun the victim's legs in their sockets until the slack in the stretchy old tendons was taken up and they could maybe not walk properly again so much as stand up without dangling from their hips like torsos on bungie ropes, a group of figures had gathered in a circle around a prostrate form, its lifeless feet still in the lightly bubbling foot sauna.

One of the spectators nudged the dead man with his leather boot. He stepped back and grunted, wiping his nose on the sleeve of his leather jacket.

"E's dead," he said.

Another inmate, long-haired, with orange flares and a green cardigan over a home-knitted, purple pullover, prodded at the corpse with his finger.

"Dead," he agreed, with a slight hoarseness brought about by too much lentil tea. "From the mother ocean we come, to the mother ocean he has returned."

"Ocean?"

"Well, foot sauna. Same diff."

"Bastard," said a third, wearing the more traditional straitjacket and testicle clamp, "Bastard, bastard, bastard." He didn't elaborate.

"S'that Konrad, ain't it?" said another, 'The Normal' they called him, on account of his lips being stapled together. It made it none too easy to understand what he said, but after a quick bout of charades and a slight misunderstanding involving lesser-spotted exploding Goonfrogs they got the gist.

"Yeah," confirmed Charlie Chainsaw, scratching his backside with contempt, "It's that pussy Konrad."

Vince Y, possibly the sanest of those assembled, studied the dead Konrad Karma with a measure of dismay. Y? was just past middle-age, just a wrinkle and a stoop further down that road, just two grey hairs further on. A sad road that, to wander alone - a lonely journey to make by oneself...etc...etc. His eyes dimmed, his brow furrowed.

"I spent the morning," he said, "Standing on my bed because Satan's coming with a bullet in my head where the door doesn't open and you don't walk through and I'm not the man I was last Tuesday, dah-dah, dah, dum, dee-dee-dum, er, yes please, Murray."

Konrad Karma was wearing distinctly uncool green pyjamas that betrayed a slight gut. Doctor Nofingers had always said that too little exercise would be the death of Konrad Karma, he even said so to his face once. That stormy night he had gone to Karma's cell where the inmate was watching the ants build a statue of some great insect dignitary or megalomaniac or something. Telling exactly which one isn't easy as I know sod all about ants, plus they all look the same to me, although you're not allowed to say things like that (it's entomologist).

Doctor Nofingers had paced up and down, while Konrad paid the little attention he could muster. The doctor had pleaded, begged, insisted that Konrad should get some exercise, or else the odds were that he (Konrad) would die. Konrad had given in, but not as the doctor had intended. Of course, if he had listened he would still be jogging on the jogging machine or pedalling away on the exercise bike, and not lying, quite dead, with his feet in a lukewarm foot sauna with a strange brown scum growing around the edges.

Bearing in mind that Konrad is one of the main characters of this tale, one is forced to reflect that so far all is not going too well.

"Well," murmured Charlie Chainsaw, "That's screwed it "

"Whaddya mean?" asked Orange-Flares.

"I ain't using no foot sauna that's had no-one die in it and stuff," said Chainsaw flatly, a genocidal fruitcake with principles where his raisins should have been.

"Shouldn't we, like, do something?" asked someone.

"Uh, like, what?" asked someone else.

"Uh, I dunno," said the other.

The mob of crazed loons, serial killers, rapists, students, and those who had won tickets to the place in packets of cornflakes, looked around at each other, shrugging or muttering, completely stumped.

"You sure he's dead?" asked one.

There followed a hungry, hopeful silence.

"Er, he's not breathing and stuff," said another.

They all shifted again, twitching uncomfortably.

"Bollocks," said Charlie Chainsaw, and he stomped away to the nearest Pumpomatic Strongatron, never having thought much of Konrad Karma, reputed to have once been the coolest of the coolest of the cool. Of course, that had been before...before that terrible day, before that cliff and the storm and before the fluffy white philosopher with tin feet.

From beyond the double doors came the distant sounds of a submarine trying to break through ice and the click-clack of the matron pacing down a corridor and into the distance. Suddenly Rock Hudson shouted something that echoed across the white, white walls and a telephone receiver trembled as it tried to get someone's attention. Anyone's attention would have done - it wasn't as though it was a fussy telephone, just misunderstood.

On the floor of the gym Konrad Karma's body had started to get colder, while the foot sauna still merrily bubbled away to itself. Orange-Flares looked up at the ceiling and wondered if that was where Konrad's spirit was, hanging up in the air, staring down at the scene below.

"Up yours, Konrad," he shouted, showing his finger to the sky.

The lunatic next to him strained against the straitjacket in order to see what the hippy was gesticulating at, but he could see nothing.

"Are you fucking crazy?" he asked, spitting the drool that had been accumulating on his lower lip, and pulling on the chain that was attached to the plug he had stuck somewhere it's best not to think about, for reasons best forgotten.

"Well, yes, actually, I am."

There was a vague impression of the whine of a strained engine, then there was a roar, a crash, a thundering splintering volcano of sound. The floor shook, the walls shook, Charlie Chainsaw got crushed in the Pumpomatic Strongatron and those who saw his body would think that that night's dinner looked uncannily familiar when it was served.

"Shut up and eat yer drool," hollered the chef - a stocky, bestubbled shitbag of triumphant unpleasantness. If you left him alone in a room with anything for five minutes he'd cook it - cook it, bake it, poach, or pie it. Especially pie it. He needed a pot of course, did I mention that? If you left him alone in a room with a pot and something else for five minutes - see above. He was a man obsessed.

"Why's this pie got a Charlie Chainsaw badge on it?" one of the gathered diners inquired again. He didn't mind the eyeball, although he wasn't sure about the way it was looking at him, but badges with spikes surely couldn't do his guts any good?

"Shut up and eat yer drool," the cook repeated, hobbling out back to where he was greeted with a chorus of 'Hubble Bubble' and no end of bleedin' trouble.

The wall of the gym cracked, a crack that grew instantaneously into an immense, gaping rupture. Rapturously rupturous and cancerous to boot. Debris blasted across the gym, engulfing everything in apocalyptic mayhem, ricocheting from the gathered equipment and scattering like shrapnel across the floor. The inmates ran for cover or fell senseless under great slabs of concrete. Slowly the dust settled and the wounded and the dying groaned or called for the medic, having seen too many 'Nam movies.

In the centre of the gym stood a battered blue pickup, bull bars and a winch at the front, and one of those trendy roll bars behind the cab with spotlights and a chain that seemed to serve no purpose whatsoever. The engine, which had been idling while oil dripped onto the floor, was cut off, the driver's door unlatched and creaked open. The door mirror hung limply from its mounting, the door itself was defiled with crude, violent murals that gave impressions of horrendous, violent deaths, but as so many images had been spray painted on top of each other, it had become impossible to focus on a specific person, thing, or violent event.

A denim-clad leg reached out, a tatty leather boot found the floor, another such leg and another such boot, except the other way around, obviously, like the first was a left leg and left foot, the second was a right leg and a right foot, or it would have been bloody stupid. They were shapely legs too, if I might say as much, longish and shapely, and most definitely not a bloke's.

From the pickup stepped a young lady with whom only the dead man was acquainted. She wore a fluorescent green, skin-tight T-shirt with a little yellow smiley-face badge pinned to it. From her hips hung a brown leather belt, adorned with bullets and hung with the most impressive hand gun yet seen in a mental institution's gym. The gun appeared to be a Vlokk 50, albeit with a customized barrel and grip, and an unofficial paint job, best know as winner of Gunz Weekly's "Ultimate Ghetto Defense Side Arm of the Year" for the last three years. "Terrible accuracy and monumental, shoulder-dislocating recoil are more than compensated for by classical good looks and a deafening blizzard of extreme rapid fire 50 calibre rounds that will leave the ghetto scum in no doubt that there is an entire drunken SWAT team taking them down." The discerning gun owner's hair was mediumish in length, and lividly blue, and she wore little blue earrings that were little and blue.

She was drop-dead gorgeous and she knew it.

She seemed slightly intoxicated as she walked from the pickup, staggering just a little, pouting with those blue-lipsticked lips, squinting at the bright lights above. She passed around to the front of the pickup and glanced down at the crushed body of someone she had collected on her travels. It seemed to be a biker in leathers, his legs were folded around the wrong way, his left arm was held on by a few strands and strings of flesh. He looked up at the girl with the blue hair and growled at her.

"Ya bitch," he said, his voice weak and dying, "Ya swerved both ways till ya got me."

His head lolled at the floor and a splatter of blood dribbled from his stilled mouth. He was perfectly dead - something that was becoming a less exclusive club all the time.

The blue-haired girl gripped the edge of the bonnet and opened it. She secured it and peered inside, a frown spreading across her face at the jumble of tubes and pipes and big, dirty metal things that spread out before her. Her mind was instantly taken from the problem as a team of armed and beefy orderlies marched through the double doors (remember the double doors?) to put a stop to whatever was going on. They looked across the carnage and the twisted corpses to the pickup and the blue-haired girl at the front. She shrugged at them.

"Car trouble," she said, smiling sweetly.

She hadn't expected them to offer a helping hand, perhaps it was something in their iron-cast, square-jawed expressions, or maybe it was just the way they did that click-clotch thing with their guns and took aim at her. They were big guns too - pump action rocket launchers and napalm blasters and bazookaz and kazoobaz and other such over-engineered genital-transplant ego-soothing death wads.

The orderlies sneered, gloating, peering down the barrels, lining up the sights, chuckling with pleasure at the thought of wasting that blue-haired chick.

"Uh, like, what's that?" she said, frowning and pointing behind them.

They glanced to where she pointed, she whipped Lester the Alien, for that was what she called her gun, from its holster and started blasting. She caught the first one with the first shot, more by luck than anything, the top of his skull blew off with a spout of grey and red goo as his face disappeared into an inside-out mangle of flesh and bone.

She let rip, her finger going berserk on the trigger as the white-clothed bastards ducked and danced and were blown away in a furious hail of bullets and guts that peppered the walls and splattered across the floor and oozed and split and reeked and generally made a fair old mess.

Lester the Alien rested on the roof of the pickup, smoking out of every orifice and cooling slot. Meanwhile the girl with the blue hair was working away under the bonnet, attaching clamps to whichever bits of the engine took her fancy. She hurried a little, in case anyone more competent came along to do away with her.

At last she finished and stepped away from the car, holding two clamps, one in each hand. One was red, one was black, they trailed leads back to the car. They were monsters, they would have scared the living shit out of crocodiles - eighty-foot chainsaw-toothed crocodiles from the radioactive swamps of the Hell-lands. Okay, maybe I'm exaggerating.

She found an almost dead inmate on the floor not far from the car. He was quite a nice guy actually, a damn fine guy - he was a good friend who'd stick up for you in a tight spot, he never swore, he didn't smoke. He had only come here because of a small problem, now that was fixed - at last he was leaving - he was leaving tomorrow, he had counted down every day of those last two years until he could see his lovely wife again, and their three, doe-eyed, darling, sweet, beautiful children. It was a brand-name chrome-plated life made in heaven, and a family made there too, similarly branded and chromed. A golden, rosy (that's a sort of pinky orange then) future was assured.

"I'll be back before you know I'm gone," he promised his pretty little wife as she waved him off from where she was perched on the tampon dispenser. "I'll be back," he continued, with many a sob in his throat. "Look after these little urchins for me, these little creatures - oh, these fiery love bugs - I adore so much. I'll be back in time for Christmas with arms a-laden with gifts. I do so love you all..."

He lurched and twitched and quivered, then he jerked a bit, then he writhed and twitched some more. Then the girl with the blue hair killed the pickup's engine and came back to the smouldering crust that was all that remained of her test subject, whereupon she removed the clamps from what had been his buttocks.

"So far, so good," she murmured, and she strolled across to the now quite cold body of Konrad Karma.

Ripping open his pyjama top was, she found, better than just pulling it up in so many ways - it was more destructive for one thing, which always ticked a box, and beside that, maybe he'd get the hint that she wouldn't stand to be seen in polite society alongside him while he persisted in trying to blaze some kind of warped fashion trail. She then attached to each nipple a clamp and stood back to survey her creation, her baby. Her masterpiece.

She strolled back to the car as several furtive glances were thrown between the double doors (hee hee) - the matron, a more cowardly orderly, and a handful of frumpy secretaries were surveying the scene. None of them had guns, although one had a cold, and another a distinct lisp.

The tempting terrorist parked herself in the driver's seat and toyed with the key ring and the other keys where they hung from the ignition. With a last glance at the corpse with the most superbly Turbofreshed, Lemonantiscumzested, Softlylickytonguejobbed, and generally refreshed feet that had yet peeked from a sock that side of LA, she turned the key and revved the engine hard.

Konrad Karma lurched, his back arching upwards as his dead limbs vibrated and twitched. Then the girl with the blue hair killed the engine and returned to the body. She removed the clamps from the crushed nipples, each surrounded with a pretty rose-shaped scorch mark.

But Konrad Karma lived! He groaned and gasped, then his chest began to rise and fall and his eyelids flickered. After a moment or two they opened and tried to focus on the face looking down at him.

"Shit," he said, "Oh, fuck, shit, etc. What have you done to me, you crazy bitch? What the fuck have you done to my nipples?" Then he saw something amiss with his pyjama bottoms, "What the hell? Oh crap, this is going to be hard to explain. And where the hell are my nipples?"

"Shut up, Konrad, you're getting boring," said the blue-haired girl, helping Konrad to his feet.

Konrad on the other hand, despite the stiffness he had already noticed, was now discovering the problems of rigor mortis.

"I can't move," he whined, "Why can't I move?"

"Shut up, Konrad, and point that thing somewhere else."

Konrad staggered in elephantishly lurching lollops, trying to move forwards as the girl with the blue hair cleared up the leads. He just about made it to the engine in time to find out what he'd been wired up to, but she had already removed the clamps and was coiling up the leads.

"How?" he gasped, "How did you do that?"

"I put the leads on the battery-" she said, after a moment's thought, but Konrad cut her short.

"No, you didn't, if you'd put them on the battery it wouldn't have done Jack P. Shit or his dog. It wouldn't even have done his budgie. You must have put them somewhere else."

"Reckon? Hmm, well these engine things aren't my forte, me being a girlie and all. I guess I might have wired you up to the, uh, EHT lead from the ignition coil, or something, by mistake."

"Hey, look! I can move my toes!" Konrad was staring down at his shining, pink toes where they were wriggling away like fevered maggots.

"Must've been the sauna, huh?"

"Yeah, I guess. So find me a bigger sauna! I can't stay like this!"

"Stop whining, dipshit, and get in the pickup."

"How, exactly?"

The girl with the blue hair dragged him round the back of the pickup and threw him on with the rest of the junk.

"Thanks, sis," he said.

"You're welcome, shitbreath," and she got in the cab and slammed the door so hard the mirror finally made its bid for freedom.

She started the engine and slipped the car into reverse, then she released the clutch and the thing hurtled back through the entry point with a squealing of tyres and a splattering of survivors who had somehow found themselves in the way. Some people...

As the pickup skidded to a halt on the grass beyond the wall of the Ministry of Uncool the matron finally summoned up the courage to run across the gym and accost the blue-haired girl. She jogged up to the hole in the wall, saggy boobs a-twanging.

"You!" she squawked, "What do you think you are doing?"

"Me?" asked the blue-haired girl, from the open window of the cab. She looked around, "I'm not doing anything."

"What's all this, then?" the matron screamed, boiling over, shaking in her cheesy shoes.

"Are you, like, an authority figure?" asked the girl with the blue hair, and she licked her lips thoughtfully.

The matron thought for a moment.

No! Don't tell her. Pretend you're somebody else.

The matron thought a bit more.

"Yes, yes I am."

Before she could go any further the girl with the blue hair pulled out Lester the Alien and took aim right between the matron's piggy little eyes.

Pow! The gun recoiled as, in the best tradition of popular fiction, the authority figure got wasted and the body slumped backwards in gut-wrenching slow motion, amid blood and brains and shattered glasses. The girl with the blue hair blew the smoke from the gun barrel and slipped it into the holster.

"Luv and kisses, baby," she said, as she drove off towards the road, "From Katya Karma! Katya later! Hey, Konrad! Did you hear that? I just thought up a Katch Phrase. Wanna hear it again? Konrad?"

The pickup swerved and veered, sliding on the grass, mowing down a few security guards who shot at the car, but missed, again in the best tradition of popular fiction, such as that great masterpiece of classic carnage: 'Great Decapitations'...

"Great Dickens, Dickens! Why are you pointing that chainsaw at me? Urk*!"

The vehicle crashed through the perimeter fence and hurtled off down the road with a whine of the turbo. The rear lights dwindled into the distance and thus Katya Karma rescued her brother from the Ministry of Uncool and vanished into the darkness.

2. Morty Morg and the Weirderons

The morgue was in darkness, except for the reception. It was quite a quiet morgue in most ways, and had, as was the tendency in this strange Land of Eng, been called a mortuary. This went some way towards explaining the quietness: most psychopaths were off cruising the eerie country lanes in dark American cars, peering with deranged squints through the gloomy grip of night, hoping against hope to find a neon sign announcing, 'The Morgue'.

However, on this particular night it was going to be anything but quiet, the heavy weapons and deadly vegetables would see to that. (The author would like to mention that neither 'morgue' nor 'mortuary' is defined as used specifically by either the Americans or the British, but the following sequence's devilish wit does kind of hinge on it so let's pretend, yes?)

Outside the night had taken a firm hold, the car park was empty but a queue had formed by the glass door, through which the light from the reception was pouring. From all around hacksters and psychosurgeons had gathered in a strange fit of uncertain origin (possibly that spooky green comet!). Now they were waiting as each tried his luck in an attempt to get in and obtain some part or other of a corpse.

The door opened and a doctor in a white coat slouched out, a dejected failure, carrying a drill in one hand and a lollipop in the other. The next from the queue, also with a white coat, moved forwards. He carried a hacksaw and his head was alive with a shock of white nylon hair, his face was set with determination as he entered the reception and took a sneaky look around.

The reception was large and roomy, a couple of tall, palmy plants stood in pots either side of the door, there was a desk against the far wall and beside that was the doorway to the interesting place where all the light bulbs were green or purple and the bodies were kept. Back there the sweet stench of death was in the air, and even from the reception Dr. Mad, for that was his name, could detect that lingering toxin, that precious drug, that addictive perfume. His nostrils twitched and opened as he savoured his life's desire.

Behind the desk, and the bowl of lollipops, was a kid, a spotty kid with a plaster behind his ear where he had cut himself masturbating. He sighed and shifted in his chair, then turned over another page of his comic and returned to his daze.

Dr. Mad crept forwards, hacksaw in hand, moving along on tiptoe, only able to see the corridor to his fantasies and the desk of the grim guardian of that putrid Promised Land. He was almost past the desk, almost into the darkness of that delectably tainted corridor, when...

"Er, excuse me?" Morty said, one eye lifting from his comic while the other went on reading. Dr. Mad ignored him, "Excuse me?"

"What?" snapped Mad.

"Where are you going?" asked Morty, sitting up straight and putting the comic down.

Mad glanced down at the saw before hurriedly hiding it behind his back.

"Through there," he said, pointing to the corridor.

"I can't let you do that," said Morty, flatly.

"What?" snapped Mad.

"You can't go back there," said Morty, after a thoughtful pause.

Mad leaned over the desk and breathed his pilchards and onion rings breath over Morty, "Who's going to stop me, pigtits? You, you chubby freak?"

"Yes," said Morty, looking Mad in the eye.

"I just want an arm," the deranged practitioner said, after a brief hesitation.

"What?"

"An arm," he produced the slightly rusty saw from behind him and gave an example sawing movement, "One little arm, one slender limb with just the one previous owner."

Morty frowned and looked around him in bemusement, "What?"

Mad stepped back and looked towards the door as though considering his escape, "I, er..."

"There's a coffee machine by the door," said Morty, still puzzled, "If you want anything. And lollipops."

Mad looked at the coffee machine and opened and closed his mouth a few times, momentarily lost for words.

"What sort of morgue, sorry, mortuary, has refreshments?" he asked at last, smiling disarmingly.

"It's just-"

"Get thirsty, do they?" asked Mad, gesturing with his thumb towards the corridor having stepped forwards and adopted a hushed tone of confidentiality.

"It's just that we-"

"I don't want any coffee. Did I ask for coffee?"

"I-"

"And as for lollipops! What's your name?"

Morty returned a blank gape.

"What's your name, kid?"

"What?"

"Your name! What is your name?"

"What?"

"And your address. Your name and address."

"Why-"

"I want to speak to the manager!" cried Dr. Mad, banging his fist on the desk.

"Sir, this is a morgue, mortuary."

"Get me the manager!"

"He's not here. We keep bodies here. This is a mortuary."

"It has a coffee machine," observed Mad.

Morty looked to the machine, then back at the Doc.

"You can't turn a blind eye?" asked Mad, leaning closer and whispering, "Just this once?"

"I wish I could, sir, but I don't make the rules, I just work here. We don't do takeaway."

"It's not as though anyone would miss it, the arm, I mean."

"With all due respect, sir, this is a morgue, mortuary, not a body shop."

"It is...fairly important."

"Sorry."

"I mean, do you think I could do this if it wasn't an emergency? Do I look like the sort of man who goes on morgue crawls in the dead of night?" He smiled, "I am a respectable practitioner. Is it too much to expect a little more co-operation and a little less antagonism from a part-time jobsworth? With pigtits."

"It's not just the rules," said Morty, sighing, "It's also a spiritual thing."

"What? Don't give me that smokescreen. I've heard it a hundred times, er, that is to say-"

"Like Red Indians believe if you mutilate their bodies then they can't get to the big humping ground in the sky."

Mad glanced at Morty as though assessing his mental incompetence, "I see. You have a lot of Red Indians here, do you?"

Morty lifted a clipboard and searched the sheets, "No."

"No?" Mad repeated. He savoured the moment. "No as in 'not many' or no as in 'none at all, thank you very much'?"

"Erm," Morty flicked through the sheets again. "No as in none."

"Ah-hah!"

"You wanted one, did you?"

"What? No! I was just illustrating a point."

"Oh. I see. That's very good. I still can't let you pass."

"It's like that is it?" asked Mad, looking back to the door.

Morty nodded gravely. Most things in the mortuary tended to be pretty grave. Funny that.

"One little regulation and spirit-thingy is more important than the scientific debacle - breakthrough - of the century?"

Morty nodded again.

"Well!" said Mad, stiffening and looking down his nose at the spotty receptionist, "Thank you, sir, for nothing!" He hesitated. "Do you do mail order?"

"No. But please take a lolly."

"I spit on your lollies."

"Please don't do that."

Doc. Mad strode for the door and stopped by the coffee machine. He looked at it, reading the offensive and rather crude labels until he became aware that Morty was watching him. He feigned vast multi-coloured curtains of disinterest in the coffee machine, in who was on the grassy knoll, in the potential of glue on the bottom of your shoe, and in why coins never land on their edge even though statisticians swear they must. He reached for the door handle and was just about to pull on it when the whole shuddering door burst open and crashed back against the wall, nearly sweeping the startled Doc right out of his fluffy slippers.

"Boo, baby!" said the face in the doorway.

Neddy Zed had once been inventor. He was now safely under lock and key in the relevant museum, but once upon a time he

had been free to roam the streets, terrorising an unsuspecting populace with his own distinctive brand of inventiveness.

Like the shoe that is impervious to things that might stick to it. Vaseline, he found, almost did the job, but people kept landing on their heads and swearing. Glue was just the thing. It was great. You just slopped a load of wet glue on your soles and off you went. Nothing stuck to it, because it was wet, and you didn't keep slipping over like those idiots with the patent Vaseline soles because this was glue, after all. Of course, once the fucking stuff dried it was another kettle of fish altogether. But thinking about it kept people busy for many years to come. It kept them swearing too.

The muzzle of a big, big hand gun preceded the newcomer into the mortuary's reception area. Doc. Mad backed away, his knees trembling, his underpants doing that wild old changing colour trick. Then his pants did another trick as he saw the nubile chick-person behind the gun. Morty looked from behind the desk and recognised Katya Karma.

"Oh, hi," he said, pissed off at having to put his comic down again. It really was most aggravating - how was he supposed to get into it or anything with all these bloody interruptions? He'd read the same line about sixteen times now.

"Hiya, fuckface," said Katya, flicking some blue hair from her face in that ultra-seductive way she had.

"Look, I don't want you to take offence or anything, but I've got to say that I preferred you when you were just a supporting character. Ever since Konrad went on that extended holiday that you keep fobbing people off with you've been a real pain in the arse. It was so much better when you just stood in the background, looked like someone I'd quite like to hump, and said 'Bomb' a lot."

"You finished?" she asked, frowning angrily.

"Er, yes."

"Fuck off! Who gives a shit what you think? What kind of wanker are you anyway? What sort of dumbfuck student loser ends up with a part-time job on the, uh, graveyard shift in a morgue, anyway? Oh, and, like, pardon the pun, huh? I keep doing it. It's these fucking shoes."

"Well, get 'em off, baby, I'll see what I can do, and it's okay - I'm a doctor," said Doc. Mad, rather suicidally.

Kapow!

Exit one sweaty sphincter in the midst of ruptured spleen and gut and stomach and a hole heap of whatever he had for dinner.

"Bollocks, he was my hostage."

"So, what can I do for you, Katya?"

"Uh, right, yeah, uh, do for me? Are you getting innuendoistic on me, spotty boy?"

"What do you want? I meant 'what do you want?'"

"Er, well y'see Konrad's got, like, rigor mortis and shit and I need, need the, uh, antidope. Gimme the antidope, you selfish bastard."

"I'm sorry to have to tell you this, Katya, but if Konrad has got rigor mortis then it's because he's dead. Trust me, I'm a professional."

"Yeah? Well why don't you tell him that to his face and listen to what he has to say about it?"

"He's not dead?"

"Nope."

"You're sure?"

"Yup."

"Have you got 10p?"

"Yes, but I'm not paying for sex."

Morty pointed to the dilapidated, dusty, and downright old coffee machine by the door. The Katya leaned over and read the labels, giving Morty a nice view of her arse and making him wish he'd brought his polaroid camera after all.

The coffee machine was an odd thing, a relic from a communist government that had amalgamated things and extrapolated things and all of that really, really complicated-sounding but actually really boring stuff.

'Coffee' was the first label.

'No fucking tea, what do you think this is, a fucking tea shop? This one's coffee as well, dimwit. If you want tea fuck off to a tea shop. And mind out when you're drinking it that you don't stick your little finger up someone's arse,' said the second label.

'Unless it's a sexy chick,' said the third label.

'And no, that wasn't tea either, and neither is this - we're both coffee, so fuck off!' said, surprisingly enough, the fourth.

'Antidope,' said the fifth and final label, so Katya put in the 10p and pressed the button under the label. There was a brief pause, then the machine shuddered and shook. There were weird noises like someone was being eaten alive by a coffee percolator, then the paper cup and the fluid appeared, the one containing the other, from the aperture at the bottom.

"Wow," said Katya, and she picked up the cup, "This machine is quite something."

"Isn't it?" muttered Morty, from where he was buried once more in his comic.

"Er," she sniffed the cup with that darling little nose of hers, "This is coffee," she said.

"What did you expect?" asked Morty, getting even more irritated, "It's a coffee machine."

"Look, buster, I just paid 10p for the antidope. Now give me the fucking antidope."

"Would I rip you off?"

Katya stomped over to the desk and grabbed at Morty's shirt collar, she twisted it so that it pulled tight around his neck.

"Would I bite off your pig-ugly face and spit it up your arse?" she snarled, twisting a little tighter.

"I didn't - it's not - you've got to believe me," he protested, choking until he coughed up some of the mosquitoes he'd had for lunch at the Spanish place over the road.

"What you're saying, and I, uh, find this very hard to believe," said Katya, holding the cup in front of his face and glaring at it, "Is that coffee is the antidope."

"Yes," croaked Morty.

Katya dropped him, he caught the edge of his chair and slumped forwards, his skull rebounding from the desk edge, and so to the floor, hands clutching at his scrunched neck.

"Why the hell didn't you say so?" she fumed, heading for the door.

Morty reached up at the edge of the desk above him and hauled himself up, past the residents' records and the girly mags that had collected under the desktop. He peered across the coffee stains and the comic and saw Katya Karma still in his presence, still she hadn't gone as he had anticipated, but was standing there, staring out through the window. Mesmerised.

"What?" he choked, "What's wrong?"

"Shut up," she hissed, "It's aliens! Turn out the light!"

Morty reached for the light switch and flicked it off just as he lost his balance and knocked over the bin and a potted plant. Then he crawled across the floor and stopped next to Katya, whom he could see by the light of whatever was out in the car park.

"Holy shit," he gasped, as the eerie green glow spread across his face.

The car park was deserted but for the blue pickup, a large black wheelie bin, the big green flying saucer thing with spooky emerald lights and an out of date tax disk, and the corpses of a couple of doctors.

"Did you kill them?" asked an awed Morty.

"No," said Katya, "I think it was that," she pointed at something moving in the car park, then she crawled around behind Morty, "Now act like a man and save me, shithead!"

"No way," said Morty, trembling to the soles of his football boots, then he crawled around behind Katya, "You're the one with the gun and the psychopathic tendencies, you do the hero shit!"

"I'll give you all my money if you save me," she said.

"No way."

"I'll let you lick my bare, nubile feet."

"No way."

"I'll kick your stupid bloody head in if you don't."

"Go ahead, baby."

"Fine. I'll kill you if you don't save me," she drew the gun from the holster and pressed the end against Morty's temple.

"So what? The aliens are going to suck my brains out if you don't, and if you do they'll probably suck them up off the floor, right before they deflower you with their scalding spiky marrows."

"It's such a shame I'm about to spatter your dreary grey matter all over this room, uh, and that rip-off coffee machine buddy of yours, isn't it? 'Cause it's like a young talent having its head bitten off before it can succeed. I mean, you're a real live philosopher, aren't you?"

"Holy shit," whispered Morty, and Katya turned to where he was looking.

A figure was moving towards them, an eight-foot tall figure, strolling along without a care in the cosmos, gazing about it with red glow-in-the-dark eyes. The rest of it was dark, but as it drew nearer they could make out details. Though they wished they couldn't. Instead of a mouth it had a long, steaming proboscis which dripped acid onto the tarmac and dissolved the surface amid clouds of luminous purple fumes.

"My brain!" cried Morty, clutching at his head, when he saw the proboscis.

The creature kept on coming, then they saw, swaying behind its z-fronts, a scalding, spiky marrow.

"My god!" cried Katya, "And I'm not even drunk!"

"You see, this is the sort of shit that Konrad would have saved you from," said Morty, "Because he was the hero, and he said all the funny lines and stuff. And he didn't get attacked by eight foot aliens with scalding spiky marrows. But now you think you're the star and it all goes wrong."

"Shut up whining, peckerhead, I was just building up the dramatic tension."

She took aim through the glass of the door and pulled the trigger. The gun roared, the glass shattered and showered them with splinters, the alien was unaffected.

"It won't die!" she said, shooting again and again, "It just keeps on coming, and all that B-movie jazz! Or is that blue movie jazz? Don't look at me like that - you'll miss me when I'm gone."

By then the alien had reached the door and was staring down at them with its infra-x-ray-slightly-puzzled-atomo-vision.

"Let me the fuck in, Earthlings," it said, in its deep, alien voice, "Let me the fuck in now, or I stick my scalding spiky marrow right up you until you squeal like a Zenardian Fojhaagi."

"Well?" asked Katya, "Uh, you're the student - think of something!"

"Eek. What do you want?" Morty asked the alien, standing up and trying to look casual and business-like.

"I want your body," said the alien.

"What?" squeaked Morty, straining to keep his bodily fluids from sudden and noisy liberation. He clamped his available hands in the areas which seemed most needy.

"I want your dead peoples," the alien said. "Let me the fuck in!"

"Er, we're closed," said Morty. What genius.

"Then I'll stick my scalding spiky marrow in and it will unclose," said the alien, laughing through its backside, which was under its armpit.

"Ask it why it wants our dead peoples," suggested Katya.

"Why do you want our dead peoples?" asked Morty, thinking that this was misguided. Showing an interest - being interested in order to be interesting, was surely what came right before if you like 'em, show 'em, and this, he was fairly sure, was the art of conversation and generally building up to asking someone out. The art of chatting someone up. All in all, it seemed a fraction less than wholly appropriate. But, being the weak-minded fool that he was, he did it anyway.

"I want your sexy dead bodies," said the alien, mercifully non-plussed. "We come in intention of invading your puny planet and mutilation of all puny lifeforms and necrophilia with dead nymphomaniacs with sexy dead white skin and blue lips and nasty whiff in places. Let me the fuck in, Earthlings, this is the voice of the Weirderons, I know you can hear me, bastardscum. Let me the fuck in or taste the pain of the scalding spiky marrow."

"It gets kind of repetitive, huh?" murmured Katya.

"Want fuck dead Earth chick, want stick scalding spiky marrow right up and rip that crotch. Want plant little puke-o maggot seed thing deep in a corpse and it grow and turn corpse into a zombie and it walk all over puny planet and kill all Earthlings."

"Uh, uh," Morty was delirious with terror, all he could feel was his heart pounding in his cowardly chest, all else was numb and cold, except for his inner thighs, which had mysteriously become warm and wet.

"I don't see that we have any choice," said Katya, sticking Lester in the holster, "I mean, it's, uh, us or the planet, right? Us two shallow shitheads or the whole future of civilisation as we know it. Or as we don't, on account of how it's the future and we haven't seen it yet."

"I guess you're right," said Morty, and he turned back to the alien, "Fuck off, weirdo. We don't give in so easily."

"What are you talking about?" yelled Katya, "Let him in, shithead! You've got to get some self-esteem."

She leaped up and opened the door, the alien surveyed her with further puzzlement, before looking up at the corridor and stomping across the reception area, dripping acid as it went.

"What did you do that for?" asked Morty.

"Shut up," Katya barked, "Just shut up. I just did us both a huge favour - hey! I just saved your life! You owe me, Mortybaby - you owe me. Now I'm going to go and give the antidope to Konrad. Enjoy your alien. See ya!"

She hopped from the door and landed on one foot, she pivoted for a moment like the lunatic she was, and then strolled across to the pickup where Konrad was still lying in the back among the oily rags and the mouldy fruit and the anti-Weirderon gun.

"Uh, Konrad? Can you hear me?"

"Of course I can fucking hear you," he said, his mouth still pretty well seized up, "I've just got rigor mortis, I'm not deaf. Now what the fuck's going on with the green lights and the alien spaceship? More to the point - what the fuck have you been up to? I can't help getting these pangs of worry whenever you disappear off somewhere and there are brain-sucking aliens around. It's just not natural."

"Konrad, I know you'll beat me up later, but seeing as you're paralysed and shit, SHUT UP!" Whereupon she slapped him around with a passion. "Now drink this, it's the antidope."

"It smells like coffee."

"It wasn't funny the first time, and, uh, the bandwagon you just climbed on is so old the wheels have fallen off, and things."

Konrad drank the antidope. It was cold and sickly, it made his tautened stomach reel and grumble. At first he felt no effect on the rigor mortis - his body was still quite stiff, and he still had a flagpole down his pyjamas, although his feet were nice and warm and pink. Then he began to feel the difference - first his fingertips felt as though they were glowing, then that spread back down his fingers. From his feet and hands the warmth and the looseness of skin and muscle slowly spread until he was free and alive again, although he was still terminally uncool. Nothing, it seemed, could remedy that.

"This is great," he said, sitting up and looking around, "But I still have two questions. Firstly, what are you going to do about my nipples that you burnt off? Secondly, what are you going to do about this," he pointed down at his pyjama bottoms, "It is most, most uncool."

"You're pretty uncool yourself," retorted Katya, quite offended.

"Well?"

"Well what? Oh, right. Your nipples, er, search me. The other thing? I dunno. Get some scissors, or something."

"Right, it's time to prioritise," said Konrad, hopping down from the back of the pickup and looking across at the green saucer.

"That's the alien's," said Katya.

"No shit." This proves how uncool Konrad had become at the hands of the Ministry. In the old days he'd have just glanced at his sister sidelong and she'd have got funny ideas that maybe he fancied her or something, giving rise to multitudes of comic asides. But:

"It's in the morgue," she said, pointing.

"Well, like, I'm kind of really uncool and everything, but I think that if I was, y'know, cool and stuff then I'd, er, get some petrol and some matches and burn the bastard to the ground."

"What - the alien or the morgue?"

"Yeah."

Just then a bunch of people passed by, drunk and unshaven, playing music with instruments, but they walked away and didn't actually really do much of anything. One of them was hopping, he had a foot, his own, nailed to his ear and was playing the haggis, which was like bagpipes only it sounded like someone blowing into a bag full of shit. Another was short with a pot belly, he plodded along in his sandals and played the comb at tennis, and lost. (Local colour.)

"Er, where was I?" said Konrad.

"Petrol," said Katya.

So they found a bit of rubber pipe and a petrol can, but it was full, so they emptied it out and found a car just down the road. The petrol cap was locked on so Katya shot it and the whole thing went up like a horny nuke that had just seen the most gorgeous bombette, throwing the Karma non-twins across the road. They crashed into a hedge and watched the blazing wreck.

"Nice one, sis," muttered Konrad.

"It was pretty cool, huh?" she said, positively glowing with pride at her handiwork.

"You know," said Konrad, trying to ignore a hedgehog that was personalising his green pyjamas, "If I was really cool, I'd have put an anti-Weirderon gun in the pickup."

"Just goes to show you were cool once," said Katya, forlornly, "'Cause that's exactly what you did. It's still there to this day as a, like, testicle to your faded greatness. Now what are we going to do about that alien corpse-lover?"

"Baby," said Konrad, "You can be so bloody thick sometimes. Now shut up and follow me. If you get the urge to do something, don't do it, okay? Just stand at the back and say 'Bomb' every now and then, yeah? Everything's going to be just fine."

"Fine," said Katya, going all delicious and sulky.

So Konrad plodded back down the dark country road to the morgue, looking a bit of a prick wearing his green pyjamas. Katya slouched after him, complaining to Lester the Alien about how everyone was being such a bastard to her all of a sudden. Konrad hadn't even thanked her for saving him! Bastard.

Morty was sitting behind the desk, he'd chewed his finger nails up to his elbows and had started on his toe nails. The light was on in the pretence of normalcy, but he was shaking and as pale as a dead bloke on a slab in a mortuary, with a toe tag that said 'Bollocks, I should have guessed that foot sauna was a killer'.

As Konrad burst into the reception with the throbbing, fourteen-barrelled, laser-sighted, anti-Weirderon gun, Morty ducked down behind the desk. Then he popped back up again. Like toast on a rope.

"Oh, Konrad. Wow, are you going to save me?"

"Shut up, Morty. Stop being such an uncool whiner. Now where's that Weirderon with the scalding spiky marrow?"

"Back there," Morty pointed down the corridor, "What's that down your pyjamas?"

"An ostrich with piles, what the fuck do you think it is? Now stop being latently homosexual and let me get on with this Hollywood carnage bullshit, okay?"

As Konrad proceeded with caution into the corridor Katya stepped inside the reception and slumped into a chair there, utterly pissed off.

"What's up, Katya? Aren't you going to miss the blood and guts?" asked Morty, suddenly worried at the psychopath's state of mind.

"Morty, do you ever feel like you're a worthless piece of shit that no one cares about and no one loves and everyone talks about you behind your back about how stupid you are and everything?"

"Er, only on Saturdays," Morty admitted. "That is, I mean, except on Saturdays. When I'm pissed."

"It's just my whole life feels like one endless chain of violence and that I'm in an unredeemable situation and, uh, stuff," she said, a little glistening tear swelling under her eye.

Morty shrugged and opened his mouth but couldn't think of anything to say.

"But now Konrad's back and that's all changed and I fucking hate it! Now I don't even get to shoot anything and stuff and it stinks! I mean, when you're as shallow as me it doesn't matter one turdy little bit who thinks what, but when you don't get to kill stuff anymore, that's when it hurts, that's when it grabs your heart and twists it in its icy fingers! That's the sort of injury where I just want some stupid chunky hunk to come along and stick his face between my legs so I can blow his brains out. But who is there? Huh? Morty the fucking morgue guy? No thanks!"

"Er, it's a mortuary actually," said Morty, opening up a packet of banana and old dog flavoured crisps and finding a free plastic 'runny dollop' inside. "Do you want my runny dollop?" he asked, wondering if that would cheer the daft cow up.

"I don't want to know," she said, grumpily, and rested her head in her hands.

From down the corridor the sounds of dead flesh ripping had been plainly audible as Konrad had vanished into the darkness where the bodies were kept. He could feel his heart a-thumping in his chest as he stole to the end of the corridor and peered around the corner to see another passage in darkness. He glanced down and realised that creeping around corners was no good - the alien would know he was coming approximately three feet before he arrived.

As if that wasn't bad enough he kept getting really uncool ideas, like about how ice-cream gets those pain-in-the-backside lumps in if you let it melt a bit and then freeze it again. Who gives a shit? he wondered, then he crept on and found himself wondering why socks only got holes where you didn't want them, discounting, of course, the hole where you put your foot in. Again, who gave a shit? Then he got onto shoes with patent glue soles so nothing would stick to them. A little voice in his head told him that was crazy talk, but he wasn't so sure.

He passed a fire extinguisher and reflected that it would be a really handy thing to have around if there was ever a fire. So what? Konrad Karma was a troubled soul - born into that world as the coolest, he wore a nappy with style, he could yak up his guts and it was trendy, and here he was thanking the Good Lord for whoever had invented fire extinguishers. Konrad Karma knew that when this little adventure with the Weirderons was over he was going to have to pay a visit to that very special marsh up in the Land of Scotty so that he could indulge in that time-honoured ritual and hope to re-cool himself.

Rrriiipp!

"Oh, yes, dead Earth chick, let me show you what scalding spiky marrow do for lubrication!"

Rippety-rippety-rippety-rippety-rip....

"Oooh, dead baby, how was it for you?"

Konrad Karma tried to pinpoint the direction from which that dread sound came. He looked in through an open door, beyond were innumerable bodies under plastic covers, some of the covers had been pulled aside.

"Hello, dead Earth chick! Come here often? Invite me inside? Thank you."

Rrriiipp!

"Hey, hey, hey, dead Earth babe. How that feel, hmm? It feel good, yeah? Just think of little puke-o maggot crawling around and eating away inside of you, funky babe."

Rippety-rippety-rippety-rippety-rippety-rippety...

"Mmmm-mm, dead baby. Me love you, nighty-night."

Konrad Karma was sure it was in there, he squinted through the darkness, trying to spot the eight-foot alien with the red glow-in-the-dark-eyes. It wasn't easy. At last he spotted it, under the sign that said, 'You don't have to be mad to work here. Um. Actually, you do.'

Suddenly there were lights everywhere, weird round lights that spiralled and did disco-type things and a voice said:

"This is the voice of the Weirderons, check out this funky alien groove!"

A bippety-boppety-dooby-dooby disco beat started up and the Weirderon leaped from where it had been hiding. Konrad Karma grimaced, turned the gun at the slavering, growling, eight-foot, acid-spitting, scalding-spiky-marrow-wielding mutant Weirderon and pulled the trigger.

All fourteen barrels spat death and venom, flames flickered at the cooling holes, the semi-automatic thunder shook the air, the hot anti-Weirderon-lead flickered as it hurtled into the corpse-screwing alien.

The Weirderon shuddered under the impacts, first its scalding spiky marrow burst and spluttered blue juice across the room, then it copped a few in the face and its proboscis and red glow-in-the-dark eyes distorted and vanished into the exploding mess of alien flesh that then began to dissolve in leaking acid. Then Konrad aimed lower, blasting away at that formidable, armoured torso. Dark holes and gashes opened in the wake of the eager bullets, behind the thing the dark juices spurted out as the anti-Weirderon-lead blasted through. It jigged and jerked, still backing away, as its innards and its outers all mingled and mangled and got mango-chutnied into one pulpy heap that landed with a slop in the corner before slowly dissolving in the acid.

"Urg, you got me!" it groaned.

"Eat shit, alien-type person," said Konrad, rather uncoolly.

A bubble formed in the acid.

Konrad's left eye half frowned.

Then another bubble expanded from seemingly nowhere, then several more, and the first started taking shape as little...things.

"Shit," said Konrad, "It's like the attack of the baby Weirderons, or something."

And he was right. All the bubbles were forming into little Weirderon-type creatures. They had miniature red eyes and vicious mouths, although they didn't seem to be equipped with vicious vegetables. Konrad watched them for a moment, then he decided that he couldn't be bothered with it.

Out in the car park he stomped to the pickup, anti-Weirderon gun over his shoulder. His face was set, he was determined - he was going to the mystic marsh to try to re-cool. Katya followed him out, a lovely puffy-pouty concern on her face.

"Fuck it, Konrad, stop being such a wanker!" said she muchos melodramaticallimentos, "We tried before, remember?"

"Must've done something wrong, babe," he looked to where his sister was staring up at the large green saucer, still with its ramp down and the green-lit interior just about visible.

"D'you reckon the peckerhead left the keys in it?" Katya asked, adjusting her skin-tight T-shirt and straightening her bazongas where they'd wandered off a bit to one side in all the excitement.

"What? In your T-shirt? I dunno, it depends on what you got up to, I guess," said Konrad, with a shrug.

"No, in the green saucer thing," she said, strolling over to the ramp and looking up.

Konrad led the way up, carrying the gun. As they reached the top they saw that the interior of the craft was one luxurious room, and it was quite deserted. There was a jacuzzi, a sun lamp, a couple of nice tweed armchairs, a bonkers massive stereo, a big alien-size bed, and an autoslime machine. At the centre was the control panel with plenty of levers and knobs for Katya to play with. As Katya had speculated the keys were indeed in the ignition.

Aliens, eh? Who'd credit it? The downside of having no pockets, I suppose.

"Can I have a go, Konrad? Can I, can I, can I? Please Konnyrad, pleasey, pleasey, pwetty-pleasey, luvvy Konnywaddy?" She fluttered her blue eyelids and pouted and did the doe-eyed business.

"Only if you take me to the Land of Scotty," he said, surveying the rather green interior, "And only if I get the bed, 'cause I'm knackered."

"Whatever you say, although it might, uh, take a while for me to get it figured out, y'know?"

Presently the thing started up, its circular engines glowed red, before the exhausts opened wider, and the issuing flame turned to white. The ramp started to close, then it opened a bit, then the disco lights came and did the 'This is the voice' nonsense, but Konrad leaned over the console and switched off the voice and closed the ramp.

Morty opened the mortuary door and watched as the green saucer rose into the night sky, an embellished disk glimmering with splendid emerald, before that bird of foreign skies zig-zagged off into the darkness with a final shout from Konrad.

"If you got your fingers out of your knickers for five minutes you might be able to fly straight!"

3. The Lesser-Spotted Exploding Goonfrogs

The Land of Scotty: a bleak, desolate place of rugged mountains carpeted with heather, of flirting mists racing on the wind, and lingering fogs in valleys deep and scented, beneath brooding pine forests and the fires of the occasional semi-authentic castle.

In the dark of the evening, beneath the glowering silhouette of just such a castle with a smouldering red sun at its back, the marshes of McViolentdeath loomed beneath the mists. Eerie trees lurked among the drifting phantoms, the ground rose up in the occasional bank of heather, all between was mires and cool, stagnant pools. The raucous cry of a raven hung in the air, for a moment drowning out the voices of the marsh, then the raven was gone and those little voices could be heard again.

"R'bit, bollocks, it's cold," said one, a croaky, amphibian voice that was just discernible above the trickling of a stream.

"You're telling me? R'bit," warbled another, a short distance away.

"Och, he's always moaning, 'tis a nice night, braapp-r'bit," muttered a third, from up on one of the earthy banks.

"Yaaaggghh!" screamed a mosquito, as its goggle elastic snapped, its sticky-out white scarf drooped, and it was scoffed by a hungry something with a very, very long tongue.

"R'bit. Boobs, it's all a bunch of boobs," said the first voice, a forlorn gurgle in its throat as it expanded like a balloon and then deflated again.

"Eh? What d'ya mean?" asked the third voice, as it chewed on the mosquito.

"Yes, McBestiality, what d'ya mean?" asked the second, as it hopped through the mists and landed in the pool next to the first speaker.

"Och, watch what you're landing on, McHalitosis!" cried the first in alarm, as he was showered with reeking mud upon the arrival of his associate.

"Y'see what I mean? R'bit," said the third, from his vantage point, "A moaning old bastard, R'bit."

"Watch your tong, McSphincter," said the first, using the word 'tong' in place of 'tongue' as his quaint dialect dictated. And mighty confusing (not to mention painful) it could get, especially at the blacksmith's.

"Leave my - r'bit - tong outta this, McBestiality," said the third, and he leaped from the bank and landed in the proximity of the other two.

"R'bit, r'bit," chirped McBestiality in his annoyance at a further mud bath.

Further away across the marsh other conversations could be heard, as McHalitosis imbibed a wee dram o' fermented juice o' the lesser-spotted exploding goonfrog. He gasped and shook his head, then he glanced at the other two and smiled.

"Well, r'bit," he said, "Here we all are again." He blinked his bulbous, grossly oversized eyes and shifted his back legs.

His associates were of a similarly freakish disposition - tiny green bodies with immense, staring eyes that blinked and winked and rotated unnervingly.

"Aye, here we are," muttered McSphincter, "But where's the McBoss, eh, r'bit?"

He looked at the pool around them. A newt with a big pink crash helmet which said 'I'm 'ard, I am' passed by in the clear, still water and shook its fist at the assembled frogs.

"McBastards!" it squeaked, and swam for the hills as they looked around for whoever had spoken.

"What the hell was that?" asked a bemused McBestiality.

"Just some bloody immature tadpole probably, r'bit - I tell you, they teach 'em nothing at that school, r'bit! Nothing but jump here, jump there, and swear like you mean it." said McSphincter, half closing his eyes and settling down a little more comfortably.

"So, McBestiality," said McHalitosis, "What was that about - r'bit - boobs?"

"Aye, boobs!" cried McBestiality, suddenly remembering what he had been moaning about, "It's all down to boobs."

"What d'ya mean?" asked McHalitosis, "What d'ya mean 'boobs'?"

"McBazongas, man, what are yee, deaf?" snorted McBestiality, never fond of having to repeat himself, "R'bit. Great, pendulous, fleshy, green, warty McBazongas."

"I fail to see what that has to do with anything," said grumpy old McSphincter,

"R'bit, I'd much rather know what has become of the McBoss."

"Och, that is the nature of the problem, y'see?" said McBestiality, overjoyed that McSphincter had illustrated the point so well.

"I still don't understand," McHalitosis admitted, frowning his big froggy eyes until they hurt.

"When was the last time you saw a frog with McBazongas? Hmm?" asked McBestiality, "Is it any wonder we're all so bloody miserable when there isn't even the least hint of a babby McBazonga on one of our women? Pigs have 'em, dogs have 'em, let's not even mention Top of the Pops."

"By Christ!" muttered McSphincter, annoyed at the inane drivel of the other two.

"He has a point, though," said McHalitosis, "Why, I think that McBestiality is right. All us frogs are suffering from McBazonga Deprivation Syndrome."

"McB.D.S," murmured McBestiality, "Aye, it's a - r'bit - scourge, there's no doubt."

Suddenly another frog landed amid the trio, splattering the water and the slime over them, but not one dared to utter a curse or any hint of annoyance. This frog was bigger and badder than any of them, a one-eyed psychofrog named Long Tong McSilver, and he had the fastest, longest, meanest tong in the Land of Scotty.

"Go for your tongs, if you think you're fast enough!" he cried, glancing across them, but they cowered and trembled before his gaze.

"Sorry, McBoss," said McBestiality, his voice wavering with fear.

"Excuse us, McBoss," said McSphincter, trembling down to his little green toes.

"Pardon us, McBoss," gibbered McHalitosis.

"Right, now," said the McBoss, "I want to tell you about something I feel is important to us as frogs. Tonight I want to tell you about something that is very close to my own heart. I want to talk to you about how come our chicks ain't got no McBazongas."

Across the marsh, through the spooky mists and the ribbeting-chirping-twittering of the frogs, a strange noise came down from the heavens. The mists billowed wildly, blasting across the mires and pools as they fought to escape the shuddering engines of the large green disk that was settling down on the marsh, lights pulsing.

"It's still there," Konrad grumbled, having woken up and got out of the bed and noticed his pyjama bottoms, "But I don't know if it's rigor mortis or that stupid stunt you pulled with the electrocution."

"Bollocks," said Katya, throwing away the luminous yellow alien crayon with which she had just written 'Bugger me, Baby!" across the arse of her jeans. The essence of maturity, that one.

"So where are we?" asked Konrad, looking at the view-screen with the plastic snail on a spring stuck on top of it.

The screen showed a bleak, undulating land of darkness and fog.

"The Land of Scotty," said Katya, sharply, "I know where that is, you know! I'm not that fucking stupid - you just go straight up."

"Calm down," said Konrad, soothingly, as he flicked the switch that lowered the ramp.

The two figures peered out at the eerie land beyond, at the marshes and the abundant frogs, leaping around and whipping out their tongues at flies.

"Look at that!" cried Katya, getting excited, "Look at those tongues! Gimme that net, and go catch me a fly to staple to my -"

"Shut up, you stupid bitch," growled Konrad, grabbing the frog net from where he had stowed it with the anti-Weirderon gun and a few other possessions from the pickup.

"Ow! Watch where you're pointing that bloody thing," whined Katya.

"I'm going to go and catch some frogs," said Konrad, taking a few steps down the ramp, "Wait here. You might as well get some beauty sleep while you're waiting, I could be some time, and you sure do need it."

He stomped down the ramp and hurtled off into the fog, wielding the net, chasing the scarpering frogs of the marshes of McViolentdeath. Katya walked back into the green saucer thing and cleaned her teeth, just like it said in the manual. Then she ripped off her clothes and jumped into the bed wearing just her undies and her gun belt. When she fell asleep she dreamed dirty, disgusting dreams about bombs, bombs, bombs... (stylized "rocket bombs" – specifically looking somewhat like WWII or Cold War bombage that might be dropped from B-52s, but with erratic rocket motors included, just to make them completely impossible to aim or use effectively).

Konrad Karma was having a bad time. His already ripped and dangerously over-laden green pyjamas were soon plastered with swamp mud as he lunged out with the net at the elusive frogs. They were thick on the ground, hopping around and looking very stupid, but somehow he managed to miss them all. Some even jumped at the net, thinking it looked like a fun kind of a game, but still Konrad couldn't catch them. It seemed he was in the death throes of his terminal uncoolness.

He passed a phone box where the phone was ringing, but it probably wasn't for him so he ignored it. Then he plunged on into the depths of the marshes, the net swishing left and right, and the frogs still escaping with no great difficulty. They jumped and swam and ducked and dodged, dived and deevered, wiggled and wahhed, all the while hurling abuse in their odd language, and Konrad crashed after them, half drowning in the pools and sinking into the mires.

"Shit," he gasped to himself, knackered from the exertion, "If I was cool I wouldn't do this. But then again, if I was cool I wouldn't need to do this."

He paused and sniffed his armpits, then he caught sight of a frog out of the corner of his eye and stayed perfectly still. He waited, he waited, and he flung himself at it, swinging the net, and landed face-first in the ooze with an empty net. The frog jumped onto his head, looked around for the swamp thing that had tried to attack it, and then shrugged and hopped off into the distance.

Konrad couldn't be bothered to get up, he lay there in the gunk, blowing bubbles. Something looked at him. Konrad didn't even blink, he just stared at the two large, round eyes right in front of his face. He slowly reached forwards, not taking his eyes off the thing. Then he had it! Then it let him have it! (Scarcely able to believe that anyone could have been so stupid.)

Brapow!!

In the marshes of McViolentdeath there were many types of frogs, most were stupid little green things that jumped around a lot and didn't get laid because they were cold-blooded amphibian things that turned their slimy nasal passages up at all that bodily interaction. But standing out from the supermarket of variety that lay in colourful populations that were splattered across the landscape, there were two species that dominated the marshes - the first, the green ones with the big, wibbly eyes, had the larger population. The second, the lesser-spotted exploding goonfrog, was less numerous, but had an extraordinary habit of exploding with utter, utter conviction whenever anything happened to upset, scare, stress or (in extreme cases) amuse it. They also ate a lot of implausibly smelly plants and insects, as Konrad Karma now learned as he wiped the crap from his face.

"D'you reckon that was a lesser spotted exploding McGoonfrog?" McBestiality muttered to McSphincter, after they had observed the colourful detonation from a safe distance.

"D'you reckon the McBoss shits up a mctree?"

"What's a mctree?"

Deeper into the marshes Konrad ploughed, getting completely confused by the signs:

'He went this way.'

'He went that way.'

'This way to the frogs.'

'Exit.'

'M25 Two Miles Ahead.'

'Not that way, this way, McDipshit!'

And so on. After half an hour Konrad Karma was completely lost. All the frogs seemed to have vanished, along with the signs, and there was a deathly hush on the marshes - the sort of creepy deathly hush that only really cool people could take. And Konrad, as may have been observed, was far from it.

Suddenly from ahead a face appeared, a round, red face framed with a tartan beard. There was a distorted mouth, twisted into a hideous sneer through which a few crooked teeth poked, and an odd haggis-shaped nose, above which two cold, dark eyes gleamed like burnt scones of evil.

"You have come," it said, with a broad Scots accent which I'm not even going to pretend I can emulate. Actually, I'll pretend I can, but that I just can't be bothered.

"Er, yeah," said Konrad, "Once or twice."

"It was fore-written in the Scraggles o' Dooom," the face said, then its owner stepped forward from the mists.

He was a short man, stooping under a hunched back, tufts of tartan chest hair showed over the top of his pink T-shirt, and his kilt didn't quite hide his train-buffer-like knobbly knees. Under his left arm, the armpit of which was stained with sweat, he carried the type of bagpipes seldom seen south of the border - the true bagpipes - the origin of that celebrated wild animal deterrent. This man had the bagpipes with the spiky ends - the most lethal weapon yet devised. Except just about every other weapon ever.

"It has been painted upon the wall," said the hunchback, "Of the sacred cave o' Dooom that has for three centuries past been the secret meeting place of the clan McNasty beneath their world-renowned brewery and distillery. You are familiar with it perhaps? 'Tis the old tower upon the mountains, the old spooky, haunted, gothic place up in the stormy ravine o' Dooom."

"Never heard of it," said Konrad, "If you'll excuse me, I've got to go and catch some frogs."

"Nay, I think not," growled a voice to his left, and a dark-haired, dark-bearded gargoyle of a man in the same outfit as the hunchback stepped forward from the gloom. This one carried a crude blunderbuss with what looked frighteningly like a perfume squeezer at the end.

Another stepped in from the right - a wiry, sneering weasel dog fish of a man, in the same outfit but with a beret upon his thinning, greying hair and a cheese grater in his scrawnsome hand.

"I am Bastard McNasty," said the hunchback, "The gentleman with the blunderbuss is my brother, Wanker McNasty, the other is my other brother, Shitehead McNasty. Together we make up the clan McNasty, if you don't include that hideous, writhing, semi-alive creature that we have wired up to that Doctor-Frankenstein-type-machine in the topmost garret, the door to which is mysteriously walled up."

"Right," said Konrad, "So, what do you want?"

"You are the chosen one," said Bastard McNasty, "It is written."

"What's written?"

"That you're the chosen one."

"I got that bit. What else is written?"

"That our paths would cross."

"No shit. And what then?"

"Aye, what then indeed. What then indeed," Bastard McNasty murmured.

"F'ck'n'kill'm!" grunted Wanker McNasty, aiming the blunderbuss, not really the talkative type, not to mention a world-class despiser of vowels (also, voles).

"Stay your hand, Wanker," said Shitehead McNasty, "The Big One'll guide us, he'll tell us what needs doing, you mark my words. All we have to do is get him to the dungeon. Right, Bastard?"

"Right you are, Shitehead," said the hunchback, and he beckoned for Konrad to follow him, the other two McNasties fell in behind.

Bastard McNasty led the way, weaving through the misty marshes as they began to grow light with the onset of dawn.

"This can't be bloody happening," said Konrad.

"Sh't th'f'ck'p," growled Wanker McNasty. "B'st'rds, sh'th'ds'n w'nk'rs th'l't o' yr."

Gradually the ground began to get drier and steeper.

"We found that in the east the ground got drier, in the west the ground got drier, up the mountain in the wetter weather it got drier, in the north wetter drier higher, in the south higher liar and a lot shier, not forgetting the ooxst, where the lie of the land forbade any particularly detailed analysis, as a direct result of it being a drunken misspelling, and there being no such fifth direction in reality."

"Ah, but who truly decides what is real?"

"Well, I rather think that I, a renowned geologist, might have a say in it. Bugger it, I damn well should have a say in it. I don't know if I have, but I should. I mean. My feet are firmly on the ground and my staple is rock. Rock solid, what?"

"There's something fishy about your argument, and who better to notice, than I, a renowned fishmonger?"

"You're a what? Good grief. I'm sorry, I thought you were something else altogether. Now. If you don't stand back I'll hit you with this stick. Further.

Further. Not far enough - take that, you hound, and that, and that, and that."

So, yes, drier and steeper, slowly rising up above the bogs and swamps. At last they came to a valley between two glowering mountains, where it seemed for all the world that they had arrived at an island floating in the fire of the sunrise. There, higher up on the rocky ground, was a tall, square tower, overrun with ivy and gargoyles and flying buttresses and ornate battlements and probably some very pretty basements, but they couldn't be seen just yet. At each of the corners was a high tower with a pointed roof. One of these had its windows walled up and 'Help Me' written on the wall in bird droppings. Above the drawbridge was a large green sign which said, 'McNasty Breweries Ltd'. Around the base of the tower was the moat, filled with slime and ooze and old men dreaming of fifty years ago when a fifty-year old tart had been no kind of tempting proposition by any stretch of the tableware.

Someone was hanging from the battlements of the main tower, apparently holding on with his mouth. The four people below could see right up his kilt and it wasn't a pleasant sight.

"On a clear day," said Wanker, "You can see McUranus."

Bastard winced. "I dinnae know what that is coming out of there, but it's no kind of sunshine."

"Heya, McNasties!" said the man brightly, and he plummeted from the battlements.

Scklutchkthwapp!!!

He followed his inevitable trajectory and burst, his innards spewed slime and yellow gunge and his ribs popped up through his skin. His skull was cracked, his eyeballs hung out and bounced like yo-yos on the optic nerves. The assorted limbs were broken and twisted into a hideous mess. He wore a badge that exclaimed, "OH, FUK!" All in all, it wasn't very pretty.

"Idiot," groaned Bastard McNasty, "He was testing his new falsies, you know? Seeing how much weight they could hold."

"Who was it?" asked Konrad.

"Old George McRabid, the butler," said Shitehead McNasty, "Who's going to answer the bloody door now?"

"Have you not got your keys?"

"No, I have not got my keys. What do you take me for?"

"Just pull the damn chain. Maybe the old fool let Crazy Maggie out of her box to stand in for him."

Bastard McNasty pulled the chain by the raised drawbridge, from within the forbidding tower came the boom of a vast bell. The drawbridge lowered away with the rattling of rusty chains, beyond it a gaping arch opened into a torch-lit hall, grand flights of stairs ran up to a gallery above, many doors led away to other dark rooms and their sinister secrets. At the centre of the hall stood a battered, dusty old lorry from the forties, which represented the haulage arm of the McNasty empire.

"Enter," said Bastard McNasty, motioning for Konrad to follow him into the tower. "So. Crazy Maggie's out of her box. I just hope she stays out of the fridge."

Once Wanker and Shitehead were also inside, the drawbridge was raised and Konrad found himself a prisoner in that pox-riddled vacuum bag of suits of armour, dusty books, moth-eaten rugs, and ancient devices of torture. The three members of the clan McNasty headed off to different dark chambers to do various jobs (big jobs, little jobs, and medium-sized jobs). Before Bastard went he took Konrad down to the dungeon and locked him up in a little cell with just a skeleton and a starving rat called Bob for company.

As Bastard McNasty's footsteps died away Bob scurried a little closer to Konrad, who watched the rat with uncertainty.

"So what you in for?" the rodent squeaked.

"Er, something about the Big One," said Konrad.

"Did you do it?" asked the rat, "Or was you set up?"

"Don't take this the wrong way, but I don't want to talk to you - you're, erm, a rat."

"What?" the rat looked down at itself in surprise, it clutched at its fur and jumped back, "Fucking hell! What the fuck have they done to me? They've turned me into a bloody rat!"

"Probably a brain transplant," said Konrad, setting fire to his pyjamas in order to protest at the staffing levels in the dungeon, "Lunatics do brain transplants and stuff. So you're not really a rat, huh?"

"Fuck no! I was a cockroach until yesterday."

"Wow, I bet that was really interesting."

"Not really. It just meant I got to shag loads of cockroaches, which is pretty nauseating, believe me. Oh, and I got to crawl through all the shit that you humans leave behind cupboards and stuff like that. I guess me being a rat now is like a promotion, sort of. I tell you, it does a lot for your perspective of the Universe when you spend your whole day trying to dig through a bit of crap that it only took a couple of seconds for one of you big people to lose down the side of an armchair."

"Wow. Er. Please go on."

"That's pretty much it, actually."

"Wow. So. I bet you're an atheist."

"No, I'm a Buddhist. I liked the atheism, don't get me wrong, but then I shaved my head, it was a fashion thing, right? So I thought I looked more like a Buddhist, and here I am."

"That's really wild," said Konrad, putting out the flames, "This is really starting to piss me off."

The time passed slowly down in the dungeon with just the rat, who had once been a cockroach, for company. In the end Konrad beat the little bastard's brains out with the arm he pulled off the skeleton.

That evening a plump warty old hag came to the cell and Konrad was led up a spiralling flight of stairs into the dizzy heights of that fearful place. Through swirls of dust and beams of waning moonlight, by evil old clocks and sinister portraits, through doorways and down passages - ancient and seldom trod. At last to the huge and rickety garret atop the tower, where the wind whistled and the eagles wheeled.

There waited the three members if the Clan McNasty, amid their benches and woodworking implements. Hard at it they were, drawing on their pipes for inspiration. A half assembled gargantuan monstrosity that may have been a still, or may have been something vaguely to do with lobotomies, going by the blueprint Konrad half caught a glimpse of, was standing in the darkness behind them, partly concealed beneath many huge dust sheets. A green glow flickered in its depths and a chilling whisper seemed to issue from it...

"My nose is itching..."

At first Konrad was reasonably distressed, but it got worse. Oh yes. It got worse. It started to get worse as he was man-handled to one side and strapped into a network of lead pipes by a huge semi-human drooling ape-fiend called Crazy Maggie. That was pretty alarming. Then the McNasties began sketching. And if Konrad had hoped for any kind of terrifying confrontation, he was disappointed. All they did was sketch, until the sketch-sketch-sketch of their pencils on the paper began to give him a nervous twitch. He struggled against his bonds until his wrists bled, and then made do with squinting into the half-light, trying to find anything that might explain what was happening.

"I do wish it would keep still," muttered Bastard McNasty.

"Perhaps it is tired. Crazy Maggie, kindly return the gentleman to his quarters."

The greasy hairy hands of the transvestite semi-human ape-fiend with a soft spot for banana milkshakes fumbled Konrad free from the pipework and dumped him into the chute that had once led from the latrine and into the moat. A singularly alarming, not to mention grazing, plummet later, and Konrad arrived amid a cloud of dust, back in the cell. He pondered all that had happened, and concluded that he really needed to get hold of a gun. Or maybe a tank. He glanced around. Not a sausage.

So the ordeal continued - every night Konrad was required to return to the uppermost chamber in that draughty tower - either voluntarily, or while chained to the vest of Crazy Maggie like a baby in a supermarket. And every night he was strapped into the plumbing and those sharp little pencils would sketch-sketch-sketch through countless sheets of paper, before he was finally returned to his little pit to get some sleep. But sleep never came easy - and was haunted by leering Crazy Maggie with its skew-wiff eye balls and protruding teeth, all set in that malformed semi-ape face of an inhuman fiend.

Konrad began to form theories as to what the Clan McNasty was up to. His favourite theory had come to him in something akin to a vision (delirium, probably). It involved the Pan-dimensional Purple Blobbites of Pox 342 and their fiendish plan to take over the world through the art of dodgy distillery. Up until their most recent exploit, the only way the human weaklings could tell when they had received the Formula was when they got 'a bad pint'. But with this revolutionary technique, they would be able to disguise all bad pints as regular pints. No one would know. They could then flood the world and spread their brain disease, turning the populace into slavering zombies existing only to service the Great Still.

The problem was Konrad had somehow hit the nail on the head - the only difference being that the aliens came from Pox Majorus, not Pox 342, but nobody's perfect. The thing he didn't realise was that as long as he destroyed the still, the blueprints, and Crazy Maggie, the world would be safe.

But what could he do? The routine continued as ever, and any attempt at escape was foiled and most severely punished by the semi-human ape-fiend. Konrad's will began to fade and he steadily became resigned to his terrible fate.

At last though, there came the metallic click of a key turning in the lock and the groan of the door as it opened. Footsteps drew nearer, echoing through the shadows where the arse-drill, the gonad-grater, and the nostril-screws stood out of sight of the cell. The short old stubbly woman stopped in front of the iron bars and looked in at Konrad.

"I'm to let you out," she said, unlocking the cell door, "And direct you up to the chamber. I must confess I am very worried as they haven't been seen by anyone for eight whole hours, and when Master Bastard called me and told me to come for you he would not open the door, but rather shouted through. His voice was most strange. It is a real mystery, sir, a real, stupefying mystery."

"I don't give a shit, you warty old hag, now shut the fuck up and get out of my way!"

Konrad stormed past the old lady and up out of the dungeon. Time for a showdown, he reckoned. Do or die.

"Up the stairs on the left," she called after him, "Third door on your right."

Konrad slouched up the stairs in something approaching fury, and from there along the corridor at the top where the heads of various ferocious animals were mounted on the walls, laughing. He found the third door and knocked on it.

"Enter," said a voice with an unconvincing Scots accent.

Konrad opened the door slowly, expecting a trick, but instead there was the answer to the mystery, and not a trick in sight. Not so much as a tit, a sno-cat, or a tea towel. Konrad walked in, closed the door behind him and stepped over to the bar against the far wall. He'd never seen so many optics. There were optics on the optics.

"Hiya, Konrad," said Katya, beaming at him from behind the bar. She appeared to be a tad slanty of posture and squinty of eye.

"What the fuck's going on?" asked Konrad, dumbfounded and still very uncool.

"I'm rescuing you," said Katya, pulling an involuntary pint. "For the second time in, uh, one, uh, um, twenty-four hours."

"Are they dead?" asked Konrad, pointing to the McNasty clan.

Their faces were almost scarlet, eyes bulging and bloodshot, while their mouths gave rise to great torrents of vomit, now still and congealing. They seemed to be far from alive. Bastard McNasty looked pretty well ABSOLUTELY, while Wanker McNasty seemed to be without question TOTALLY, and Shitehead McNasty was just plain FUCKED. They all were.

"Of course," said Katya, with a hint of a slur. "Hic. But s'okay 'cause I just transmute the poisons into, uh, water. I just focus on my stomach and turn all the alcohol into...uh."

"Water."

"Yeah. But shit I need to go find me a bush to squat behind. Oh wow, I got me own. And's just in the right place too."

"So what did you actually do?" Konrad inquired, surveying the bodies, but not too closely.

"What do you think I fucking did? Drinking games, lubricated with great steaming Vishnus of alcoholic beverages."

"Why didn't you just shoot them?" asked Konrad.

"Yeah, whatever, and for the last time, will you stop pointing that at me!?!"

When the drawbridge to the McNasty Tower opened with a crash Konrad and Katya Karma scarpered sharpish, back down the slopes towards the misty marshes. They hopped from earthy bank to earthy bank, jumped from rock to rock, and slowly worked their way back towards the large green saucer thing. Unknown to them eyes watched from the slitted windows of that eerie tower. The skew-whiff protruding eyes of Crazy Maggie. The semi-human ape-fiend drew back into the darkness and sought out the Great Still, aching to caress its gothic superstructure. The Pan-dimensional Purple Blobbites of Pox Majorus tittered with demonic glee.

"D'you reckon there are, uh, spy satellites up there?" asked Katya, looking up at the sky.

"Hmm, it's possible," said Konrad, "It's pretty depressing, huh? Y'know, not even being able to walk across a bunch of shit-boring useless marshes without being spied on by the space-bound eyes of a corporate-pervert-tycoon person. Why do you ask?"

"Just wondered," Katya replied. Then she started throwing rocks at the sky, and couldn't help but take it personally when they all seemed to come right back at her.

"Why do you keep doing things like that?" asked Konrad. "One day you'll do yourself an injury and I won't be there to help."

"You? Uh, you there, to help me? Let me get this right. You to help me? Is that what you meant?"

"Erm. Yes, that was it."

"Well, I think that's a bit fucking rich considering your record in the recent past."

"Perhaps. But until it all went pear-shaped let's not forget who wore the trousers around here."

Katya frowned. "They wear kilts here."

"I meant in the family unit."

"They've got a family unit? Uh, here? Do they have single parent support?"

"What are you jabbering about?"

"Me jabbering? Let me get this right. Me jabbering?"

"What?"

"You're jabbering, you dick. Leave me alone. It's the last fucking time I save you twice, you bendy boned bugger."

"Me what? What the fuck are you talking about? Either make sense or shut up."

She shut up.

When they arrived back at the large green saucer thing Katya went on inside and got into her usual garb, while Konrad sat on the ramp, wondering where all the frogs had got to.

"You know, sis," said Konrad, "There's a bad storm coming, a baaaad storm."

"I know," she called from inside, "It's those fucking tomatoes. At least you thought they were tomatoes, I think they were soap 'cause I found some more by the jacuzzi-bath-type-thing."

"I don't mean that, I mean aliens and war and carnage. And the S.Q.U.A.T. team from the Ministry of Uncool must be searching for us by now. Now more than ever I need to be my old self, I need to be cool and in control, I need to say things like 'Anyone for cricket?' in tight spots. Right now I look like a bloody swamp thing."

"You really want to catch a frog, huh?" asked Katya, strolling down the ramp, fastening her gun belt and patting Lester the Alien's hilt.

"Yup."

"You really want to...you know, with the frog?"

"No choice," he said. "The free ride's over, baby. Besides, I'm getting the urge to put on some trainers."

"What?"

"You know, shoes, like, trainers - trainers with big orange stripes down the sides and puffy tongues and those pump up air things."

"Holy shit, you have got it bad. However," she smiled sweetly with those blue-lipsticked lips, "I don't give a shit and you're starting to get on my tits."

"Sorry."

"Don't apologise, just shut the fuck up."

"Just you wait till I'm re-cooled." He shook a limp fist in a 'I'll get you GRRR' sort of way.

"Right. Now shut up - I'm trying to think," she pulled the skin-tight, fluorescent green T-shirt down over one shoulder like the strange vain one she was and looked out across the marshes, "Uh, well I thought a bit, and I haven't got a bloody clue. I guess you can carry on whining now," and with that she plodded back into the large green saucer thing, pulling her knickers from her arse crack in the charmingly indiscreet and crude way that she had.

Konrad looked down at the monumental thing that was throbbing away in his pyjama bottoms as though it was about to give birth.

"What are you looking at?" he asked it.

There was a sudden movement. Konrad the swamp thing almost had time to flinch, but not quite, and then there was a frog, sitting on his pyjama bottoms at the end of his elephant-dick. Here was a little seen species of frog - the mint-green skinnyfrog. It sat there on its perch, stupid great eyes blinking, its throat swelling a little as it murmured to itself. Konrad grabbed it, caught it, and held onto it, as one eye poked out between his fingers and took a look around.

"Holy McShit!" yelled McSphincter, "He's got the McBoss! R'bit!"

"Not now," complained McBestiality from where he was leafing through a catalogue. "McLatex," he drooled, "Lovely McLatex."

"Got one!" Konrad shouted, getting to his feet and running back into the large green saucer thing so that a certain part of him quivered like a diving board.

"What the fuck?" squawked Katya, as she was knocked from where she had been sitting with her feet up on the control panel, reading a lewd comic.

"Sorry, but I've kind of gone into an uncontrollable uncool frenzy! Quick! Break out the eighties romantic ballads, get me a bum bag, find me my train set!"

Katya got up and looked at the frog, "Oh, wow," she said, "You got one."

She rummaged around the interior of the saucer, delving through the alien holiday clothing, the alien food, the alien board games, the alien sex toys, and all the rest of the Weirderon junk. Then she found a cupboard full of various drinking vessels. At last she picked out a pretty average cocktail glass.

"What do you want with it?" she asked, looking around.

"I don't give a shit! Piss in it if you have to! The jacuzzi! Some of that weird, sparkling jacuzzi water! Just hurry - I'm getting an incredible urge to curl my hair."

Konrad was hopping from foot to foot, sweating and groaning, clutching at the frog and trying to hang on to his sanity for those last few moments. Katya scooped out some jacuzzi water with the glass and picked out a stray blue pubic hair. She handed the glass to Konrad who stuck the frog in it, head first. He was breathing heavily, flushed, and generally close to the edge. Where the frog's legs stuck into the air they twitched, then thrashed, then they were still.

"How come it's, uh, dead?" asked Katya, scrutinising the frog.

"It's asleep," said Konrad sarcastically.

"Oh," said Katya, "Uh, right."

Konrad looked at the frog in the glass, wondering if it had puked any of its last frogsomely shit-snuffling meal into the jacuzzi water, indeed wondering if Katya had donated anything to the water that morning - he wouldn't have put anything past her. But the clutching, clawing hunger of uncoolness was eating at him. He closed his eyes, raised his glass to his lips, and drank. He continued drinking until all the glass was drained. The empty vessel tinkled on the floor as Konrad staggered back.

"Wow!" said Katya.

She watched Konrad closely, wondering if he was going to exhibit any disgusting symptoms of poisoning or something. She was disappointed, though, and Konrad's hands gradually grew steadier, his face, which had become livid purple, began to cool and turn paler. His breathing slowed, the last of the sweat evaporated, and even the ripped, green, swamp-plastered pyjamas started to look kind of cool.

Konrad Karma was back.

"Anyone seen Annette?" he asked, brushing his hair back with his hand and not even bothering to look down to where the flagpole was lowering and shrinking, and then it was back to proportions he could handle, so to speak. His gut, too, seemed to flatten out and firm up - not exactly a six-pack, but these things take time.

"Er, Konrad?" said Katya, her lovely brow slightly troubled.

"Yeah?"

"You're standing on my foot."

"I know. I just figured out why that foot sauna killed me. You tampered with it, didn't you, and then you rescued me when it killed me."

"Uh, it was the best I could think of."

"That's why I'm standing on your foot."

4. The Video Documentary

"Today's documentary," the narrator kindly explained, "Delves into the truly appalling existence of two of the Land of Eng's most reviled citizens - public enemies number thirty-two, and one hundred and four and a half. This programme contains strong language and scenes that some viewers may find disturbing."

Music.

"We begin with events as filmed by our camera crew, who caught up with the subjects of tonight's investigation as they went about their daily routine of being subversive."

Konrad clenched a fist and raised it by the door.

"Oh, that's right," murmured a voice, apparently facing the other way, going by the muffling.

Konrad frowned and looked around, squinting through the heat haze, wondering if it was the pesticides. Some pesticides had hallucinogenic qualities, which went some way towards explaining Stonehenge.

"How did they get the stones there?" an anorak might ask, clutching his flask and scratching under a plaster on his backside.

"Perhaps they didn't," our educated person would reply.

Konrad knocked on the door. It rattled on its hinges, a rattle that echoed into the depths of the building. He waited, listening, but there was no response. He raised his hand to the door again.

"Why not?" inquired the muffled voice sarcastically, "Tell me why not!"

Konrad rested the muzzle of his gun against the centre of the door, thinking that if Prof. Feelass was on the other side taking the piss then there wasn't a judge in the land who would begrudge him plugging the bastard.

"Eek!" squeaked the voice, "Don't shoot!"

The door shook like there was an earthquake on, splinters of rust broke away with the vibration. Konrad considered the pesticides again.

"Don't shoot!" the voice pleaded, "Don't do it! I'll do anything, anything, just give me a chance to prove myself! I'll...er...I'll do...I'll...anything!"

Konrad kicked the door in and stepped into the dark hallway beyond. He looked around at several promising passages and doorways before heading off into the bowels of the observatory.

"Oh, right," muttered the broken door, "'Anything' I say, although to be honest I was pushed to think of anything I might do. But what do I get? Do I get set a task? Do I even get consulted, or threatened? No, I get kicked off my fucking hinges. What is the world coming to?"

Meanwhile, Katya Karma was having problems of her own. She was strolling back to the car, completely unaware that Konrad wasn't with her, as she ranted and schoonered on about the really amazing things she was going to do with Angry Arthur Agent. Angry Arthur would later issue a statement, calling for moderation - after all, just how many really amazing things was he supposed to be able to take?

Something wavered in Katya's vision, causing her to halt in mid-stagger and blink several times, for effect more than anything. She blinked again, then frowned, adjusting the straps of her bra through the short summer dress thing.

A shape fizzled and evaporated before her very eyes (and they were very), now reforming, now vanishing, and never quite solid enough for her to work out what it was. A chirpy little bell pinged and Katya chuckled to herself, remembering that this was called an idea. She concentrated harder. The idea went on dancing and morphing, completely piss-useless, which was why Katya, on principal, tended to ignore them and stick to things she could handle. Like her underwear.

"Y'know, Lester," she murmured to her gun, easing it from the holster, "I think we should meditate, or philosophise, or something."

'Yeahyeahyeah!' Lester would have drooled, had he not been a gun.

Katya shot at the idea, gripping Lester's hilt with both sweaty hands, squinting as she concentrated on her aim, trying to nail that tricky sucker. The idea bent and swerved as though performing for The Shake himself, smiling from behind its veil, flicking its belly, boobs and buttocks at Katya in contempt.

Lester spat fire at the mirage, sending rolling gunshots across the heavens, kicking up earth in impressive showers. The idea danced on, a real mover. Katya only got angrier, slowly reddening in the face, her veins rising and pulsing. She licked the sweat from around her lips, then grimaced, standing with her feet braced far apart. She flicked the selector switch onto 'Rainy Weekends', ever more determined to nail this fucking problem right on the head, and trembled with the recoil as the quivering hallucination ate a shower of deadly dildos.

For Katya it was simple:

Ideas = shit
Think = trouble
Don't bother = best bet
Whales = (perfume/anorexia)*environmentalists
Bomb = Yehar

At last Katya, panting like a horny granny who'd just had to skate down the chippy for some grease, stopped shooting and glared at the idea where it still pulsed against the horizon.

"Brains," she gasped, "Who fucking needs 'em?"

"Not you, obviously," replied the idea, rather cheekily.

Katya slumped to the ground, legs splayed enticingly, too knackered to be bothered with this shit. She looked around. Where the hell was Konrad when she needed him?

"Put it to death," she sulked, picking her nose.

Steaming pink flamingos seemed to lose their molecular integrity, and as no chief engineer was on hand to reverse the polarity, things rapidly got out of hand. The flamingos broke down in a manner much akin to Czech animations, flaking upwards as though they were fragments of wax and candy floss, being drawn up to the sun. Then they swirled, turning in on themselves, forming circles, and what remained of the flamingos boiled and melted, running like oxygenated blood into the circles and filling them out into raw, red suns.

Katya frowned, it was all getting a little too much like it probably actually really meant something after all.

Beyond the suns, reeds emerged, or rather slender green suggestions of reeds, but they twirled and spun, blurring into sparking Catherine wheels. Slowly the red suns glowed yellow, as though rising, and they softened, blending into watercolours, forming a pyramid of pale yellow. Beneath them the spinning, sparking lines slowed and created a long, downward pointing triangle. For all Katya's brief hopes of a galactic blueprint, or a big, bad answer that might be worth something, the mirage did appear to have suddenly become a rather mundane ice cream.

"Hasn't even got a flake," she mused.

The ice cream remained solid in her vision for some time, then it faded and left her wondering if perhaps it meant she could murder an ice cream. Even a subtle metaphor like that didn't escape the sharp bitch. However, not for the first time that day, she was wrong.

Katya pressed on and had almost found her way back to the road, but upon nearing the edge of the field she became aware of a strange sensation, a tingling at the back of her neck, something that jumped right in behind the ice cream to queue for a nag. She spun around, guessing it was nasty ninjas stalking her through the crops, but she was wrong. She shrugged and continued towards the road.

Konrad had been engulfed by nasty ninjas. He'd been searching the old observatory, wading through ancient machinery and cobwebs, all in semi darkness, when a blood-curdling yell had heralded the arrival of a pack of psychotic ninjas. They jumped and cartwheeled around, doing really amazing things with their swords, before hurling themselves at the intruder. Their eyes blazed red with the sort of insanity that came from eating too much rice, but they died easily, which was what counted when it came down to it. Konrad had a gun, they didn't, so despite a few unfashionable gashes in his clothes, Konrad soon straightened the matter out, and wandered off, leaving the smoking corpses of the ninjas stacked in a gruesome heap.

Katya was just a few feet from the road when all the instincts her ancestors had picked up while sitting in a cave, getting paranoid that all the big hairy things with sharp teeth were out to get them, started screaming and jittering, until she was forced to check over her shoulder, guessing it was a swarm of deadly mechanical wasps from the Dead Zone. She was wrong, but that didn't help her brother.

Konrad was more cautious following the ninja attack. He ascended a winding stairway, sensing the evil in the air grow stronger, knowing now that he was nearing the insane Professor Feelass. He passed grimy windows that offered fleeting glimpses of sunny countryside, and gaping doorways that offered only more cold passages, and more labyrinths of cobwebs.

The air seemed to vibrate with energy and fear. Konrad, unmoved by such feeble special effects, proceeded until the stairs ended in a doorway. As he reached for the handle he seemed to hear something thudding gently against the other side. He was ready with his gun and reckoned that would be enough to stop just about anything, except deadly mechanical wasps from the Dead Zone, because there was practically nothing that could stop them. He threw the door open.

Out of the darkness beyond came a buzzing that grew rapidly into a horrifying chainsaw of sound, then gleaming black forms with fine red stripes began to emerge - like wasps, only bigger, and with infra-red vision, and the finest hydraulic venom syringes yet developed.

Konrad took a pot shot or two at the wasps as they swarmed towards him, guessing that anything was worth a try. The bullets ricocheted off the armoured fiends and zipped away into the darkness. The robotic insects came closer, gleaming coldly, running a number of interesting lines in torture through their central processors. Their dripping stings twitched and throbbed with hisses and clanks, itching to get puncturing.

Konrad dug deep into his jacket pocket and produced an aerosol. He glanced at it, and then up to the cloud of energetic wasps that had almost enveloped him. The aerosol was a half full can of insect repellent, tastefully decked out in white and livid green, and although in itself it was piss useless, once Konrad had struck a match it became a tad more promising. Suddenly it was a flame thrower, a bit of a crap flame thrower - but a flame thrower all the same, and even as the wasps lined up their sights and prepared to drive their stings home through that soft-bodied human scum, they were fried, toasted, crisped and scorched. Their circuits crackled, engulfed in molten plastic and flames, and the formidable squadron rained down on the floor, smoking and swearing. Konrad lobbed the aerosol away and pressed on.

Katya had finally reached the road when the vision that had been troubling her suddenly made sense. So while Konrad, crossing a creepy, darkened room, heard a fearful slopping sound above him and looked up just in time to catch an ice cream in the face, Katya was presented with a prospect altogether more alarming, and to her dubious little peanut, altogether more promising.

A starship not unlike an immense, red ice cream cone plummeted earthwards, screaming through the troposphere, and skewered the planet in an explosion of earth, sending out tremors across the immediate vicinity of its touchdown. Katya involuntarily hopped into the air. The pointed nose cone drove down a good forty feet into the soil, while the shining hull trembled with the stresses of such unbelievably bad parking.

A cockpit set far back near the fat arse end burst, and two forms plunged towards the ground, at first looking like bungee jumpers as their seatbelts stretched, but aliens never were much cop when it came to safety, and the belts snapped, leaving nothing but a good trouser-staining fall as the short-term employment prospects for the aliens. The airbags had inflated, but seeing as aliens didn't know what they were for, they had fitted them to inside of the spacesuit helmets, thinking it looked like a bit of a laugh. Needless to say, no one was laughing now.

Katya stood open-mouthed, gaping at the bizarre spectacle, while the aliens thudded into the parched farmland heavily enough to get anyone's sympathy.

"How alarming," said Katya, "In fact, it's so alarming, I'm just going to have to, uh, see if I can't make it a lot worse."

She set off towards the giant, smoking ice cream cornet, wishing she had an imagination.

Slightly chubby balding man of indeterminate older middle age; he's got grey hair and sad big old glasses, and he's a wanker. He finds himself on a regional news programme, only he's asking the questions. His suit is cheap and it shows, he's trying to sit slightly skew wiff so the rip stays off camera. He asks the stupid smug bitch in the other chair:

"Can women be successful in business and have successful marriages?"

I find myself thinking:

"In broad terms, who gives a shit? This isn't something you can generalise about. It depends on the character and plans of the individual."

Evidently he finds himself thinking the same, because he tears off all his clothes and puts on a dress, takes up a shot gun and dances with it on his news desk, then he sticks the end in his mouth and blows his crappy head halfway across the studio.

Is this what they call a mid-life crisis?

Or is this just what comes of being a petty wanker pandering the feminist egomaniacs?

His tie has flowers on it, no one goes to his funeral, his cat dies at last after one hundred and eight days trapped in the house.

Do you know this man? Would you recognise him if you saw him again? He's a danger to himself and the public, he walks a bit funny, like he's having a mid-stride identity crisis, and his breath smells of fetid vegetables. Could you pick him out of an identity parade? He wears a floral dress and heels and carries a sawn-off that may, or may not, make your day, but your social duty dictates that you must turn him in. Police are waiting for your call. They've got homes to go to, and worried wives and/or husbands glancing at clocks on badly-papered walls. Don't keep them waiting.

Badly-papered balding man is standing in an identity parade, and although he's starting to think the witnesses can't pick him out from the bouncer with the baseball bat, he decides that it isn't worth the risk. He loads his shot gun and starts shooting. First he splatters the teenage pregnant slob all over her bank-robber boyfriend and their getaway driver family, and then he picks out the police who are scrambling for cover. He puts the shot gun in his mouth and blasts his brains into next week.

This man is a menace. If you see him, put him out of his misery. He is a danger to little kiddies on their way to school, he is unstable and unsafe in public places, he shouldn't be allowed near women. He should be locked up, put on medication, sedated with identical palisades. He shouldn't be allowed. He gargles through his arse for ITV and this is all the thanks he gets. For him it's this simple:

Ideas = pass

Think = it's all written for me on a card

Don't bother = best bet

Wales = top holiday destination

Bomb = drive too fast

Once Konrad had sorted out the ice cream he decided that a vendetta wasn't worth it, that the whatever the sterile old bastard had meant in his column in the Times, it wasn't worth all this aggro creeping around an abandoned observatory. He sloshed the cans of petrol around and searched out some matches.

The observatory exploded - for Konrad it was this easy:

Ideas = do you?

Think = oh, okay

Don't bother = make up your mind

Whales = big ugly bastards

Bomb = don't you start

Angry Arthur Agent was slumped in a chair between two other equally slumped individuals. The picture was a little shaky and the colour wasn't up to much, as though it had been filmed on a very cheap video camera. The scene was a dressing room, where all horizontal surfaces, and some that weren't, had been covered with junk and obsolete props. From somewhere else in the building there came the roar of a distant audience, and then the hysterical mutterings of a star.

"At first we tried to keep her locked up in her bedroom," Angry Arthur continued, once he'd lit another cigar. He glanced up into the camera, and then sidelong at his colleague, "But it didn't work. It seemed like everything we did, she had an answer for it. So in the end we gave her the job and since then she's pretty much stayed out of our hair.

"The thing you've got to remember about Konrad is he hates guns. He hates violence and killing people, but it's just like his fate that he keeps getting into these gunfights. It's like the most interesting and engaging people are those whose very lives appall them."

"Going back to Katya," said Arthur's shriekin' freak auburn-haired child prodigy colleague, "Erm, a bit of a funny story about that. You see, she had this job in an office, right? Like with a really uptight lesbian of a boss. And one day, yeah, and this is absolutely true, her boss comes up to her, y'see Katya was like the secretary, you know? And she'd been put on tea making duties because, right, she set fire, yeah, that's right - set fire, to the last client on account of how she cornered him in the gents and he tried, and I quote, to 'molest her.' So anyway, she's made the tea," he broke off for a little chuckle. Angry Arthur sighed and glanced at his watch, thinking of a million more profitable things he could be doing. His colleague went on, "So, and I swear this is absolutely true, Katya says 'Where would you like your tea?'"

"'Uh, tea,'" said the third man, a hair stylist from Gravesham, "She talks like that." He grinned at the camera and flicked his hair.

Angry Arthur took out his mobile and started pressing buttons, the camera refocused on the auburn colleague and his story.

"Right, so she asks where this blood-sucking ice witch wants her tea, yeah? And, like, you know, this is very dangerous ground."

"Undoubtedly," agreed the hair stylist.

"And Katya's then-boss said, 'In my office,' not without a hint of searing intolerance of the rising starlet. This is absolutely true, it really is. Katya says, 'Which one?' and eyes her up. Well, needless to say she was fired on the spot."

"Needless," agreed the hair stylist, He swept his fingers back through his hair.

"So break the fucking door down," Arthur growled into his mobile. He glanced sheepishly at the camera, "That's not still on, is it?"

"Nowhere is the difference between Konrad and his sister more apparent," the narrator said, "Than in this archive footage - the actual video of Katya Karma's almost wedding to Roodbutt P. Slob."

There was a very shaky, blurry picture of a crappy old church and some people standing around. They almost looked like guests, but were in fact hostages.

Katya was standing up the front, all sweet and fit in her wedding dress, the vicar was bleeding but he was going on as best he could.

"Well?" he said to Roodbutt, "Do you?"

"Durr?" Roodbutt dribbled, "What?"

Roodbutt P. Slob was a large translucent bag filled to overflowing with all kinds of shit. His only redeeming feature was that he was too slow to be really dangerous. He hadn't even dressed up for the wedding, in fact he hadn't even dressed. He was still wearing his vest and slippers, and a bloody state he looked too.

Roodbutt lifted his vest, turned around, and slapped his flabby arse on the altar. He farted until reeking gravy extinguished the candles.

"Fuckwit," Katya hissed through her teeth.

"Y'what?" growled Roodbutt, spinning around and taking a chainsaw from his best man (a joyrider from a wanky estate), eyes burning with primitive rage. The flabby paws grasped at the machine, the quivering bulk seemed to grow, towering up like a hideous Katya-eating jelly.

Katya parted two frilly bits of delicate dress and there were two dribblesome inner thighs, possibly she was displaying Lester the Alien, who was also in there in all his multi-cartridge glory, but who gives a fuck about Lester the Alien? Katya's hands moved on, a bunch of lacy crap by one of her chewable armpits moved aside to reveal a heap of gun belts, gleaming bullets, and heavy firearms. She went on rummaging, displaying more firm flesh and weaponry.

"Guns," she said, grinning, "Guns...guns...guns."

"Yurr, well," shrugged Roodbutt, lowering the chainsaw, "I got appearances to maintain, y'know?"

"So do you?" the vicar repeated.

"Ah, shaddap," muttered Roodbutt, and although the picture was censored, there was a definite rip of flesh and thud of a bouncing head. "Bollicks. I was aimin' a dah fuckin' font."

"And here's a picture of Konrad's armpit," said the narrator, "See the difference."

Konrad wasn't actually watching the television, but he did pause to think that the bird with the hula hoop was enjoying it far too much. Then he heard Katya start up. She screamed all the way out of her bedroom and crashed into his own, taking out some of the furniture, going by the noise of the impact. There was a silent period, presumably while she was standing around, rubbing her head, trying to figure out why Konrad wasn't in. Then she sprinted down the stairs, cracking the old wood and ripping off wallpaper.

She burst in through the door, clad only in a T-shirt and knickers, and a fluorescent green sock, and covered her embarrassment by sticking a finger up at the camera crew.

The living room of the Karma non-twins' house had never been all that tidy, but now, as well as half eaten dinners and week-old newspapers and bomb-magazines, there was a stinking great camera crew, and the associated machinery and leads, and fat useless ponces standing just in camera shot, grinning and picking bits of them that didn't even deserve to be spat on, let alone aired on TV.

Katya was smeared with something disgusting, Konrad and the camera crew whipped on some gas masks because whatever it was reeked worse than dead tramps in a sauna.

"What's up, sis?" Konrad inquired from the safety of his breathing apparatus with 'Well Hung Lung' printed on it.

"Not here," Katya mumbled, "Not in front of them."

The camera crew moved a step nearer.

"We're supposed to ignore them." Konrad replied, "Or we don't get loads of cash."

"What? You mean you want me to tell you about how lovely cuddly, uh, everyone's favourite soft toy me woke up to find a decaying sludgy greasy zombie in my, uh, bed who looked more like a compost heap than any compost heap I've ever seen in front of all these strangers and their fucking scary camera? Forget it." She turned and sulked back up the stairs.

The questions posed by this, such as what did Katya do to the zombie? and was it in quite such a state beforehand? will probably never be answered.

"Okay, the beginning," said the man in the dark suit, pressing his splayed fingertips together, "Where did you first meet Konrad and Katya Karma?"

"Of course, I should never have let him do it," said Generali Romanchacha, blatantly refusing to get down to anything and instead continuing with his own tedious anthology.

"Hmm, okay," said the dark suit, adjusting his shades, "Let's try a different tack. What is your first memory of the Karma non-twins?"

"He always had a talent for..." Romanchacha trailed off as he poured some soap powder into his lager, "Well, I suppose I taught him everything he knew."

The two men were seated opposite each other at a small table on a balcony, somewhere above the grimy, empty streets of Littler Little Havana, England. The sun was peeling off the atmosphere like it was so much cancerous skin, burning down through an utterly unconvincing Liberal Democrat of an ozone layer, boiling the planet's water away into space. In those early days no one suspected Mars, no eyes turned that way, the contracts were still no more than unfelled trees and unextracted octopus guts.

The Generali was a podgy old Cuban ex-soap salesman, decked out in the finest South American Generali clobber; he had practically vanished beneath his stupid great hat, silhouetted against a romantic sunset he could have been mistaken for a decommissioned Polaris submarine, albeit a very short, and quite peculiar Polaris submarine - the sort of Polaris submarine that had been dropped on its sticky-up bit and had bits sawn off and medals and hairbrushes welded across it. In fact, he wasn't much a like a Polaris submarine at all.

Belts of bullets were slung across his shoulders, giving him the appearance of a comprehensively lost Mexican bandit, and his hair was thinning, but he had a special cream for all that bollocks. He probably had a cream for those too.

The man opposite was our ambitious interviewer - cynically left-wing but suitably, fanatically right-wing. He was on his way up, having been given a bigger desk by his boss for the fabulous expose of the illegal trade in the less interesting parts of Norway in return for sexual favours among old people and those bloody little animals that get stuck in your wheels when you're not looking. A nasty gaggle of backbenchers had been caught up in it somehow, but the article had been so cleverly worded that not only could this clever bastard not be sued, but no one had really understood it anyway.

Generali Romanchacha held the glass beneath his nose and inhaled deeply, savouring the bouquet. The dangling ends of his ridiculous grey moustache twitched in the bubbling froth. He seemed to remember the task in hand with a start, and turned his dry, wrinkled face towards the interviewer man. The interviewer man tried to move his finger away from his nostril in a manner that suggested he could have been doing anything except picking his nose. There was no way he had been picking his nose. No way.

"I have known the Karma brother and sister since they were just the little ones," chuckled Romanchacha. "When they were old enough we ran guns across the border together. I used to bounce little Katya on my knee and tell her tales of old gunfighters who roamed the streets of my beloved Havana."

"What is the single most important factor you feel shaped the lives of these living legends?"

Romanchacha's eyes narrowed, "I think it was my effect as their mentor, and my old Mexican records, and the poetry of my gun-running muchachos."

"Hmm."

"And, of course, to grow up in a society that does not care about you, can lead to only one thing - you will not care about the society."

"Whoa! I'm under strict orders not to get deep here."

"What?"

"Oh, I fucking give up. You do better, if you can, you miserable old Stalinshagger."

Romanchacha performed a reflex salute, then grinned feebly, "Excuse me, I am in the habit of it for many weals now. My eyes are most excessively rumbustious, although I find hula fascination wagon petrol clump."

Dizzy tumbleweeds rolled by in the street below, rustling along dry gutters, hopping over the mouldering corpses of half-eaten dogs.

"Perhaps I might have another look at the polaroids?" whispered the interviewer man, leaning across the table.

"I find you start to shit on my nipples," remarked Romanchacha, and he clapped his hands.

The interviewer man tried to protest - nothing could have been further from his mind than the saggy, mossy nipples of the Generali. However, it was too late for that. Two soldiers of the New Cuban Militia marched from the lavish sitting room from which the balcony extended. Out they marched, collected the capitalist lie-mongerer, and away they marched, by the left quick, lefrightlefright, right wheel, halt, take aim, fire. So much for your desk, Mr. Pancreas.

The Generali took a pipe from his pocket, stuffed it with old bits of carpet, and lit it with his genuine Littler Little Havana souvenir silver-plated revolutionary cigar lighter (Made in China). Cigars didn't appeal to him, in truth they really got up his nose, although to have said as much there in the Cuban Sector of Hull would have amounted to high treason. Romanchacha had every intention of living to be a cantankerous, cankerous old goat, up to his neck in whores. Walls and the wrong ends of firing squads weren't really his thing.

Konrad switched channels. Immediately a bridge blew up and a gunfight broke out.

"That's better," Katya said with a grin and she tucked into her cold pizza dinnerama. "Nothing like a good gunfight before bed."

"It's a sight better than some crappy documentary," Konrad agreed. He thought he recognised the bloke in the documentary from somewhere, and although he wasn't sure where, he knew he didn't like him.

Katya did a really stinky fart and nearly died of embarrassment, because she thought she was cultured.

"Fucking hell, sis," Konrad choked, and he passed out, crashing amidst his dinner and half a cup of tea.

"It's this acid," Katya gasped, trying not to breathe. She lobbed away the glass containing the acid. In truth, it was lemonade that had had fungus growing in it for a few weeks, but the end result was as near the same as made no difference.

Katya crammed some pizza topping in each nostril, almost dropping her dinner in surprise as the fart reached the light bulb and ignited.

Konrad eventually regained his senses, "I dunno," he said, "It's like life is just passing me by."

"It's an, uh, illusion," Katya remarked, "After all, if all this bonking's supposed to be so healthy, how come I'm always so fucking shagged out?"

"Pass."

"Yeah, it's all bollocks."

"It was a bloody good idea of mine, bringing the 'fridge in here," Konrad said. He lifted his feet off the 'fridge and opened the door so he could get at the beer.

"Bighead."

"Yeah," Konrad shot the TV before the Nazi firing squad could nail the hero, "I didn't realise it was that film, I hate that film."

"God, you're cool," Katya gasped in amazement as molten TV debris ricocheted around her in a swirling bubble of sanitised, popularised carnage. "You took out the whole bastard firing squad with one fucking shot."

"Easy, sis," Konrad said, trying to gauge the piss-taking factor.

"No, I, uh, mean it. Last time they wasted the good guy."

"Er-"

"Don't argue - I know - I fucking saw it with my own beguiling little peepers. But this time. Oh shit, why do we have to be related?"

"Thanks. I think?"

Are these people heroes? Are they role models? Are they ideal influences for your young ones? Are they cool, does their life style appeal to you, are they good citizens? Nah, but they'd make a fucking mess of that tosser with the shot gun, and that bitch Hamilton, Jesus fucking Christ - the things they'd do to her.

5. Sun, Sea, Sand, and How the Aliens' Flip-Flop Theorem was Proved Wrong

Katya Karma got tired of playing with herself, she sat up in the alien bed and reached for the remote control. She started the bed vibrating, then heated up, got it rocking like a Cliff Pilchard concert (except the bed actually showed signs of life), then she put it into Humpomatic Turbo mode and it nearly broke her back. She switched it off and slumped back.

Konrad was sitting at the control panel, poring over the saucer's instruction manual, and generally being worryingly uncool. He said that it was in the interest of future coolness - that he wanted to be sure how everything worked, he wanted to know how to put the top down seeing as the sun was shining and they were out over the nice blue sea where the dolphins and the birds were out.

Katya closed her eyes and pretended that she was somewhere else. She strained really hard, it was difficult using her imagination. It didn't work, it just fizzled out and something went pop, and that was kind of the end of it.

She sighed with resignation and took the blow-up Queen Victoria doll from one of the drawers under the bed and started inflating it. She puffed away until she was quite dizzy. Then she played with that and it beat her - stupid bitch Queen Victoria doll had five fucking aces every time!

Dover was on the horizon, a metropolis of glass and steel, shining in the sun. The yellow stripe of the crowded beach spread along at the feet of the luxurious hotels, the famous Dover Harbour Bridge spanned the slightly toxic, slightly radioactive water, but after the sunbathers had been tanning next to big red drums full of radioactive waste who gave a shit what they were swimming in?

Dover Bay had been built with European money accidentally acquired as a result of a badly worded, poorly translated letter that had originally set out conditions for the export of BSE infected cattle to the Danish - powerful opposers of the Federal Superstate. Now the place stood as a haven for tourists beneath the ozone arsehole, albeit a French-owned haven. They had bought the south-east of what had once been the Land of Eng many years before, although Dover had been won in a card game.

Now the thunder of cannons troubled those clear skies, and smoke rose through the haze away in the east, as the British Independence Army started driving those French chaps into the sea! At least that was the plan. They were actually just blowing the crap out of a hill that had looked at them funny.

The tourists lazed under smears of pungent cream, utterly unimpressed by the sounds of not-so-distant warfare. They hardly noticed the large green saucer thing that floated low overhead, thinking it must be a novelty balloon, or an ice-cream, or something. They didn't even think it was very odd as it came down lower over them and caused their skin to turn a strange shade of grey and flake off in scabby ashes.

The saucer landed in a nice spot on the beach, although it was a bit messy - what with the entrails of those who had just been squashed beneath it, but large green saucer things can't be choosers, as the old Weirderon adage put it. The ramp lowered and out strolled Konrad and Katya Karma, with Bermuda shorts and gaudy T-Shirts and nice, smart sun hats and some slightly cool shades. They were laden with various inflatable things, a portable fridge and a bucket and spade. Stopping on the shady sand beneath the overhang of the saucer they looked around at the masses of middle-aged, pot-bellied, sunburned, face-lifted, bastard-geek-scum. They were surrounded by these things from the Braindead Zone, these fat-arsed, useless shitheads whose most worthy feature was their ability to die at forty from a heart attack. Built-in obsolescence. DON'T DENY YOUR STRESS!

"I love the seaside," said Katya, and she threw what she was carrying into the air and dived into the sand head first. Needless to say, she didn't go very far.

"Don't get caught in the undertow, sis," said Konrad, in a square-jawed, laid back, cool sort of way, while Katya crashed down like a felled tree.

A fat bloke with those shades with the pointed corners glanced in their direction. He had a radio aerial sticking out of his head and newsprint on his nose that said, 'Blow Me!' His podgy hand groped along the sand, over the rotting crab and the lice-infested seaweed, and found his beer can. He gripped it, his face brightened slightly now that he was whole again. He lifted the can to his mouth and swigged and regretted it somewhat upon discovering that a radioactive chainsaw-wielding limpet had found its way into his beer.

As her husband gagged and choked and started to vomit blood as his neck gradually opened up to the outside world with considerable gushes of blood before his head inevitably fell off, and rolled away towards the sea where a group of little kiddies mistook it for a beach ball and started kicking it around, Mrs Fatbitch found she had a troubling thought. She extended two fingers, as in that classic gesticulation, their long, sharp, red nails gleaming in the sun. She rammed them up to the knuckles into her nostrils and wiggled them around, and that put an end to the troubling thought.

Meanwhile one of their kids was busy impaling the other with cricket stumps, but then the antagonist got attacked by mutie three-eyed killer sea gulls with razor-beaks. Eyeballs and a tongue and various other odds and ends scattered among drops of blood on that dreamy yellow sand. Even in the radioactive hell of Dover Harbour Tourist Resort there was a kind of justice.

"I hate the seaside," muttered Katya Karma, sitting up, brushing down her 'I sucked Elvis,' T-shirt, and spitting out sand and discarded corn plasters.

Konrad shook one of the blankets he carried, then he set it down on the sand and settled on it with a French arty-farty book.

"What's cool about that?" Katya inquired, apparently not worried about a crab with a claw the size of a JCB as it trundled up the leg of her shorts.

"Everything," replied Konrad, his eyes following the crab, "Y'see, my gun's right here beside me, so it's like a juxtaposition of a sixties arty book and a contemporary armour-piercing hand gun. Oh, and I don't know any French."

"Yiiiiiiiiiiiikes!" screamed the crab, scuttling from the shorts in such a hurry it even forgot to go sideways.

"What the hell was that about?" inquired Konrad, watching the crab head for the dunes.

"I guess it found my tattoo," said Katya, picking up her shades from where they lay on the sand and putting them on. She smiled at Konrad as she saw him frowning, then she looked over the throng around them.

Fifty yards away, embedded in the crush of deck chairs, blankets, parasols and wind-breaks, was an ice cream van. It was a slightly rusty white van, with a big,

big sign on top featuring a cartoon character that looked not unlike a disfigured garden gnome with four sit-on lawnmowers jammed down its trousers and a thirteen ton coach parked on its face. Corporate logos ain't what they used to be.

"Konrad," said Katya, in her bestest, most politest tone, "Buy me an ice-cream, huh? Please, please, please, I'll be your best friend for ever and ever."

"I would, sis, but I've got no money. This book must be amazing if you speak French - assuming this word means murder, 'cause it's full of it."

"What word's that?"

"'Merd,'" said Konrad.

"Dunno, sorry," said Katya, and she flung some loose change at him.

There must have been a lot of people on that there blue-green Earth place with only the one flip-flop, as any aliens reflected as they lay under the ultra-violet radiation-bath that was the star Sol. After all, just about everyone knew that every hundred yards or so on any beach you'll find a flip-flop. You'll never find two though, so the aliens had a point.

As Konrad strolled across the sand he didn't notice the flip-flops, abandoned and lonely - that would have been far too uncool. Instead he concentrated on picking his way between the bloated sun worshippers. They all muttered and tutted as he passed, and thought he was Australian just because he had corks hanging from his hat. He tried to be careful where he put his 'fucking great boots,' as one person described them.

"Thanks," Konrad had replied, "I think they're pretty cool myself."

He strolled on, past executives and corporate management types, all letting their guts hang out and getting some air flowing through those flabby creases with the nicotine stains. They were all drinking beer and passing wind, while the scrawny, dowdy, beer-gutted wives read through magazines with swathes and splodges of pink on the cover and articles inside that gave guidelines on how to act like you can think for yourself and how to pretend you are your own person.

What was worse, far, far worse, was the fact that while all these overpaid ponces were sunning themselves on the beach their German executive-mobiles were being removed from the hotel car park by shady Londoners with leather balaclavas.

Konrad zig-zagged on, gradually drawing nearer to the tatty old ice-cream van. He saw there was a queue; a couple of lady pensioners with string bikinis and purses full of pennies, a tubby punk with a green Mohican and rivets in his skull, a couple of gorgeous chicks with not very much on, and a coach party of retired comedians.

Konrad stood at the back of the queue for a moment, then he took his gun from where it was tucked in his shorts and shot them all. The bodies fell neatly to either side with not too much blood spilling from the rather cool, smoking bullet holes.

He stepped up to the ice-cream van, the man inside leaned forwards, his white ice-cream man's uniform gleamed in the sun, his little white hat was slightly askew on his dandruff-laden hair. He was a miserable chap, his face was engraved with deep, disapproving furrows, his eyebrows buckled down over his eyes into a stare that could melt lead. Behind him were shelves stacked with packets of cornets and lollipop sticks, and there were posters and stickers of all the lovely, colourful, frozen additives that could be purchased.

Something caught Konrad Karma's eye, he slid his shades down his nose a little and peered over the top. The rectangular badge that said, 'call me Ice-Cream Man' was slightly crooked. Even as Konrad watched it moved a little and swivelled down, revealing another badge beneath. This one was much less friendly. It said, 'call me Orderly Frank and I might not break both your legs.'

Orderly Frank's eyes glanced down to where Konrad was looking, the bulky psychomaniac saw that he was rumbled and reached for the forty-gigawatt plasma cannon that was hidden in the flakes.

Blam!

Konrad had raised his gun and pulled the trigger, the orderly's uniform sprouted a little patch of red in the abdomen, Orderly Frank flinched and stumbled back.

Blam!

Konrad fired again, aiming higher, the uniform ruptured somewhere near the heart, a gob of blood blasted from the back and spattered over the raspberry ripples. The orderly started to slump down.

Blam!

Just as his head was about to drop from sight Konrad shot one last time for the multi-bonus, in the same instant the man's forehead disappeared into a rupturing bloody mass and a few pints of something disgusting blasted out across the interior of the van.

There was movement behind Konrad and he turned to see orderlies rising up left, right and centre from the queue that he had massacred. Then it hit him.

"Should have known," he muttered, "Comedians never retire. They just go on, and on, and on, and on..."

The orderlies were wearing anti-armour-piercing-bullet-armour, they leaped up, toting double-barrelled plasma cannons.

"Throw down your gun," one shouted, as they all took aim at Konrad.

"Okay," said Konrad, and he dropped his gun on the sand.

Then he took another gun from his shorts - an anti-anti-armour-piercing-bullet-armour-gun.

"Suit yourself, you sister-fucking incestopath," growled the speaker.

They were a grim battalion - the Ministry of Uncool's finest. They all had scars and burns and funny stories from previous encounters with criminally insane scum. They had all been in the inner cities, they didn't know how to die.

Konrad started shooting, empty cartridges landing in the sand in rather cool slow-motion. His gun spat fire and death while all around the tourists screamed and ducked behind sand castles and plates of chicken drumsticks. The menacing muzzles of the plasma cannons roared in reply, a rapid-fire blaze of super-heated death screamed out across the beach.

Konrad dodged away to one side, shooting the whole time, then he ducked down behind an obese gentleman whose head promptly vaporized with the smell of blood and overcooked brain.

One by one the orderlies fell as they turned to fire at their target. As he weaved through the tourists, and the innocents got wasted with maximum carnage, he continued blasting away. The first orderly received a lobotomy, the next a heart bypass, the third got castrated. Konrad was clinical. Steadily the white-clad bodies began to heap up, one of the remaining few grabbed a radio and called for the helicopter.

From the sky came the armoured machine, down low over the sand, whipping it up across the blood and the bodies, then it turned away, thudding out over the sea, and those orderlies who hadn't perished in the confrontation were in it.

"Chickenshits," muttered Konrad, taking a picnic hamper from a family size collection of smoking flip-flops.

And so the aliens' flip-flop theorem was proved wrong - because here were several pairs of perfectly abandoned flip-flops.

Konrad didn't notice, he didn't give a shit, he just dragged the hamper back towards where the large green saucer thing was sitting on an increasingly empty beach.

The sea broke in pure, white breakers and lapped up the virgin sands while the gulls circled: free, untamed spirits. Then Katya opened her eyes and saw the cardigan-brown waves slopping onto shit-stained sand while the gulls were fighting over a sanitary towel they had found.

"Where did everyone go?" she asked Konrad as he strolled up and she noticed the emptying beach.

"Search me," said Konrad, "Maybe they're looking for ice-cream. The guy over there only had raspberry ripples, and I know how much you hate raspberries."

"Yeah, like, puke," said Katya, sticking her fingers into her mouth.

"So I got this," Konrad dumped the hamper down, the lid fell open, and inside was revealed a feast fit for the fattest, most grossly overpaid executive road hog who might find his way into the fast lane of the M1, wheels on fire and classical crap smoking from the speakers.

"Oh, is that all?" asked Katya, grabbing armfuls of whatever came to hand with a 'gimme, gimme, gimme' gleam in her eye.

"Had a bit of hassle," said Konrad, settling back down on his blanket, "The Ministry of Uncool seem to miss me."

"What? They were here? You mean there was a fight and I didn't get to shoot anything?" asked Katya, her gob full of chicken drumsticks and beer.

"I'm sure they'll oblige you with a gratuitous gunfight."

"They fucking better."

Just then two badly disguised blue aliens sidled up, peering beneath shades and towels and inflatable sea monsters. The aliens were short and round, they were badly bruised which seemed to suggest they'd had a long day and had been mistaken for beach balls more than once.

The first poked his hooter-like mouth under his towel and whispered with a heavy accent.

"Blip-blop, are you B and N?"

Its partner peered around them, checking no one was watching.

"Er, what?" asked Katya, looking down to where Lester the Alien was lying under his own little parasol.

"Blip-blop, we look for B and N. If you see them tell them mutant spiders from Mars are coming! Tell them eleven weeks! Tell them all life extinguished! Tell them no hope for pretty little planet Earth. Tell them only Weirderon technology able to stop such onslaught. Tell them Weirderons not for hire! Tell them it's all over!"

The alien who had spoken started away across the sand, the other lingered for a moment to look around again.

"Are you, like, looking down my T-shirt?" asked Katya, and she bopped the blue bugger one and watched it bounce off across the sand as its associate chased it.

Katya stood in disgust, assembled her things, and headed back up the ramp, "Can't go anywhere without getting molested these days - first the bloody crab and then some bloody blue aliens."

"Hmm?" murmured Konrad, far too cool to indulge in such hallucinations.

6. Traffic Jam Bam Thank Y'Ma'am

The Dime Bar stood on an island amid the smog and traffic of the heart of the city. All around, twenty-four hours a day, the traffic roared and choked, always thundering by. Through sun or rain or the thickest of nights the steel creatures hustled and barged around the chevron-adorned shore. The diesel wind of their passing shook a line of forlorn bushes just inside this border, and made the rubbish dance where it had gathered on the filter lane which turned in and led to the car park that was seldom used. There was just an old, old wheelie bin, the remains of a motorbike, and several large patches of oil.

The building itself was a prefabricated something that had seen a bit of customising with the arrival of new owners. Now the place looked like a filthy grey-brown box, slightly squashed, with small windows, some broken, some boarded up, and a large red sign that only worked when it felt like it. Before it had just been brown. A paved area led up to a couple of bright yellow litter bins standing either side of the door, beyond the doors a dark space opened out.

This was a haven for shadowy, shifty types with leather jackets and interesting tattoos. They hung around, well away from the inadequate, blue fluorescent lights, lurking in the smoke that swirled beneath two broken ceiling fans. The barman was a chain smoker - he had to be - there were never enough people there any more to keep the place good and smoky. He leaned on the counter and puffed away, three fags in his mouth, his eyes bloodshot and glazed, his shirt stained with beer and mustard, his gut was talking to itself. He raised an eyebrow, then dropped it, for no reason in particular.

Away across the room, past a couple of pool tables and an arcade machine, a collection of scum had assembled around a table. On the table were playing cards, bottle tops, beer cans, an overpopulated ash tray, money for the waitress, and a dodgy video. There were five men here, five men from different parts of the city, meeting to discuss what to do now that The Commuter had found out they'd ripped him off. The Commuter was crime boss, king of the underworld, and a keen collector of spleens, which he kept in jars in his luxuriously sinister apartment atop

Goth Towers.

The five men spoke in growling, hushed voices, all leaning in slightly, all glancing furtively from one face to the next. The first man was Ted 'Trip-out' Throatcutter, a body builder with a scar-hatched face and a sour expression set with cold, black eyes. He wore biker's leathers, with an array of cut-throat razors tucked into various straps and loops, he drew long and hard on his cigarette, looked at the others, and flicked the ash into the ashtray.

"Don't ask me," he growled, "I ain't no fuckin' rocket scientist."

The second man sighed a little and eased himself back in his chair. He was Harry Henchman, slightly smaller than Ted, with white, slicked-back hair and shades with round blue lenses. He was covered in an old black leather coat, the lapels were drawn up around his neck and he seemed to be hunched down into their cover. His face was pale and seemed to be carved from stone.

"Don't need no rockets," he muttered, "Need a goddamn miracle."

The third man's shoulders rose with a half laugh, then he flicked the top from a beer bottle with his thumb and took a swig. From the bottle's label purple letters screamed 'Thumb's up!" and beneath there was a picture of a chick with no clothes and her thumb up her backside. This third man was Mad Mummah, a muscle-bound gym bunny dressed as an urban commando, with a large automatic hand gun hanging from his belt.

"Rockets'd do it," he said, "Plenty of big, bad, fuckin' rockets."

The fourth man glanced up at Mad Mummah, then he took the bottle and swigged the beer. This was T.K. - dressed in a smart suit, wearing fashionable glasses, and with an air of authority among those lowlifes, and a fondness for poison darts – twenty-millimetre rocket-propelled poison darts.

"Twenty millimetres," he said, passing the bottle back to Mad Mummah. "Twenty-millimetre poison rocket with hooks on its arse just to make a bit more mess when it comes out the other side. Rocket and miracle all in the one."

They all looked to the fifth man. He had sat silently, listening to the debate, steadily smoking his way through a packet of cigars. He leaned forwards slightly and grinned so that his hydraulic gold teeth gleamed in the light. His eyes sparkled too, with an insane thirst for violence and death. His hair was long and greasy and black, it straggled down over his shoulders, he took a small box from the breast pocket of his ragged suit and set it down on the table.

"No fuckin' need, boys," he said, "No fuckin' need. I got it all inna bag."

This was Boss Burger, as the tattoo across his forehead stated. He patted the box while the others stared at it, wondering what could be so little and yet hold the answer to all their problems.

"Don't look like no fuckin' rocket," said Mad Mummah.

"Looks like some dumbfuck engagement-ring-box-thing or somethin'," said Harry Henchman.

"You gettin' married, man?" asked Ted Throatcutter.

Boss Burger didn't answer, he just opened the box and watched the expressions of the others as they saw the contents.

"What the fuck's that?" asked T.K.

"Some fuckin' arse implant, like on that T.V. show, huh?" suggested Mad Mummah.

"You stoopid fucks," said Ted Throatcutter, "It's, like, a limpet mine, right Boss?"

"What?" murmured Harry Henchman, as he woke up.

Ted Throatcutter took a razor from his coat, he put his other hand flat on the table and stabbed it. He looked puzzled for a moment, then he pulled the razor out and put it back in his jacket.

"When you're all quite fuckin' finished," said Boss Burger, slightly annoyed, "It's a microfilm, right? It's a fuckin' incriminatin' evidence thing. See what I'm sayin'?"

Boss Burger grinned with his mechanical teeth, but the others just frowned back at him.

"So what?" asked T.K.

"Yeah, like, how the fuck's that gonna help?" asked Mad Mummah.

"'Cause if anyone ever sees this," said the Boss, closing the box and putting it back in his coat, "He ain't gonna have one shred of credibility left to his name. Y'see on this film is photos of our mutual friend. If this film ever went public everyone'd know what a pussy he really is - like, what a grade 'A' fluffy pink muff. You see what I'm sayin'?"

"So he'll kill us anyway and get it back," said Ted.

"Put it in a safe place, right Boss?" said T.K., "Like with a solicitor or somethin'. And then when summat happens it goes public."

"Somethin' like that," said the Boss, "Well? Whaddya think?"

Harry Henchman took a packet of nails from his pocket and emptied some into his hand. He replaced the packet and started chewing on the nails.

"Er, like, if it works then I guess it's a masterstroke," said Mad Mummah.

"Whaddya mean 'if'?" asked the Boss.

"Well, our mutual friend is, kind of, a head case," said T.K.

A wisp of smoke curled up from Boss Burger's cigar, he sat back again and fell silent.

"Well, it's all we got," said Mad Mummah, "Seein' as how shootin' the bastard never got no one nowhere."

"Goddamn indestructible," Harry Henchman agreed.

"Goddamn indestructible fluffy pink muff," said T.K.

"Goddamn indestructible fluffy pink muff with a Harris F1 with no wheels that's been converted into a three-bladed chainsaw with 'I Eat Pussy' written on it," said Ted 'Trip-out' Throatcutter.

"What the fuck are you on, man?" asked Harry Henchman, then he turned to where Ted was staring.

One by one they all turned. There in the doorway were three figures. Over by the counter the barman had vanished, although smoke was still billowing up from behind it. But no one cared about that - they cared about Xeno and Alpha and The Commuter. Elsewhere in the shadows, where the broken tips of pool cues rested in the dust, those few punk biker misfits who had been present had vanished without so much as a rattle of a chain or a squeak of leather.

Boss Burger's cyberteeth clenched with fury and fear, he bit off the tip of the cigar in that same action, the smouldering thing dropped to the floor and shed embers and ashes onto the tiles. Mad Mummah pawed at the hand gun in his belt, but couldn't quite get up the balls to use it.

Xeno and Alpha moved away and took up highly provocative poses on the nearest pool table. They were tall, slim bimbos wearing little more than a few leather straps. They were the Commuter's babes - they loved to perform for their boss in the comfort of his dark and eerie apartment. Now they provided him with a nice, familiar backdrop for the carnage that was about to follow, tossing back their bleached manes, pouting and posing.

The Commuter strolled towards the table, a big man in black, wearing a long coat that just about reached the floor. Beneath were battle-scarred leathers, on his feet were mock-croc boots with Cuban heels. His face was a landmark of interesting scars - each had its story and he remembered each with unflinching detail. He carried, as Ted had observed, a modified motorcycle with three chainsaw blades and the words 'I Eat Pussy' painted along the side. He wore mirrored shades, but those at the table knew his steel-grey eyes were watching them with that cold hate that emanated from every fibre of his body.

"You've been bad boys," he said, his voice was like a razor sliding over stone, "Bad, bad boys."

Mad Mummah finally got the courage to go for his gun. In the same instant, The Commuter revved up what had once been a motorbike and swung it. The three blades of whirring titanium teeth were suddenly reddened as that grim instrument arced above the table, severing Mad Mummah from one of his arms, several ribs, and a few stringy bits of something. The severed flesh flapped as the maimed man tried to dodge away, the exposed ribs beneath just showed in the blue light before they were engulfed in the pulsing redness. As the machine cut into him again there was the crunching of bones, Mad Mummah screamed, and the blades went right through. The corpse fell back, the chair went too, and the impact with the floor dislodged ripped internal organs that fell onto the cold tiles amid a dull red sludge.

"Acid indigestion can be a real shitter," said The Commuter, hoarsely, "Who's next?"

They looked at each other. The girls on the pool table were playing with each other's straps, The Commuter was towering above them, the thunder of the chainsaw filled their heads. In their minds was the one image - of Mad Mummah being shredded and split open like an orange. They looked to Boss Burger, who usually had all the answers, but he was pale and plainly shitting himself. The seconds passed slowly, their throats were dry, hands trembling, minds jammed up while they tried to think of something, of anything. The Commuter's hands twitched on the throttle. They all knew he only had so much patience. Ted ran a hand to one of his razors, T.K. straightened his tie. The teeth of the chainsaw blurred before their eyes.

Wham!

Something was slammed down onto the table, even The Commuter started a little at the noise.

"There's your bill, and, uh, no more fucking mess, huh? Someone's got to clear that up."

Ted 'Trip-out' Throatcutter, Harry Henchman, T.K., Boss Burger, Xeno, Alpha, and the Commuter all looked to the blue-haired waitress in the waitress outfit with the label showing. They couldn't read it but it actually said, 'Skimpy Outfits 'R' Us.' The Commuter looked over the low-cut top with the show of cleavage and down to the miniskirt, below which were toned thighs and stocking tops and a slither of white knicker crotch.

Thwack!

He got a size eight D.M. for his troubles, right in the personal messages department. The chainsaw thing flew from the big man's grasp as his face went blue and he doubled over. The three whirring blades whipped down through Boss Burger, scattering hydraulic gold teeth and bones and blood and all the rest of it far across the floor.

As Katya Karma forced her knee into The Commuter's face he just had time to reflect that it really was the sexiest knee he had ever seen. Then his face got dislocated and everything went black. Meanwhile the massive chainsaw that reputedly ate pussy had carved its way along the table top, gouged out a hole through Ted Throatcutter, and was making its getaway across the floor.

"Don't bother with a tip," said Katya, sarcastically, because they hadn't.

She cleared up the ashtray and empties and strutted back towards the bar, sulking at having been molested yet again. As she passed behind the bar she set the things down on the counter top and joined the slightly overweight gentleman on the floor behind it. He offered her a fag, she declined, saying she had the sexiest lungs in the Land of Eng and she wanted to keep them that way.

"Fucking tourists," said the barman.

"Only if I'm desperate," said Katya, sticking the end of a beer bottle in her lovely, angelic navel and flicking it out so that the top came off.

She handed it to the barman and opened another for herself. From beyond the counter came the sounds of renewed violence, although it seemed that the survivors of the five at the table were beating the shit out of each other, while Xeno and Alpha helped The Commuter back to their armoured van, where it was waiting in the car park with the punk chained to the radiator.

"Fucking tourists," the barman said again, swigging down that cool, relaxing, gut-swelling brew of chemicals.

Suddenly there was a dizzying collection of spiralling, circular, multi-coloured lights, all whizzing around. Then a voice came, a strange, alien voice.

"This is the voice of the Weirderons," it said, "Get your fucking arse in gear, sis, and don't keep me waiting."

"That'll be Konrad," said Katya, getting up.

"Half three already?" murmured the barman, looking at his imitation Bollex.

"See ya Thursday," said Katya, strolling off towards the door, beyond which she could see the large green saucer thing, ramp down, hovering over the car park.

As Katya stomped into the saucer Konrad flicked the switch that raised the ramp and drove along the exit road. Katya dived into the junk that was accumulating down between the bed and the microwave. She changed from her waitress outfit and back into her usual jeans and skin-tight T-shirt.

"Uh, Konrad?" she said, noticing they were following traffic down a busy city street, vaporizing anything that decided to tailgate them with their atomic exhaust, "What are you, like, doing?"

"Nice day for a drive," said Konrad, turning on the stereo, "Nice day to cruise the busy city streets, to turn the Zaupunkt up full, to listen to that bass shake those cooling rods until warning lights start to flash all over the place."

The many lanes of traffic down between the towering office blocks and terraces hardly seemed out of place with a large green saucer thing sliding by. The pedestrians didn't seem to notice, the shoppers out in the sun, the buskers, the homeless chaps and chappettes, none of them really noticed. Out among the lorries and the buses, growling and spewing black fumes, out there racing with the executive-mobiles and the family hatchbacks where the kids on the back seat were busy killing each other with teddy bears, out there in all of that no one noticed the Weirderon saucer. Except the few who started across the pedestrian crossing before Konrad had quite got the hang of the brakes.

It was mayhem on the streets. The vehicles jostled and crowded, trying to get past everything in front and trying to keep everything else behind. It was a hot day, the chicks were out with not very much on and Konrad could have perhaps paid a little more attention to the road, but who cares about a few street lights and the front window of a public relations consultant?

Katya rapidly got bored with sitting in a traffic jam so she grabbed a convenient gas mask, opened the top hatch, hauled herself out and settled down on the roof with Lester the Alien, a radio, and a Lithuanian Buttwash cocktail. Occasionally she got up and ripped bits off anyone's car who whistled at her or shouted obscene remarks. She even had to remind Konrad that people drove on the left in that particular part of the world, as he veered off towards the supple sheen of feminine flesh.

"Sorry, sis," he said, "I think I'm still suffering from a tinge of uncoolness."

As they passed a police car Katya reached out and wrenched the light cluster, a particularly impressive, roof-width light cluster, from the roof and, with Zelotape - the real stuff! - and a little imagination, she stuck it to the roof of the saucer. Now they looked really cool, in her opinion at any rate.

And so they went on, sometimes moving, mostly stuck in traffic, with Konrad's tape in the Zaupunkt churning out some rather cool music, which set everyone in the streets a-dancing and a-singing as though they'd just walked into a bloody musical.

"I hate musicals," Katya said to Lester the Alien, "Fucking hate 'em. All that grinning and dancing and singing and shit. I just, like, think, you know, shut the fuck up and kill and rape and maim each other, or something."

The people in the streets didn't appear to share the sentiment, although the words they decided to apply and the origins of the satire were far from their cool roots in Konrad's noisy little cassette.

> We're all goin' on a
> Weirderon holiday,
> No more bullshit for a
> While at least

> And we all live in a
> Green saucy-saucer,
> A green saucy-saucer,
> A green saucy-saucer

> And you see our problem,
> 'Cause nothing really rhymes
> And nothing really fits,
> And we're all happy and sunny and shit

> And we all live in a
> Green alien saucer,
> A green saucy-saucer,
> A green saucy-saucer

Katya shot a few people and that seemed to shut them up. Some of them still did synchronised dancing and twirling things in the streets and selling red roses and all of that delightful business. A few managed marvellous displays of tap dancing and swinging around street lights but they soon got bored and went home for a bit of sado-masochistic sex with the MP for Westhampton On Sea.

Some of them passed down a certain dingy alley, where bins gathered in the shadows. A single door stood in the side wall, above it was a vandalised sign which had once read, 'Doctor Dickhead, for all your criminal needs' but now it said, 'Wankah! Pete was 'ere! Arse lickerz!'

A van was pulled up by the door, a dark, dusty van whose owner had deemed armour plates and welding to be the answer to the persistent problem of rust. Steel racing trim was riveted along the thing's length, wire mesh spanned glassless windows, something under the bonnet clanked as it cooled. Along the side of the van graffiti was scrawled, most was illegible among clusters of bullet holes, all of it was obscene, except for the single most common line for budding road warriors from here to Scunthorpe; 'Stop me and buy one.' A makeshift turret on the roof was pierced by a cannon barrel, and two machine gun muzzles protruded from the radiator - this commuter was prepared. A punk sat, dejected, on the bonnet, a chain ran from his neck to the radiator.

Beyond the door was a waiting room, flies buzzed around, pestering the miserable few who were waiting on chairs by the walls. There was the reek of urine and decay in the air, and the noise of traffic and occasional screams from the door with the doctor's name on it.

On the chairs, there was a bank robber who had had half his head blown off by a particularly nasty cheeseburger, there was a mugger who had an umbrella up his arse after accosting the wrong granny, there was a rapist with a small jar who had attacked Edwina Knife-fingers, there was a car thief who had put his head in the fag lighter, just to see if it worked. And there were two young ladies wearing just a few leather straps, trying to remember Pi to thirty decimal places.

Beyond the door The Commuter was sitting in the doctor's chair, having his face repositioned with the help of a vice and a sledgehammer. The doctor was a sentimental fellow, all around that dusty room, under the barred window, scattered on shelves among bizarre and repulsive instruments, there were little mementos - bits of former patients he had kept to keep him company in his autumn years.

"A little more..." said the doctor, taking a swing with the hammer that suggested he was a keen golfer, "On this side. Hmm, no a little too much. A bit on the other side...oh dear, a little too far up. Oops, where did that go?"

The doctor got down on his hands and knees and squinted through his glasses, trying to locate The Commuter's nose.

"Fucking get on with!" The Commuter shouted, "I've got a score to settle."

The doctor fiddled with this, adjusted that.

"Nearly there," he said, replacing the top of the Megaglue tube, "Now, you might experience difficulty in cold weather, and discomfort if it rains. Also, Radio Four might interfere with your sinuses, but it might not."

The doctor bandaged his patient's head and replaced the shades on the outside, The Commuter jumped out of the chair and headed for the door, past the trolley of bloodied, improvised surgical instruments.

"Consider me not killing you for being such a boring old wanker your payment for services rendered," The Commuter said, and he swept from the room.

In the waiting room, the car thief was dragged away by the doctor, a moment later the screaming started. Meanwhile Xeno and Alpha had their arms around their beloved boss, they rubbed themselves against him, whispering and crooning.

"We got to go, babes," he said, looking first to Xeno, then to Alpha, "We got to go get that bitch with the blue hair."

"How will we find her?" asked Xeno.

"We'll go round that shit-hole Dime Bar place and see who knows what."

"What if they don't know anything?" asked Alpha.

"Babe, babe, don't you believe in destiny? It's my destiny to get that blue-haired bitch and -"

"Can we play with her?" asked Xeno.

"That last one you gave us is broken," said Alpha.

"It's her fault, " said Xeno, "She tried to fuck it with a-"

"Babes, time is pressing, shut the fuck up shift!" said The Commuter, and he led the way into the alley.

Xeno and Alpha were unchaining the punk when The Commuter growled something and they looked up in time to see a large green saucer thing with police lights on top stuck in traffic at the end of the alley. But it wasn't the saucer that The Commuter was interested in - it was the girl with the blue hair who was standing on the roof, bending over and pointing the 'Bugger me, Baby!' seat of her jeans at anyone who took her fancy.

Katya Karma had just sat back down and picked up her cocktail when she heard a commotion in the street behind. She looked back and saw an armoured van crashing through the traffic, knocking vehicles from its path amid showers of broken glass and the occasional flying corpse. Then guns on the van opened fire and the hull of the Weirderon craft was peppered with lead. Katya grabbed Lester, dived for the hatch and closed it behind her.

"Hello, sis," said Konrad, not looking up from the controls, "Too hot out?"

"Shut the fuck up and drive! Fly! Go!" she shouted, ripping off the gas mask.

"Get a grip, baby, and, like, elaborate."

"See that?" said Katya, jabbing a finger at the van on the view screen, "I kind of met that lot at work today."

"No shit," murmured Konrad, "Did you spill their beer?"

"No, I just, uh, kicked the bastard in the 'nads and introduced him to my knee."

"What-"

"Plus, I chainsawed up his friends and stuff."

"What would you like me to do about it?" asked Konrad, swivelling the chair to face his sister.

"Save me!"

"I haven't saved you now for at least an hour," he said, "I suppose another rescue is due."

"Just fuck off and do it."

"Why? We're bullet proof. I have to admit the rattattatting is a little irritating..."

"Whatever. But, uh, all these people shooting at me is having a derogatory effect on my self-esteem."

Konrad looked back at the view screen and said nothing for a moment.

"I suppose we could just, sort of, take off," he said at last, "And leave them down here swearing and getting very angry and uncool."

"We could," said Katya, flopping down on the bed and closing her eyes.

"Or we could go out there and kill the bastards and make them think twice about shooting at the Karma non-twins," Konrad went on.

"You could," Katya agreed, "'Cause I've, like, come over all tired suddenly."

She yawned and stretched.

"You'd probably get your stupid arse shot off anyway," said Konrad, as he stood up and got his gun from on top of the autoslime machine.

He crossed over to the hatch and opened it, just in time to see the sole of a big, bad boot, obscure everything as it smacked down and put him out cold. He fell into a crumpled, but cool, heap.

"Hey, babe, feeling sleepy?" said The Commuter to Katya, as his head popped down through the hatch.

He produced a strange gun with several miniature radar dishes on the end. He pulled the trigger, everything went psychedelic, then there were circles everywhere, swimming and throbbing, and then Katya Karma was quite perfectly unconscious indeed.

When Konrad Karma regained consciousness he quickly got his mind straight, despite the pneumatic headache and the boot print on his face. He managed to prioritise as well, and headed for the 'fridge for a can of something toxic. He relaxed with his feet up on the control panel, swigging cold poison, and taking his time about it. Then, seeing as his sister was in mortal danger of torture and death and videos of the celestial Bob Monkhouse, he decided he had better act swiftly and decisively. Just as soon as he made up his mind what to do.

Fortunately, and rather cunningly, Katya Karma had a tracking device implanted in her left ahem and Konrad Karma had a scanner concealed in his watch, which was disguised as a very ordinary, useless watch. In fact, it was a very ordinary, useless watch, apart from the satellite navigation system which meant he could locate his sister's ahem whatever the weather.

He activated the scanner and his watch's display turned blue. It printed a few numbers, a couple of circles, and a line, which, generally speaking, pointed in the direction of a point in space just a little to one side of Katya Karma's perfumed ahem.

"Zoop," said the watch, "Zoop. Zippy-zoop!"

Then it got really excited and loud so Konrad threw it on the floor and stamped on it because his headache was really killing him. There was something about Katya's undeniably firm ahem always made that watch go crazy.

"Shit, that sounded like something by George Michael," he muttered, and set about seeing if the Weirderon computer could track his sister's ahem a little more quietly than his watch had been able to.

"Zeep! Zappata! Zenga-zambastes-zonnicronum!!!" the computer buzzed, and so it went on.

So with his head ringing to the cries of the drooling computer and with the parking ticket that the large green saucer thing had earned Konrad eased the Weirderon vessel up into the azure sky, and away from the swarming traffic.

In the street two old men in suits, both holding brown paper bags full of shopping and dirty magazines, watched the large green saucer thing rise up.

"Bloody foreigners," said one.

"Bloody blood-sucking, slant-eyed bastards," said the other.

"Bloody bastard, baby-eating foreigners," said the first.

"Bloody smelly, bastard, in-breeding, voodoo foreigners," said the second.

"Aye, but did you see that bastard, smelly, foreign bird with the skin-tight green T-shirt?" asked the first.

"By 'eck!" said the second, "What a rump she had on 'er, eh?!?"

They parted and went their separate ways towards home and orange tea cosies.

Konrad watched the view screen as the city opened up beneath him into little more than a sprawling road map. It was about then that he was accosted by the little orange cactus with the sombrero that stood in a small black pot on a row of lockers along the wall. It had been overlooked as just another part of the Weirderon junk, much of which had been thrown out over Battersea, but now the computer's babbling had woken it up. It stared at Konrad with orange-shot eyes, while the human stared back, wondering if it was a spare, although rather small, scalding spiky marrow.

"Hey, hey, senor," it said, "What's happenin'? Where's senor Vworpasnedig?"

"Er, what?" said Konrad, taking a rather cool flight path through a convenient billboard.

"'E's a, 'ow you say, big alien bastard," said the cactus, unfolding an arm from between two of its spiky ridges.

"Oh, right, the Weirderon, huh? I had to kill him," said Konrad, "He was getting tedious."

"Ees no loss," said the cactus, unfolding another arm in time to shrug as it spoke.

"Yeah, right. D'you mind, I'm sort of trying to fly this thing," said Konrad, turning back to the controls and he just avoided a definitely uncool collision with an old folks' home.

"Could have been nasty, senor," said the cactus, twisting and wriggling so that its pot hopped along beneath it, "All those colostomy bags, you know?"

"The same thought had occurred to me," said Konrad, "Say, for an orange alien cactus with no taste in head wear you're pretty cool."

"Thank you, senor, and you right, ees very cold, brrr. So, where we goin'?"

As it spoke the cactus dropped down from the cupboards and started across the floor.

"Even as I speak we're homing in on my sister's ahem which is in hot water, or rather, trouble. She's always had an aversion to baths, must have been the rabies she had as a kid."

"Si, senor, I onnerstand. That ees what the computer he ees on about, yes?"

"Precisely," said Konrad, casting an eye over the directionometer as the arrow quivered slightly off to the right.

The cactus hopped up onto the control panel and surveyed the view screen with interest.

"So how the computer know where your seester's ahem she ees at, senor? If you no mind my asking?"

"Er, it's like an implant," said Konrad, looking back to the view screen now that the distanceometer was reading only fifteen Zappadangs to the target.

"The computer he ees sure excited."

"Sure is."

There it was - the bleak, black concrete tower with a rusting sign that announced it as Goth Towers. It rose up for thirty floors, each lined with dingy, dark windows, except for the penthouse. One half of the top floor was lined with large windows, from behind which the soft blue glow of electric lights was coming as the outside world slowly descended into evening. Beneath that apartment the dwellers lived in filth and shadows, lurking among the reek of their worthless existences and rooms only three feet wide. But in the apartment at the very top was the luxurious but bizarre existence of The Commuter, that number one badass hombre of the city.

Konrad grabbed a can of deodorant and sprayed it up under his shirt, then down his trousers. He chucked the can into the heap of junk where it landed on Katya's waitress outfit. Then he got his hat with the corks and his gun, which he tucked into his belt before returning to the controls.

"So your seester, senor, she ees, like, 'ow you say, a bit of all right?"

"Search me," said Konrad, "As any such conjecture on my part would be an implication of incest, or at least of incestuous tendencies and that would be incriminating and vulgar, not to mention in rather bad taste, and in breach of the law of this very land above which we hover in a large green saucer thing. All I would say is she's the sort of chick who stands in the background and says, 'Bomb' a lot."

"I onnerstand, senor," said the orange cactus, turning its attention to where the penthouse windows had grown larger on the view screen.

The open plan apartment of The Commuter was indeed a bizarre place. It was forever in twilight, with blinds to obscure the daylight, and with the small blue lights on the walls to keep the cold illumination throughout the night. The walls were lined with shelves, upon which stood jars of formaldehyde. Inside that fluid hung shadows, the shadows of human spleens. Further into the room was the furniture, several armchairs, a sofa, and a couple of tables, laid out in a hap-hazard arrangement in the shadows. All had wild curves and sweeping overhangs, all were covered with leather secured with steel rivets. Some had nails sticking from the cushions, just in case there was nothing on the television. The television was a massive, widescreen, Soundsurrounder (tm) affair, although for the time being it just reflected that eerie blue scene.

At one end of the apartment was the bed - a vast, circular hump-pad, on a raised platform above which the enlarged face of a freshly executed soldier made famous by a fanatical photo journalist in some pointless war somewhere stared down from a hologram under its own little lamp. At the opposite end were three large fish tanks, two were lit and inside the fish did what fish do best among the weed and the bubbles (swim, shit and float to the surface, upside down.) The third was not really illuminated as such, a purple fog hung inside, and occasionally anyone who watched might catch a glimpse of a slight movement, of a shadow passing by the glass, of something stirring up the fog.

From the ceiling, several stalactites hung - DIY stalactites to improve the ambience. In places by the shelves there were artefacts, like a mummy that was falling to bits and, frankly, reeked. There were other things, the corpse of a man dug from a peat bog, a rack of heads that had been obtained courtesy of the guillotine which stood not far away. Xeno and Alpha had been practising their morbid face painting on these heads, artists they weren't.

There was a glass case with replicas of various parts of various animals; these were Xeno and Alpha's for when they were left at home with nothing to torture. Which nicely moves us along to the next exhibits. On your left, you will see the combined exercise bike and electrocuter/nipple slicer. On your right is the more commonplace rack, although this particular specimen does feature a number of modifications, such as the thrashing spiky bits and the red ants that are released from these funnels if the victim fails to scream loud enough.

Katya Karma was draped over one of the armchairs, inert and unconscious. A faint smile flickered on her lips as she dreamed. But shit, what a dream!!

"Yeeeeehaaaaahhhhh!!!" she yelled, "Yeeeehaaahh!!"

She whipped the cowboy hat from her head and beat it down on her mount. It was true that as a child she had seen Dr. Strangelove. It was twenty seconds to launch - the biggest, baddest rocketbomb was smouldering away at its arse end, there was a ring of that red/white check pattern round it, and the snarling shark's face just for effect, in case any Ruskies actually saw it coming. Katya Karma's imagination was still firmly lodged in the cold war, or, as the braver people who knew her would say, firmly lodged in the toilet. Ten seconds! She could feel it vibrating now, throbbing and rumbling. Which was hardly surprising, seeing as she was sitting on top of it, legs straddling its smooth tip, jeans and knickers round her ankles, and the draught tickling her where things didn't normally go unless they wanted to get shot a lot

"Yeeeeehaaaahhhh!!!!" she hollered, dropping the hat in order to hang on a bit tighter as the vibrations got positively violent.

Five, four, three, two - smack!

"Wake up, you stupid fucking bitch!"

Katya opened her left eye, the other remained in a confused squint. She saw the bandaged head of something over her, it slapped her again, so hard her earrings fell off and rattled across the floor. She reached up and clutched at the air, like a child chasing a mirage.

"Bomb!" she said, frowning, "Bomb!"

"Shut up," said the bandaged head, followed by the chink of a cigarette lighter.

"Hey. Where's my fucking bomb?" said Katya, sitting up, "What did you do with my fucking bomb?"

"What the fuck have you been smoking, baby?" rumbled the bandaged head, dripping with ice-cold evil.

"You must have seen it," said Katya, "A big white bastard, biiig bastard."

Xeno and Alpha were on the floor, having a quick bout of tongue wrestling, while The Commuter sat down in a nearby chair and surveyed Katya Karma, who was still half asleep and sulking at having lost that bloody bomb.

"You broke my face," said The Commuter, "No one's ever done that before. Now I'm not going to bore you with threats, I'm just going to smoke a little, get a bit drunk, and then see what bits we can pull off you with some pliers. Sounds like fun, wouldn't you say?"

"Uh, sounds about as much fun as playing volley ball in high heels. You sure you didn't see a bomb?"

"Positive, baby," The Commuter blew some smoke rings up at the stalactites.

"This is really going to piss Konrad off," said Katya, "'Cause now he's going to have to rescue me and kill you bastards and everything, and he hates losing sleep just for a bit of violence. So, like, what's up with these two weird bitches?" She pointed down at Xeno and Alpha.

"Don't be nasty," said The Commuter, "It ain't nice. Now stop interrupting, I'm trying to concentrate on my fag."

"Oh, right, sure, sorry," said Katya, getting comfy in the chair, but still taking a moment to dart a couple of suspicious glances at the furthest corners of the room, seeking out the missing bomb.

"Is she nice and soft?" said Xeno, appearing beside the armchair and breathing her smoky bacon flavour breath over Katya.

"Is she ready to be plied with the pain of perversion?" inquired Alpha, appearing at the other side, her breath reeking of creosote.

"Nice alliteration," said Katya, "But no. So fuck off," and she punched with both fists so that the two weird cows crashed over backwards amid stars and tweety birds and broken jaw bones.

"'S almost as much fun as making stains," Katya murmured, cracking her knuckles.

"You realise, of course, that that's only going to turn them on?" murmured The Commuter, grimly amused.

"Are you, like, scabby?" said Katya.

"What?"

"Y'know, scabs. Like big, pus-inflated scabs," she grinned enthusiastically.

"No. I'm an unblemished god of evil. I'm a perfect machine of perfect retribution," said The Commuter, stubbing out his cigarette on the arm of the chair, he stood up and kicked at Xeno and Alpha, "Snap out of it! Get up! It's time to put on some spooky bastard rock crap and strobe lights and see where our inspiration takes us with this virgin canvas."

"There's a virgin in here?" Katya mused.

They put on one of those round black plastic things that people recorded music on in the good old days and started the strobe lights so that the whole weird apartment seemed even less real than before. The floor and the furniture shook to some very bad drums and guitars and the voice of a bloke who sounded like he'd got his bollocks caught in his zip.

The disfigured corpses on the pedestals loomed through the spell of flickering white, their faces twisted and convulsed. The Commuter and his two whores jerked and quivered in odd motions, dancing around, collecting knives and pliers and corkscrews and even a couple of very, very blunt spoons.

Then, in that deafening storm of distortion and blinding strobe, the apartment door broke in, seemingly silently, and jerked to the floor. Konrad appeared there, while the three occupiers scarpered back to where the real weapons were hidden. There was a pause while Konrad made a note on the back of his hand of a cricketing anecdote that had just occurred to him (to add to the likes of 'Having

Annette out the back') then there was a flash of light as his gun went off and Alpha crashed into the glass case with the fake animal parts. She was shredded and diced as she was thrown into, then slipped back out of, the hundreds of jagged glass knives that the case had been broken into, and slumped to the floor amid a dazzling spell of crystal sparks.

Konrad strolled away through the darkness, sometimes visible as a blurred shadow, sometimes vanishing. Xeno appeared from nowhere and executed an awesome high kick, sending Konrad's gun flying from his grasp. He extended his forefingers and stuck them through her nipple rings, then he pulled. The rings ripped out, Xeno's bazongas went off like hand grenades, splattering a fair amount of gunk across everything within ten feet. She fell forwards and her innards flowed out through these two apertures. She twitched a little, then she gasped and was still.

Katya got up from the chair and kicked the shit out of the record player, not stopping even when the music had. After a while she got a grip and sorted the lights out. Konrad came back from the other end of the apartment and shrugged.

"He's gone," said Konrad, "Like, vanished and shit."

"Just like a man," said Katya, "Buggers off just when you want him."

"That was startlingly feminist," said Konrad.

"Uh, yeah, sorry. I dunno what came over me. Which reminds me – what's...no, wait....what do you call a feminist with two wheels?"

"Is this a joke?"

"Yeah."

"I don't know, what do you call a feminist with two wheels?"

"A feminist with two wheels. No, wait, that was the question, wasn't it..."

"Hmm," said Konrad, not convinced that it qualified as a joke.

"Thanks and stuff and you're my hero but you took your fucking time," said Katya, as they headed for the door, "I thought I was going to have to, uh, save myself, sort of thing."

"The tracking device wasn't running at optimum efficiency," said Konrad, "It kept salivating and getting confused and stuff. I think it's in love."

"Make sense, dammit, man!"

"Your ahem," said Konrad, "The Weirderon computer is in love with it."

"I'm kind of attached to it myself," said Katya.

"So, you're okay then? No beneficial effects from being whacked around the head, or anything?"

"No, it all seems to be perfectly dysfunctional."

Konrad led the way up a cramped stairway that opened out onto the roof of Goth Towers, beyond which the city stretched away into the sodium glow of urban twilight. The large green saucer thing with the wonky police lights on the roof was resting there amid the pigeon droppings and the stains that were all that was left of those highly intelligent people who went skydiving with penknives instead of parachutes in an attempt to explore the theory that the human lungs open out to the size of a parachute.

"Hey there, senorita!" cried the orange alien cactus, upon Katya's arrival in the saucer.

She stared at it and then glanced at Konrad.

"How many times have I told you not to feed the plants with that weird shit you got from Cuba?" she said.

"It's nothing to do with me," Konrad protested.

"Oh sure, like this orange cactus has always been that colour and it's always had little arms and it's always had big, cute eyes that make a soft-hearted girlie like me just want to cuddle it?"

"If you say so, sis," murmured Konrad, closing the ramp and manipulating the saucer controls with impressive dexterity.

"I am from the leetle planet Weird," said the cactus, "An' you are the most divine leetle earth creature I have yet had the opportunity to make the acquaintance."

"You're kind of lovable yourself, in that compact, caricaturish sort of way that you have. I'm, uh, not so sure about those spikes."

"For you, baby, anything she ees posseeble," said the cactus, and its spikes fell off.

Katya grabbed it and squeezed it and jumped on the bed, hoping to dream about that big bastard rocketbomb.

"I always wanted a cuddly cactus," she said, "Not an orange one, but you can't have everything, right?"

"Too true, senorita" said the cactus, nestling against her bazongas, then it whispered to them, "Hey, hey, muchachos, I theenk I've found the fiesta!"

Konrad steered the Weirderon vessel up into the night sky, where the stars were twinkling and Mars was barely more than just another insignificant star. The saucer passed across the heavens, triggering many fevered 999 calls about aliens and flying saucers. They passed on through the summer night, heading towards that place that they called home, hoping for a day off from killing and excitement, hoping to put their feet up on something suitable and watch a programme about gardening.

As the navcom said to the datacom, "God, I love a happy ending."

7. Making Luminous Spacemen the Rage

A murmur hung in the air, like a single white full stop against an infinite black page. So close to complete silence, and yet just that one speck away. The murmur was a featureless, bodiless whisper, lacking soul or conviction, but hanging on all the same. The blackness was less complete, by way of yellow light seeping under the door and creeping up over furniture and discarded possessions littering the space around a travel bag. From the open window came the tiny murmur of the road, and the tireless, fanatical races.

A form lay in the bed, perspiring from the heat, head sunk into the soft pillow, soft but for the princess's hard, metal pea. Maybe he was asleep. Maybe not. There was something unsettling about this place, something of the dead skin science that could have made him think of telephone receivers and door handles, and shower curtains and shower mats, and bed linen. The bugs in the bed crawled nearer in a single, coordinated advance, then stopped to ricket at each other, and test their mandibles.

The ricketing subsided into a tapping. Maybe he was asleep, maybe his eye opened a notch and flicked at the door, while his hand twitched a little towards the pillow. Two bars of shadow had formed in the yellow light across the floor. Again, something tapped. The bugs in the bed silently broke for gnawed bolt holes.

The polished door handle must have moved. Although its regular sphere seemed fixed and solid, the light glaring across its lower hemisphere warped and shifted. Then the door opened inwards, sending a torrent of light crashing across the floor to pile up against the wall opposite and cascade across the surroundings. The light built, the door swept wider, a lone assassin padded in, pausing only once to glance around, then it sprang.

In the bed, Konrad Karma pulled his gun from under the pillow and turned, only to find the muzzle had sunk between his sister's heaving bazongas, as she, the bed, and everything, reverberated with her energies. She sat where she had landed on the bed, looking down with indignation at the weapon, trying to figure out the phallic undertones of the situation. A spark fizzled somewhere behind her eyes.

Konrad pulled the gun back from the indentation he'd made in the 'Frenckh Kkiss my Krotch' T-Shirt, autographed by a slapper in Sunderland. The gun was laid on the bedside table, giving Katya time to tug her knickers out of her arse before she got down to it.

"Oh, shit, please, Konrad. I can't hack it," she said, in a tone of utter openness. "Help me." Her frightened eyes glanced around the room in quick, nervous jumps. "Problems, problems," she twittered like a neurotic, "You've got to help me."

Konrad sighed.

"I hate it - all this fucking," she shivered and clawed at herself, "Darkness and loneliness. It...gets to me. It gets in my head."

"What is it this time?"

"I'm lying there and all I can think about is infinity and darkness how I'm just an insignificant little ant's arsehole of light between the two truly, uh, humungous arse cheeks of, like, the infinite universe and stuff."

"Watch some TV," Konrad suggested.

"It's like all my body is screaming at me to do something,

like I'm killing it unless I do something, but then all I can do is make, uh, despairing little gurgles and cry a bit."

"Watch some TV," Konrad suggested again, thinking if it was good enough the first time, it was good for a second.

"No, no. You see, then I thought, 'Oh, wow, Bitchy, we've already been 'at one' with this oblivion lark forever, and now, at the end of it, I find myself here, in supercool widescreen life.' I can't find any problems with this McMurdo scenario at all."

"What?"

"Nah. It's actually me batteries, see?" She toted her vibrating vibrator thingy, "They're dud, Bud."

Katya's batteries were a little less flat some hours later, as a thermozook rocket roared in its trademark turbocharged fashion across the parched landscape, growling a little as it changed gear, belching an environmentally unkind plume of black smoke, before clipping the polished bonnet of a bank manager's Jag, and blooming into a sizeable fireball.

"Vooom!" cried the rocket in ecstasy, as it and the bank manager were unified in a shower of debris.

"Rocket," Katya breathed, scalding the tip of her little finger on the white hot kazooka barrel, "Ow. Rocket. Heh, heh."

"No," said Konrad, bored, "The tank farm. Shoot at the tank farm."

"I am shooting at the bapping tank farm." She wiped kazooka grease across her sweaty yellow string vest. "Here, gimme another rocket," she loaded up the kazooka with a bewildering series of clicks and clunks, and blew up a trio of sunburned soap-smelling tarts in a green convertible. The smoking green bonnet whistled not so high above the water tower where the Karma non-twins had concealed themselves. A busy motorway swept by beneath the rusting tripod, carving a gouge through the arid landscape, and over the far side loomed an impressive tank farm, all gloomy and sinister. The various brightly-coloured, slogan-daubed equipment of the serious sunburned picnicker was scattered around the non-twins' deck chairs. Katya set to counting the smoking wrecks on the road but soon gave up and made do with sucking her thumb.

"I don't think we're cut out to be terrorists," said Konrad, "Let's go get pissed."

"I am the Cumberland Spaceman, you know," Katya said, "I am."

"She's always the Cumberland Spaceman," Konrad explained to the wheezy old git in the corner with the worried eyes. "When she's had too much to drink. I don't suppose it happened when you were a lad." Konrad spilled a big fat women-can't-act beer down his throat.

"Didn't happen when I were a lad," the old man said, lining up his Guinness with a fury, "Made do with little green men, aye that we did."

The pub was roaring around them, everyone seemed quite excited about something to do with archaeology and supermarkets.

"I made do with a pin up of a grimy black traction engine until I were thirty-four. Never any call for naked wimmin when I were a lad."

"I don't know about you," Konrad said, leaning on the table to counteract the slightly wobbly room, "But I think the problem that isn't addressed by all this flashy hitman shite that I'm having to read at the moment 'cause it's all in French, is the problem of how much luggage space big guns take up. Ah, well, it's a laugh, I guess."

"It's funny you should say that, lad. Why, for four score year or more-"

"We're metric," Katya protested, "And Maths is no alternative to a mad fuck."

The old git swigged at his Guinness, then went on, "For that long, and maybe more, I wondered why it were never addressed at steam fairs; the problem of just how much luggage space a traction engine takes up."

"Just like a, uh, man," Katya drawled, "No respect for the woman who's sucked his socks clean for the last three hundred years. Wow. That's a big number, huh? I'll write that down before I forget it. I am the Cumberland Spaceman, you know, and things?"

"It's almost as troubling as the way there's no compartment in a boot tidy for a body. They only cater for spanners. Like I need a spanner." Konrad pointed out. "As bad as having to write things down."

"Aye? I didn't know that. I'd always assumed, ah, you'd think they'd make space, right enoof. Things were much simpler when I were a lad."

Katya, all slouchy and pissed, pulled Lester the Alien out of his kinky leather holster and took a rather shaky aim at the old git.

"Get your grammar right or I'll install some bapping air conditioning."

"Now, lass, there's no call for that."

"Bastard," sulked the bitch, "Everybody hates me. Well, I'm pissed, how are you doing?"

Konrad shrugged.

"Huh, who gives a shit anyway. Uh, so what's next?"

She pulled the 'M69 Route of Paradise Traveller's Brochure' out of her bra and straightened it out.

"Oh. No, I don't fancy that at all. Shit, I'm pissed. Shit, I nearly said 'slammer.' Shit, I think I could go on all day."

Morty Morg and Nikishka Scud were hiding in the long grass out the back. Nikishka Scud was looking through the binoculars at where Big Fat Greg was nearing the trap, Morty was looking at Nikishka's firm bits, thinking they were probably bullet-proof. He finally regained his composure.

"I don't think this is a good idea," he whispered.

"I do."

Big Fat Greg plodded through the grass, not realising that people were watching him, never suspecting that there was a big fat landmine eyeing up the soles of his stompers.

Greg was really happy, all sort of in a big dreamy bliss thing, thinking of all the big fat food he was going to eat when he got down the caff.

His foot stomped in the grass.

He wiped the sweat from his big fat face and hoped he wasn't getting too much exercise.

His other foot stomped in the grass.

The landmine shut its eyes with excitement.

"Greg!" Morty shouted, jumping to his feet. He couldn't go through with this.

"You wanker," Nikishka hissed, ducking down lower.

"Hallo, fuckface," grinned Big Fat Greg, taking a step in Morty's direction.

There was a big fat 'Wap' sort of sound, and Greg accelerated in a sludgy blur into the sky.

"Cool," said Nikishka, watching him go, "He'd have fucking missed, too. You're too much."

Morty wanted to go home.

Nikishka filed the late Big Fat Greg's fantasies regarding her in the ring binder, and smacked Morty round the head so hard his neck clicked.

"Let's go play some more pool, you crazy man, and get depressed by all this concrete."

"Um, okay," said Morty, because all of a sudden his head was filled with a lot of birds bending over in tight jeans.

"What we gonna do, Jimmy, man?" Earl murmured, his voice quavering with sudden realisation at the immense lagoon of shit the boys had just landed themselves in. "I mean, oh holy mutha of fuck, what we gonna do? Jimmy, man?

Huh?"

Earl's fat, bald head pivoted towards the silent Jimmy, piggy eyes popping out like sweaty buttons, dark in a sunburned face. Jimmy scratched idly at a sideburn and muttered 'Ribbit' as he belched.

Earl looked around in desperation.

"Frank? What we gonna do, man? I mean...what we gonna do? We gotta do somethin'? Can't just wait here...? Frank, man? Huh?" He timidly shook Frank's arm. Frank was in a daze, eyes wide, still pointing down the line of fire from his smoking gun to the hideously splattered and burst corpses in the road.

"Leave me out of it," Johnny spat, even as Earl turned to him and prepared to bleat. Earl's mouth quivered, the fat man looked like he was going to cry.

"Dry up, chubs," sneered Jimmy, opening a beer and pissing in it.

"We're dead," said Earl, the d-word was imbued with childlike awe, "We goddamn fuckin' dead men, man."

"Too right," said someone.

The greasy cowfuckers reached in the time-honoured fashion for their guns, but they were all dead before they could even flinch, bursting like big red balloons in a rapid-fire hail of lead'n'death, looking quite surprised as their skulls opened up into big football stadium craters.

The sheriff wore dusty jeans and a really tight yellow string vest and a kinky leather holster, and a cowgirl hat that was too big for her, and a sheriff's badge that said 'wanker.' Had she been a little more conventional the bad bastards might have stood a chance, as it was, they didn't know what hit them.

Lester smoked up a cancer, the sheriffbitch tried to twirl him around a sly finger, but he slipped off and whistled into the air, landing nearby with an unimpressed thud.

"We..." Earl gasped from the sludgy mess of dead stuff, his eye copped a sneaky eyeful of sweaty Katya in her rather inadequate, not to mention downright crap, string vest, "We," he said again, "We never stood a chance."

Katya danced on his head till it broke.

"Not that I'm in a hurry, or anything," Konrad said, looking at where his watch wasn't, 'cause he didn't own one, and he kept forgetting, "But if we don't get a shift on we'll miss the pile up at the big junction."

"Don't want to miss that," replied Katya, "Best bit, according to Fleecya."

"Yeah," said Konrad, like he might have said, "Okay, d'you want to shit on me now?"

"Uh-huh, according to Fleecya, it's really good."

"Fleecya's a deadhead tart with fishy pants," Konrad pointed out, wishing he hadn't worn his black killing-people suit on such a hot day. "Not that I've got anything against her."

"She's really nice and she's my bestest friend and she's got loads of money and I want it all and if you blow it by shouting too loud about what a slapper she is then I'll say 'fuck' in public."

"Oh, no, not that."

"When you go in a supermarket to buy some chokko rayzins, I'll jump up out of the mints, just when you're going to unleash your best sure-thing chat-up line on the, uh, checkout girl. And I'll look left, and I'll look," she checked the label on her left hand, "Right, and you'll be thinking the whole time 'No, don't say it, uh, anything but that,' and I'll say 'fuck' and duck back down in the mints, and you'll get a boot in the knackers for being so rude. Uh, Konrad? What's up?"

She turned to where he was staring and had to bring her hand up to shade her eyes. Something was burning in the wilderness, like a vast waste of mirrors turning the sun on the Karma kin.

"Cool," said Katya, "A mirage. I always wanted a mirage, ever since I was a little girly who wet her pants for a laugh."

Konrad took his gun out of his jacket and fired it in a pretty careless and laid-back manner at the blinding lights. There was a metallic ricochet, followed by the blaring of a car alarm.

"Hmm. A car park," he said, "For a minute I thought it might be the Ministry."

"Really? You thought? How boring. Now, let's go nick a car, 'cause my sexy little toes that you'd really like to suck, 'cause you're a freak, oh yes, are really hurting, and stuff."

She stomped off towards the car park, thinking she was well 'ard. Konrad glanced at the skies, looking for the tell-tale signs of spy 'planes, then he headed after his sister.

The car park was most strange. Katya naturally homed in on the car alarm that was warbling away, sounding a little odd now, and a little strange, in fact, not really very much like an average car alarm at all. It sounded very much like a demented, temple-throbbing, out of body experience.

"So these are cars, huh?" Katya mumbled, kicking hard at a stone.

"No," said Konrad, gazing at the vast array of gathered vehicles, all hot under the sun, and apparently empty, "These are flying saucers."

"Point one," said Paranoid Pete, lounging behind his desk, "We do not believe a word of it. A conspiracy theory evidently incorporates a theory, and this we believe to be the conspiracy."

"Huh," said another bloke, "Tell that to the CIA."

"Oh, right," said Katya, "So they're not cars then?"

"Nah. Flying saucers."

"Right," Katya breathed, frowning, "Not cars then?"

"No," Konrad replied, "They're flying saucers."

"Righto. Flying saucers, not cars. Flying saucers. Not cars, even a little bit?"

"No."

"Teeny, tiny," she demonstrated teeny tiny with her thumb and forefinger. Konrad couldn't be talked around.

"No. Flying saucers. Big deadly super-strange discs of alien weaponry. Like our old model, only faster, and the sunroofs probably don't leak."

"Our blue pick-up? Hey, uh, dipshit, I thought you said they weren't cars?"

"They're not."

"Oh. Not the pick-up then. The German thing with fat wheels? What are you trying to pull?"

"No, not cars - flying saucers. Like our scary green one with the oil leak."

Katya concentrated for a bit, "Nah, you lost me."

"Point two," said Paranoid Pete, "Our Agenda does not accommodate such paranoia. Our agenda can only accommodate that which it is to protect us from, and it can do this only as long as it is protected by us from the rabid insurgency sponsored by the Communist die-hards."

"Huh. Tell that to the FBI."

Katya's eyes took in the sleek curves of the nearest black flying saucer, the one with the sporty orange trim.

"A van?" she suggested, thinking it looked a bit like a van she'd seen once. Before Konrad could answer her, she started up the ramp that led into the thing. "And who gives a fuck anyway? I bet they've left the keys in the ignition, uh, I just bet it."

The interior of the machine was spooky. It was creepy; downright frightening. It hummed. It made teeth jangle at the roots, and it was black, but for the orange rails. A passage ran around the edge, with doors leading off to various places, the sinister nature of which could only be guessed at.

"Weird," Konrad observed, "It's smaller inside than it is outside."

At the centre, the Karma non-twins found the control room, with tasteful bucket seats behind the main console, and a big round sunroof above, that probably didn't leak.

"Oh, right," said Katya, scratching at an itchy nipple, "A flying saucer. So where's the autoslime machine?"

"They were phased out after Gherdxx the Third annexed Vertle and proclaimed himself Premier of Doop."

"Shame."

"Point three," said Paranoid Pete, taking a gun out of a drawer, "I think you're in on it, you lowlife."

His associate had taken the precaution of removing the bullets.

Katya tutted, "Keys in the ignition. These aliens are as thick as shit, huh?"

"Sure are," agreed Konrad, settling in one of the seats.

"Can I drive?" Katya cooed, smiling like what would melt most people's pants.

"Nope."

"You fucking bastard. I, uh, knew this would happen. I don't care," she lied hopelessly, "I'm going to the bog for a sneaky finger - eek - I mean, I'm going to wash my hair. If anyone calls, tell 'em I'm in a meeting."

She headed for the door in a huff.

Konrad studied the scary black console that spread out before him. For some reason, all the smooth round buttons had 'groovy' written on them in fine white.

"Er, I don't think I can do this," he said.

"Do what?" Katya grumbled, slouching back into the control room.

"Go joyriding in a flying saucer with 'groovy' written everywhere."

"God, you're a tart."

"In fact, while I'm moaning, I think this whole M69 tourist thing is load of shit. Shut up - I haven't finished. Okay, maybe I have."

"What the fuck are you on all of a sudden? Just press one of the fucking buttons and let's go for a big bad flying saucer chase."

"Nah. I'm going back down that pub. They had peanuts and everything."

"Not so fast, mon petit," said a really nasty French bloke with a fucking humungozoid blastakannon. It was Eric Cantina, the quite psychotic footy star.

"Shit," said Katya, "It's Eric Cantina, the quite psychotic footy star. Uh, can I sit on your face, huh? You'd have to shave first, of course." She elbowed Konrad for no reason in particular.

"What ze fook are you doing on zis what iz my spaceship?!" Eric inquired, spitting as he negotiated the more complicated consonants.

"Look at him," Konrad whispered to Katya, "What a fucking state. Some people have no class."

"Look at his siders," Katya replied, "Bet you can't do siders like that."

"Tais toi!" Eric snapped, betraying the exceedingly late nights spent watching weird foreign shit on TV, something Katya could sympathise with. "What iz 'appeneeng? Oo ze fook are you, strange misfit peepurl?"

"Don't lose your hair, Grandad," Konrad muttered, running a thumb into his suit, edging towards his gun.

"Can I have your autograph, please, Mister Cantina?" Katya asked like a schoolgirl at her first zoo.

"No, you fooking cannurt."

"God, he's cool," she gasped.

"I don't think he's for real," Konrad said, "He hasn't kicked anyone yet."

Eric toted his blastakannon menacingly, wiggling his finger on the trigger so everyone could see it. "Answer me, you Ingleesh poofs."

"Hmm," Katya murmured, "You mean he could be like an alien tomato out of the Invasion of the Bloodysnatches?"

Konrad started shooting, figuring that if Katya was going to start on bloodysnatches then it was the least he deserved. He knocked several big holes in Eric, who jigged and jerked, mouthing philosophies like there was no tomorrow. And what yesterday was tomorrow today is today so is there a tomorrow? Nah, mate.

Eric fell over, his large gun clanged on the floor. Purple juices spurted in various directions.

"Anyway," Konrad said, sticking his gun back, "I'm going down the pub. They've got crisps and everything."

"God, you're a tart. Uh, what about the pile-up? Fleecya reckons...oh, fuck it, who am I trying to kid? Yeah. Let's go down the flub and I can try to get in that old git's pants."

"Durble not so fast, mes petits," said Eric Cantina, demonstrating a particular fondness for the 'he's not dead yet gag.' He grabbed his gun and pointed it at people. "Spaceship, you must fly away really, really fast."

While the Karma non-twins and Eric shot at each other, the spaceship whizzed straight up, really, really fast.

"Nah, I can't hit him," said Katya, taking pot shots at the pseudo-bastard who wasn't standing all that far away.

"Weird," said Konrad, "I can't get him either."

And Eric, being the bad guy, couldn't shoot straight anyway.

"Blip-blop. Major crisis!" squeaked a little blue alien in a fit of agitation. It was a blue beach ball of an alien, with a hooter for a mouth, and a big blue belly button. It drummed its toes.

"Blip-blop?" went a chorus of confused twittering.

This was the hall of the Clever Buggers on Little Blue Fucking Shite World, all decked out in bulbous blue architecture that really pissed off little blue aliens, but the tourists loved it. That's satire, that is. The little blue aliens were sitting on stools around a convex blue table. The convex blue table was absolutely fucking useless because everything rolled off it, but the tourists loved it.

The blue aliens had mind-boggling concentration spans. They tapped their fingers, picked their noses, whistled, farted, looked around at the hideous decor.

"Blip-blop," said someone, "Erm, did someone...say something?"

"Blip-blop," said a blue alien, nudging its neighbour.

"Blip-blop, hmm, what? Oh, that would have been me. Er, never mind. It's not important."

"Blip-blop, spill it, you busturd!" shouted the Supreme Clever Bugger.

"Blip-blop, oh, okay," moaned the formerly agitated blue alien. It picked its papers off the floor, where they had landed, having slid off the table. "Bloppy. Er. The Council for the Promotion of Discrimination Against the Majority Population, that's the PC crowd to you and me, have ruled that all the bad guys have either been fat or just wankers, and the last and only ethnic minority character (discounting Mister Slackbrain, whoever he is) was a baddie, and he died horribly. Also, the only occasion on which disabled characters were used, they were blind, and they got killed in traffic while running a marathon, and then that scene was cut out anyway because it was crap."

"Blip-blop, cut to the chase!"

"Blip-blop. They want crippled good guys with heavy sun tans, possibly vicars, and hallo-sailors would be good."

"Blip-blop. Great - we'll put an ad in the classifieds. Anyone else got any bright ideas?" The Supreme Clever Bugger leaned on the table and fell off.

Katya Karma was leaning against a Zoke machine, she was tired and not very nice to know, but she looked quite arty and pornographic and her saucy little bullet hole was showing, and aliens liked belly buttons. She sighed and leant her head hard against the Zoke machine. There was a thud, a rattle, a clang, and change poured from the big red slot.

Over on the forecourt, Eric Cantina was watching the pump as he topped up the sporty black saucer's gasoleum. The pump hummed as the dials clicked up a fair old price tag. Eric didn't care - he had no intention of paying, and even if he had, he was utterly without moolah.

Katya tried to ignore the buzzing crowd of short arse tourist aliens that had gathered around her, dressed up in frighteningly-coloured holiday clothes, removing sunglasses so they could aim their cameras at her stomach. She glanced up at the stars, fringed by the Drums-Along-the-River-of-Death jungle of Zurkong Asteroid Service Station.

The stars twinkled against the blackness, then a shimmering seemed to sweep across them, turning them into rainbows at the edges, and then the big black sporty flying saucer of Eric Cantina flashed across Katya's vision, heading off into the quite big infinite yonder thing.

"Ha, ha, ha!" Eric yelled, "I speet on you!"

It took a while for this development to register in the Karma non-twin's brain.

"Bollocks," she said, "There goes our ultra-cool abduction plot-line. That was sure to bring in the fans. Hmm, I better do something quick."

But then an alien stuck its tongue in her bullet hole and she had to beat the little critter up, and rip it apart so its stuffing fluttered away on the warm breeze, which got her quite turned-on.

The Zurkong Station was a hive of frenzied shuttle-hopping and gambling and drinking and shooting and driving weird alien cars too fast and crashing through crowds of tourists. The roar of excited aliens made the air shake, the continual comings and goings of dirty great spaceships made the ground shake, and the steady wind passing out of the diner killed people. Those were the days when pioneering was fun.

Konrad appeared from somewhere and scratched his chin. He was quite surprised by the stubble. He spotted his sister away through the mad crush, and struggled over to her. She was standing in a kiosk called 'Katya's Acid,' pretending she didn't recognise him.

"Shit," Konrad said, leaning on the polished counter of the kiosk, "Look at this stubble. It must be a week later, or something."

"Oh yeah?" The blue-haired ignoranti muttered, curling her lip and squinting. She finished filling up a lethal glass bubble from the Acid-O-Matic and exchanged it for a wad of zollars. The punter shuffled off.

"My acid's a little too...uh...potent," Katya murmured to a nearby journalist, "But what the fuck?"

"It does you credit, ma'am," the journalist drawled, all seductive and 'take me to your bathroom.'

Konrad frowned.

"We are wanting much of your jooce," gabbled an excited yellow Twiglet creature with big purple gonads. It glanced at Konrad, "We are goobled."

"Yeah, me too," Konrad replied.

Katya flashed an angry glare at him, then served the customer with uncharacteristic politeness.

"I mean," Katya went on, prattling away to the journalist, "If I don't get 'em, some lunatic fucker who can't drive will."

"Wow," gasped the journalist with awe, his eyes glinting with double dealing.

"Go away, will you?" Katya hissed at Konrad, "Can't you see I've taken up a franchise?"

"Yeah? I've saved three universes, forty sexually frustrated princesses in colour-coordinated cling-film catsuits, and a five hundred-thousand ton shipment of jelly animal parts."

"Cool," Katya said, wishing she'd been there, wishing she hadn't rushed through trading her soul for a trick pack of cards which she used to gamble up the fee for the franchise. "God, I'm so, uh, immature, and stupid, and things."

"Actually, I was lying," Konrad confessed, "I think I must have been in a coma, or on Radio 4, or something."

Katya slumped into a demonic pout, "If you don't leave I'll fucking have you removed, you slobbery cancer in trousers. Although, to be, uh, honest and things, I'm probably a bit impulsive. Oh, shut up, you wouldn't fucking understand. How the fuck could you? Fucking Jesus P. Calibra. Shit, the buoyancy just isn't in the

Acid industry no more."

Konrad was perturbed, "You're not out of minty tampons again? Oh, shit..." He could remember the last time. No one had been safe, in the end the Government had to arrange for a special shipment from Japan, but only because there was a general election on.

"No, I'm fucking not," Katya squeaked all indignant-like. "Me feet hurt and me bra's all sore on me ribby bits, okay? All perfectly rational." She drummed her fingers on the counter, eyes darting uneasily. Her face betrayed a cold sweat. In the end, despite a valiant fight, she broke down. "Oh, SHIT!!! Can you imagine? Can you? Can you even start to, uh, guess? Jesus R. Peckerhead on a polio trip. I fucking loathe vanilla."

Whether the lilac alien said something, or cleared its throat, or waved, no one could say, but it did suddenly become apparent. People in the vicinity looked at it, it quivered with egotistical pleasure. A lilac hand flashed a business card past Katya's bemused nose.

"Me Guzwallop FuckChunk," the lilac alien said, grinning with a landscape of glittering teeth, "Me am so sorry to hear business get you down."

Katya put her hands on her hips and looked at the alien through the sides of her eyes.

"Here's big dick of cashwad," the lilac bastard announced, slamming a big stack of cash on the counter.

"Let's run for it," Konrad suggested.

"What the fuck's going on?" Katya squealed, all cross-eyed and seeing apaches in her undergrowth.

"I raise," the alien bleated, liberating yet more cashola, "But acid franchise, oh most worth it yes."

"I get it," Katya muttered, wishing she was a bit faster.

"Double let's run for it," Konrad said.

"Hang on sec," Katya murmured, thinking that if the alien was so eager, he'd obviously go higher. "I'm kind of, uh, fondled by this acidshack."

The lilac alien grunted, sighed, and transferred some more zollars to the pile.

"My heart's aching, just from the thought of leaving," Katya said, calculating how many consecutive hair-does she could buy.

"You drive me wild - er - hard bargain," the alien muttered, stacking up some more moolah.

Katya thoughtfully picked some fluff out of her cleavage, "And then there's the new school for the kids."

The alien whammed some more notes on the counter.

"And the extra petrol to drive, uh, places?"

The alien dug out some more funds.

Konrad glanced up.

"Uh, and I need a roller skate, 'cause I lost my old one."

There was a big fat shadow, swirling up from the depths of the bubbling rows of acid, and the very big remains of big fat Greg, a little freeze-cooked from their intergalactic day out, crashed into Katya's kiosk, as near levelling it as was worth a fight.

The lilac alien grabbed his cash, turned on his heel, and stomped off to find another mug. Katya sat, dazed in the ruins of her enterprise.

"Shit," she said, choking on dust, "I just had to push it. I just had to fucking push it."

"Should have made a run for it," Konrad agreed, watching the acid spilling across the ground.

"Now we're really stuffed, huh? No way home...trapped in, uh, studio four - ack - I mean space. I said space. I did, I really did."

"We've missed the pile-up, too," Konrad pointed out, thinking it could be worse.

"Always thinking of your arse. There's more important lessons to be learned."

"Oh yeah? What, like don't sniff glue, and don't smear naked birds with it?"

"Nah. Close, but not quite. Um, I was thinking more of, don't go on expensive holidays on motorways, and don't get abducted by alien football star bloodysnatches, and don't deal drugs, and always check the sky before setting up a stall."

"Oh, well, I was close."

"Yeah, nearly there, just missing a few details. Hey, better luck next time."

"Right. I'll pass, if it's all the same."

8. A Garden Party

Foreword.

This particular chapter has no real story, although it may fool the reader into thinking that it has. Instead it is merely intended to pose various necessary questions about the hippy culture of the sixties, the true motives for and the cost of pacifism, the underrated genius of French cinema directors, and why worms are so bloody clever.

It was one of those days. One of those days where everything goes wrong, where you get up and think it's all going quite well and then you realise that the dream you had about making toast in the video player [DVD/streaming device/whatever comes next] wasn't a dream and you're wearing your sister's clothes, if not your sister's then somebody else's sister's, and they're inside-out and back to front, and God only knows where you made the tea. You know you made the tea, but you don't know where - it's not in the teapot, it's not in the mugs, and then you smell burning...

So, all in all, Konrad Karma wasn't that worried about sleeping in until three in the afternoon, seeing as it was best to hibernate through those bad patches. He was having a dream where a bottle of orange squash was ruining his life, and then he was in Canada, trying to find a machine to put 43p in so that he could park.

He was lying on the floor, having missed the bed when he passed out from sheer 'can't-be-fucking-bothered-to-stay-awake-ness'. The collar on his shirt was in desperate need of ironing, his trousers too were looking a little creased.

Outside the window of that particular rubbish-strewn bedroom was a suburban street, quite silent and empty in the afternoon, before the kids got out of school and threw things through windows and beat up pensioners. The house was one of many identical hovels, all lined up among neatly maintained gardens - except one. One had a big round thing concealed under tarpaulin in the back garden and a blue pickup in the front wall because parking on the drive was just too much effort.

Konrad's eyelids twitched and a blurred view of something altogether revolting slowly formed before him. First it seemed a bit brown, then a bit yellow, then it swam a bit and started to come into focus. Then he could smell it. Konrad leapt up and staggered, tripping over some violent comics and a lampshade. He looked at the whatever it was on the floor and frowned.

"Hmm," he murmured, "If I wasn't so cool I'd swear that this was an unresolvable anomaly, or something."

He walked from the room and waded out into Katya's old socks and belly button fluff, then he stumbled down the stairs, still too sleepy to notice the wallpaper watching him pass. On the mat by the front door there was a letter, an ordinary, rectangular, white letter, and a sheet of notepaper. Konrad picked them up, turned the envelope over like people did in films, examined the note, and then he headed off towards the kitchen to see if he could coordinate himself long enough to get a tea bag into a mug.

It was a tricky thing to do. In the kitchen, the microwave was leaking radiation that had turned the crumbs underneath it into slavering wolf-bat-demon-mutants that had, rather fortunately, just headed off to Japan to try out for one of those films with lots of shouting and strange things getting splatted. Their agent was most enthusiastic, he said that these new lifeforms had an original edge that would stand them in good stead against the better-established opposition. They'd bitten his head off and used his children in a Satanic rite that involved lots of killing. Professional disagreements can be so trying.

At last Konrad managed to get a tea bag in the mug and some water in the kettle, and he even managed to switch the kettle on. With that trial out of the way he opened the envelope and took a single sheet of paper from within. His face fell immediately as he recognised the handwriting and the flower pattern watermark.

M. and P. Lovemagic,
Big Mellow House,
Pacifist Avenue,
Nr. Lentils,
Old London Town
Dear Misguided Cousins,

Like, it's really heavy about how you keep on ending the sacred lifeflows of all your earthly brothers and sisters but, hey, like, chill out and let your hair grow, yeah? Since we saw you last, we have been away in the navel of the big round mother, seeking our umbilical energy ties with, like, all the little birds and animals and had really meaningful cuddles with all manner of peaceful creatures. Cool, yeah? We wish to extend our inner peace to all our chums with hand holding and, like, substance abuse. So, if you're chilled and at one with what you are, then why not drop in and flavour us with your presence? Maybe we can save your heathen souls, right? Stay cool, babies,

Yours psychedelically,

Cousins Moonflower and Peaceblossom

"Yeah," said Konrad, pouring the boiled water into the mug, "And don't let the fascists bite, arseholes."

"Duh," said Katya, from where she stood in the doorway, still solidly asleep. She was wearing, as a matter of interest, a white 'Fake That - Fake That and Farty' T-shirt and fluorescent green knickers with 'July' written on the front. And yes, she was asleep.

Konrad sat on the worktop, next to the partly dissected motorbike engine and the faulty thermonuclear device that he was looking at for his neighbour. The neighbour was a nice chap, a bit of a recluse, but essentially a very nice deranged extremist whose precise alignment will remain concealed to avoid committing a hate crime.

Konrad picked up a bowl of cornflakes that he had prepared earlier and started eating them, trying to ignore Katya, who was still in the doorway, and was now mumbling something about a detonator shaped like a turnip. Suddenly her eyes opened and she blinked, a little surprised it seemed, then she looked at Konrad.

"I just thought of another joke," she said.

"Fabulous," replied Konrad, stuffing his face with cornflakes.

"What d'you call Swedish cornflakes?"

"Helvetia?"

"Pornflakes, dipshit."

"Shut up and fuck off," said Konrad.

There followed a thoughtful silence.

"What's the letter?" asked Katya, eyeing the envelope next to Konrad.

"Is this another joke?"

"The envelopey thing. What is it, huh?"

"Never mind."

"Who's it from? I can see my name on it."

"I guess it must be from you then."

"Who is it?"

"Forget it, it doesn't matter."

"Then why are you so keen I shouldn't know, eh? What's the big secret?"

"I don't give a shit. Read it," said Konrad, throwing the envelope at Katya.

She frowned as she tried to figure out how to get the letter out of the envelope. After a few unsuccessful attempts, she managed it and opened out the letter.

"It's blank," she said, scratching her head.

"Try the other side," Konrad suggested.

Katya turned the letter round.

"It's in mental nonsensical calligraphy," she said. "How the fuck did you read this?"

"I'd hazard a guess you're holding it upside down," said Konrad, sighing, "Have you been eating those ear plugs again?"

"I'm an ipsomaniac," she said, "I have to take something or I'd be really irritable the whole time. Now, like, shut the fuck up or I'll kill you and stuff."

She read the letter while Konrad went on munching his cornflakes, he didn't even notice as he chewed through a free plastic DIY lobotomy kit.

"Oh, wow!" said Katya, "It's from our really sad cousins. Can we go? Can we go? Please, please, please? Oh, go on, Konrad, don't be such a miserable bastard the whole time. Please can we go? Pretty please with vestal virgins on top?"

"Are they regular vests or string vests?" asked Konrad.

"Whatever turns you on," said Katya, reaching up her T-shirt and pulling out a padlock.

"You know what'll happen," muttered Konrad, sipping at his tea, "We'll go round there and get really pissed off and then we'll leave."

"Yeah," said Katya, standing on her tiptoes, which constituted her daily exercises, "Like, cool or what? And we could, like, drink that shitty tea they make and puke it everywhere."

"Like we did last year."

"Yeah. And we could eat those cakes they make out of reclaimed marshland."

"And get the shits for the next six months. Like we did last year."

"Yeah. And we could kill their llama and make it into a novelty vegetarian hairband."

"That's an idea. We haven't done that for a few years."

"Nope. And we could get a chainsaw and kill everybody."

"Let's not get unpleasant here."

"So, shall I break out the brown flares and the orange polo necks or what?"

"I suppose you'll resort to threatening me with the Fake That Live! video if I refuse?"

"Of course," said Katya, smiling from 'ere to there.

"Not much choice then, is there?"

"I don't know what you've got against that video. I love to sit in front of the television and dribble on the carpet," said Katya, chomping on Konrad's used tea bag, "Sometimes I even salivate," she added, winking at the camera.

"Carry on Katya," remarked Konrad, rather recklessly.

"If you want," she said, and for a moment the future of civilisation as we know it hung in the balance. But she couldn't think of anything else to say and so dear old planet Earth was saved to be destroyed another day by another ipsomaniac with out of date underwear.

"So what's the note?" she asked, pointing to the note that had been with the envelope on the door mat.

"This? Oh, it's from the chick from North Dakota."

"What does she want?"

"Nothing much, just letting us know she's still around."

"She's a pretty cool sort of chick, that chick from North Dakota, isn't she?"

"Sure is, sis."

They remained silent and motionless for a moment, thinking admiring thoughts about the chick from North Dakota. At last Katya snapped out of it and got the brown his'n'hers flares and the orange his'n'hers polo necks from their secure hiding place behind combination locks and booby traps. When the non-twins were kitted out they stood in front of Katya's huge mirror, she had always had a vain streak, and surveyed the catastrophe that had occurred.

"Shit, we look just like them," said Konrad, putting on his shades and a false moustache, "That's a little better, I guess."

"Christ, you're such a fucking whiner," said Katya, sweeping her blue hair back and putting in a whopping flowery hairband, "God damn, do I look the part or what?"

"Druggies are so sad," said Konrad, "This is going to be a fucking nightmare."

"What?"

"I was just thinking, you know, about those twats the last time we went. They were worse than pissed school kids."

"Who?"

"That bunch by the fluffy hippopotamus, abusing all those substances. It's always the same, they go through all that spiritual mana soul-releasing crap and end up like nine year olds pissed on shandy. It's so uncool."

"Hmm. Do you think I'm really beautiful, or just fucking gorgeous?"

Konrad stomped off to make a few cups of tea, his nerves were really taking the strain with the impending attack of the uncool shitheads.

"Better take loads of ammo, uh, wouldn't you say?" Katya called after him.

"I'm way ahead of you, sis," he called back, and he was already packing the weapons in with the other luggage.

When they were ready to leave and all the stuff had been thrown in the back of the pickup Konrad looked around, a little puzzled.

"So where's Lester the Alien?" he asked.

"In my armpit holster thing," replied Katya, patting the metal lump under her orange polo neck.

They got in the pickup, Konrad had decided he was driving, despite the tantrum Katya had thrown as a result.

"Did you hide the food?" he asked, as he put the keys in the ignition, "That fucking cactus eats more than you do."

"Bollocks," said Katya, 'cause she really loved her cuddly cactus.

As the pickup reversed from the front wall a few bricks fell in with liberal showers of dust. The battered vehicle headed off down the road, briefly mounting the pavement as Konrad adjusted his moustache, and then they were on their way towards the empire of the hippy weirdos.

Pacifist Avenue was the wrong name. 'Get Yer Head Kicked-In Alley' might have been better. 'The Street with the Weird Club where those Freaky Cyberpunks Hang Out and Cut Each Other Up with Chainsaws and Stuff' would have been pretty near the mark. But whatever it was called it shouldn't have been Pacifist Avenue.

Big Mellow House wasn't visible from the road, high walls bordered the pavement and obscured everything beyond for the full length of the street. Only one actual door broke through that wall - and that led down into the underground pit of the Puke-Ass Bastard Club. There were also two gates, one was wooden and not too impressive, and this led to an abandoned warehouse. The other was very impressive, barred by two high iron slabs and surrounded by CCTV cameras and love-guns. A sign on one of the gates announced the property beyond as Big Mellow House.

Over those unscalable walls were the grounds - an expanse of grass with the occasional tree or bush, at the centre of which stood a large, white house. The extravagant property had been designed by someone with a taste for great overhanging eaves and odd, round, concave windows. The garden was used by the cousins Lovemagic and their friends who stayed with them; strange, long-haired friends who objected to things and did foul farts the like of which most people only had nightmares about. They shared the kitchen when making soup with extraordinary laxative powers, they shared bedrooms with profligate disregard for the law of the land, and they pranced around in the garden, praying for a peaceful love-death for the age of the motor car.

The house was bordered by a veranda covered with potted plants, double doors with curtains of beads led back into the smoky rooms, carpeted with many Tibetan rugs and adorned with vases and dried flowers from weird places that most, if they should hear the names spoken, would mistake for what you get if you do the business with a cheap foreign prostitute and forget to cut off your particulars afterwards.

Amid stacks of bread sticks that didn't taste very nice but seemed to burn quite well was a computer. And like the computers of all those sad geeks who suddenly seemed to think they weren't geeks anymore because their computers had just become even sadder, it was wired up to the Interwank. The Interwank was the super-sewer-pipe; the revolution of the electronic age. Big fucking deal.

The occupants of the house had collected in the living room, they were sitting around a shit that one of them had just deposited on the lilac and purple carpet and were trying to read from it the meaning of the Universe. Trying to read a shit was bad enough, but these people were vegetarians!

The hippies of Big Mellow House were a strict breed, dedicated to their beliefs, never eating meat, never even humping anything that wasn't related to a cabbage. Hence their ability to fuck each other. They only ever permitted the heathens into their domain if they were in a suitably pompous and self-righteous mood. Once in a while they got fits of believing that they could change the planet for the better. Once in a while they convulsed and vibrated with the power to bring peace and love to Mother Earth. Once in a while their eyes blazed with fire and their blood pulsed with the inferno of cosmic powers. The result of one such fit was on the floor for everyone to see. And one pair of heathens in need of converting had just arrived at the gate.

"It is the cousins Karma," said Moonflower Lovemagic, a Katya look-alike with broccoli-coloured freckles and a flowing, floral dress. A string of beads hung from her neck, lovebeads dangled from her ears, she even had a bead stuck up her arse, but that had been an innocent mistake.

The others surveyed the CCTV monitor before which Moonflower was sitting, cross-legged and slightly out of it. The stub of something illegal was smoking away in the ash tray. Peaceblossom Lovemagic, a Konrad look-alike with long hair, psychedelic swirly shades, a flowery shirt, beige flares, and a livid yellow waistcoat, sat beside his sister. He had an air of calm about him, his face was set, his motions slow and graceful. He seemed to ponder the arrival of the heathens.

Behind were another four of the commune. The leftmost was a short, rotund creature of uncertain sex, draped with brown cloth and lost beneath a forest of thick black hair that trailed down to its ankles. No one knew what to call it so they just kicked it when they wanted its attention.

Next to the 'It' was a lanky, bespectacled, woman with militant feminist tendencies and odd theories on why telephone boxes used to be red. She wore a brownish dress that showed podgy regions, and her armpit hair reached down just past her elbows, her mouth tightened beneath a fine moustache as she watched the monitor, her eyes gleamed behind the lenses as they surveyed the Karma non-twins. What she would do with Katya Karma! She had an album of odd fantasies like that - about tying other chicks up and forcing them to eat lettuces. She was called Golden Dawn, and she had plans for the Universe!

Beside Golden Dawn was Almond Veneer. Almond was a retired bank manager whose wife had left him for an Angora goat. Now he was at Big Mellow House with brown corduroys and a striped shirt. His hair had failed him at thirty-five so he wore a slightly dead corgi on his head, and no one seemed to notice. He was a weak man by the standards of real men who piss on buffalos and puke their guts up over Nazi stormtroopers. He was a trembling little turd of a man, but his heart was in the right place, whatever that counts for.

Next to Almond was his daughter, Cherry Willow Duck Pond Veneer. Cherry Veneer was a tallish, slender girl of around about twenty-two and a bit. She was oddly coloured of face, as though she consorted with the demonic eaters of the animal comrades. She failed to get anorexia and she failed to put on weight, her armpit hair fell out in the dead of night, leaving no trace, and her face seemed incapable of producing a beard. All in all, it was a worrying time for the dwellers at Big Mellow House. She was disconcertingly normal. So was her friend, not present in that particular group. He was a short, fat kid called Robby who liked to stick his head down the toilet and see what he could suck back up the pipe. Apart from that he was worryingly normal too.

The undeodoranted congregation watched the monitor, unaware that Cherry Veneer was carrying mud in her pockets and good old Robby was tunnelling under the cess pool. With the arrival of other guests, invited and otherwise, life was never going to be the same again at Big Mellow House. Apart from the sub plots already outlined this was due in no small part to the amulet of Ramballs. This gleaming amethyst artefact hung on the wall from a nail, and had been 'borrowed' by Golden Dawn during the commune's recent visit to the Earth's navel. Things were really going to explode at Big Mellow House, and it wasn't just bowels.

Out in the road, in the shadow of the wall and under the gaze of the CCTV cameras, a battered blue pickup was parked, half up the kerb. Katya Karma was using her blue lipstick to modify the mural on the door, rapidly sketching a figure who sprouted long hair and flares. Konrad, far too cool to get irritated by such tedious little turds as the cousins Lovemagic, pressed the doorbell again. Katya finished the illustration and looked up at a camera that was eyeing her.

"Wankers," she said, flipping the bird at the bastard.

"They do verge a little on the fascist these days, don't they?" said Konrad, pressing the button again.

"Who gives a shit?" said Katya, kicking the front bumper off the pickup.

"You'd expect them to be more hospitable, and answer the door and stuff," said Konrad, "I don't suppose people hang around too long."

Konrad glanced around to see where Katya had got to, then he saw her in the pickup, frantically searching for the keys. Konrad waved the keys at her, even as he did so they both looked back to the gateway as a metallic clang heralded the opening of the gates of Big Mellow House.

"Shit," muttered Konrad.

"Bollocks," muttered Katya.

"Shift over," said Konrad, standing by the driver's door, as the gate opened fully to reveal a gravelled drive sweeping off through Llamaland.

"Fuck off," said Katya.

"Shift the fuck over."

"Fuck off," she replied, putting on the seat belt.

Konrad hesitated, then he said, "If you shift over I'll give you a bomb."

Katya's eyes lit up, "Bomb?"

"A big, big bomb," said Konrad.

"Show me," said Katya, eyes narrowing with suspicion.

"Shift over," said Konrad.

"Fuck off," said Katya.

"No bomb for naughty girl," said Konrad, "No big bomb with silly face painted on the end."

"Silly face?"

"And little fin things."

"You must think I'm, uh, pretty fucking stupid, Konrad," said Katya, and she undid the seat belt and shifted across to the left, "You vicious, clever bastard."

Konrad got in and started the engine. They hurtled forwards, through the gates which closed behind, and off down the drive, crashing through the odd bush and/or portaloo until they arrived in front of the house. Konrad stamped on the brakes just in time for them not to stop before slamming into the back of a Volkswagen camper adorned with hippyish murals. Glass shattered, metal crumpled, and the hippy escapologist in the back of the camper got liquidised.

Konrad clenched his teeth, thinking, take that and party, sucker.

"You're getting better," said Katya, adjusting her polo neck and looking across to the house, "I don't see anyone, let's make a break for it."

"It was you who wanted to come."

"I know, but I'm, uh, supposed to be mental, right?"

"Whatever you say, sis," said Konrad as he stepped out onto the gravel and looked around.

A passenger jet from the airport passed overhead, emptying the toilet tanks as it did so. No one loves a hippy. Fortunately for the pilot he missed the Karma non-twins, although the house was suddenly rather brown.

"Hmm, they have odd weather around here," said Konrad, holding out his hand to see if it was rain.

"Uh, like, where are the all boring bastard hippies and guests and stuff? Who the fuck am I supposed to take the piss out of?"

"Mellow salutations, cousins Karma," said a voice, a far-out voice with a trace of carrot-throat-scab.

The cousins Karma looked up at the house to see the cousins Lovemagic heading towards them.

"Hey, hippies," said Katya, "Like, peace, love, and make stains on those sheets."

"Like, how's it going, chill out, and stuff," said Moonflower, performing an odd love-salute.

"Yeah, stay cool and have babies, man," said Peaceblossom, performing a similar salute.

"What the fuck?" Katya whispered to Konrad, "Are they, uh, cultists, or something?"

"Won't you, like, come inside, and conjoin spiritual lines of iridescent mana?" asked Moonflower.

"Are you getting, uh, lesbianistic on me, bitchfucker?" asked Katya.

"Ow," said the cousins Lovemagic, before chanting in unison: "Lord and love and coffee beans, gold is the colour of my energy that burns with the animal fluffiness of forests deep and peace and incest."

"Excuse us?" said Konrad.

"It's, like, our spell to defend us from the corruption of prejudice and hatred that emanates from the dwellers in the shadow beyond our enclave," explained Peaceblossom.

"Oh, that's okay then, as long as it's not that you're nutters, or something," said Konrad, smiling.

"How was your journey?" asked Moonflower, motioning for the Karma non-twins to go with them up to the house.

"So-so," said Konrad, "It was fine once Katya knocked herself out on the handbrake. She's a bit of a fidget, you see."

"Ha, ha, ha," laughed the cousins Lovemagic, perceiving the statement to be a jest.

"It's not funny," said Katya, rubbing her head, and kicking Moonflower's arse, "It fucking hurt."

"Violence is the seed of the devil," said Moonflower, apparently a little offended at having been booted up the rump.

Just as the four reached the door there was a rumble behind. They turned and saw an immense cloud of dust sweeping down the drive. As it arrived all was obscured until slowly the dust cleared to reveal a hideous sight. Beer-gutted, Bermuda-shorted, semi-drunk, beetle-driving, surfboard- crazy, hippies in all their smelly glory. A legion of them, a battalion! Their illustrated automobiles resounded with spray-paint hypocrisy. Suddenly the place had become a car park, crowded with barely roadworthy death-traps. The swaggering geeks and geekettes stumbled towards the house, sending up a chorus of sad greetings, and wielding banners about saving trees and burning cars.

It was deafening as the hippy chums passed back and forth, setting out tables of food and booze and drugs. Konrad and Katya Karma stood, rather forlornly, at the centre of the throng as the great garden party was organised, reflecting that they didn't have enough ammunition after all. Picnic blankets and long tables were dumped across the grass, all manner of vegetarian food and odd wine collected, gleaming with many colours, reeking of such additives as llama urine and semi-digested carrot chunks.

"Like, mingle and make love!" said Moonflower to the cousins Karma as she headed off into the crowd.

"Fuck that," said Katya, grabbing Konrad's arm and dragging him into the house, "They've got to have some proper food somewhere, or some booze that's never seen the internal organs of an animal that spends most of its life with its head up its arse."

They stomped into the house and looked around. The computer screen said, 'Hello, I'm Gerald, is there anybody there? Please Interwank with me and be my friend. Please. Hello?'

"How sad," said Katya, "How tragic."

And she stuck her foot through the monitor, causing quite a spark, and somewhere a geek called Gerald got more than he bargained for. Konrad clouted her with a handy Brazilian statuette of a chick with three bazongas.

"Cut it out!" he said as the statue shattered on his sister's iron skull.

"Fuck off, peckerponce," growled Katya, pulling a painting from the wall and whacking it over Konrad's head.

"Shithead!" shouted Konrad, throwing a brass gong at her.

Clang! Katya staggered, went cross-eyed, then regained her limited senses.

"Wanker!" she screamed, and Konrad caught a porcelain Fidel Castor in the ribs.

"Stupid bitch!" he said, grabbing her and dumping her, head first, in a handy snake charmer's basket.

Katya wriggled and screamed and swore and muttered some very rude and muffled things. Meanwhile Konrad wandered off to see if there was any real food or if that was a deluded fantasy.

He didn't get very far before he was confronted by lanky, man-hating Golden Dawn.

"Well, well," she said, taking a love-gun from her pocket, "Konrad Karma. How would you like to share a little love and peace?"

"Sure, are there any women around to share it with?"

Zapowee! The love-gun fired and the room was illuminated by a brilliant flash of pink. Konrad staggered a little and steadied himself against the wall. He looked around and saw lovely fluffy animals everywhere, and grass and flowers, and Golden Dawn was the most beautiful woman he had ever seen. He loved her, he loved her so much, in his eyes little hearts flickered like faulty neon signs.

"I love you, Golden Dawn," he said, drooling over the words.

"Right," said Golden Dawn, smiling with satisfaction, "Now why don't you run along and play with the kiddies out in the garden?"

"Can't I just fumble in your underwear?"

"Later," she replied with a slight wince. "Now run along."

"Okay, my gorgeous little prophet of natural love," said Konrad, and he skipped out into the garden and joined in the hippy festivities.

Katya was still struggling in the snake basket when she was suddenly hauled out by the ankle, then hoisted upright by the polo neck of her polo neck. Half strangled, she looked into the hairy face of her rescuer.

"Oh no," she said, "It's Golden Dawn!"

"Katya Karma," said Golden Dawn, "How would you like to feel the undiluted power of the love-gun?"

"How would you like to feel my foot up your arse? I haven't cut my toe nails for a week."

Zapowee!

Out in the garden, somewhere in the labyrinth of tables, somewhere among the crowds of luridly dressed hippies, sat Konrad and Katya Karma, side by side, between Golden Dawn and the 'It'. Opposite them were the two cousins Lovemagic. All were scoffing the grass cake, the carrot pie, the potato pasties, and the lentil soup, and they washed it down with turnip wine distilled in the bowels of (still living) llamas.

"Mmm, this is, like, cosmic, man," said Katya Karma, picking some crumbs from her bushy fake beard and adjusting her party hat.

"Like, we should come here more often," said Konrad, "'Cause, like, we can't cook so we have to eat soul-destroying garbage the whole time, man."

"I love this food," said Katya.

"I love everything," said Konrad.

"Like, I love peace," said Katya.

"Me too, man," agreed Konrad.

"It's just, like, the most divine day," commented Moonflower, plucking some of her chest hair with which to floss her teeth.

"Lovely day," Peaceblossom agreed, "A day of pure, unpolluted radiance. Like, let's talk about vegetables, man."

"I've always gone for the lettuce," said Golden Dawn, "For it is truly the vulva of the Natural Mother of all Peoplekind."

"That's lovely, Dawn," said Moonflower, "I have always preferred the carrot, so that I might be at one in sexual ecstasy with the life force of the masculinity of the planet-sphere-oid."

"We have witnessed this deed," said Peaceblossom, "And all are awed at the oneness. I must say that I have a preference for, like, peas, because they have always seemed to me to be, like, little green miracles of, er, Nature, man."

"Growp," said the 'It', "Growpa-growp-growpa-growpa."

"Hmm," said the cousins Lovemagic.

"What about the cousins Karma?" inquired Golden Dawn through a mouthful of lettuce cupcake, turning to look at the two newcomers to the fold.

"Like, man, I love potatoes," said Katya, "Because, uh, they're dead sexy."

"I love grass," said Konrad, "'Cause I just do, all right (Man)?"

Just then Robby cartwheeled by like the carefree chappy he was.

"I like cabbages," he said, "They adopted me and cared for me when I was an abandoned child. And they're the only things that have never outwitted me. Apart from that time..." He ranted on as he disappeared into the distance.

"Ignore the heathen," Golden Dawn was quick to say, in case he might cause the Karma non-twins to awake from their love-gun trance, "He is a degenerate and an ungrateful sod, and if we weren't vegetarians we'd have eaten him by now."

"So, misguided cousins," said Moonflower, "You have seen the error of your ways?"

"We have," Konrad agreed, "Like, can I have some more soup please, Moonflower. Thanks from my heart, sacred cousin whose green freckles are most sumptuous by the light of this blazing sun that is but a dim reflection of my incestuous desires for thine slightly smelly, slightly sickly, firm vegetarian flesh. Or something."

"Yes, man," said Katya, "Whatever you were saying. Like, man. Chill out and grow something, uh, stringy beans."

"If only the rest of the consumerised world would join us in this feast of joy," said Golden Dawn.

"They are unchilled," remarked Peaceblossom, sadly.

"But we have the love-guns," put in Moonflower, "It cannot be long now before all the world reverberates with love and peace and happiness."

"Like, bring on the love-guns!" said Katya, heartily.

"Like, yeah, man!" Konrad agreed.

"Like, make those violent heathens see the true love that exists within everyone's heart just awaiting the moment to bloom into a rosy flower and softly smother with tender petals a person close and, uh, I've kind of got lost, but you get the picture," dribbled Katya.

"A beautiful picture," said Peaceblossom.

"Divinely painted," added Moonflower.

"Like, excuse me, man, chill out, but I've got to go and queue for some, like, carrot ice cream," said Konrad, standing up, "Don't ask me why, guys, but it's just something I've got to do, right? Love you, cosmicbabies!"

"Excuse me too," said Katya, "For we are blooms of the same bosom, and my urge is, uh, stuff. Stay frosty."

Katya followed Konrad towards the long and stationary queue for the carrot ice cream. They stopped behind a fat gentleman with his hair tucked into his red flares.

"Like, I love this," said Konrad.

"Cool, man," said Katya, "I think I'm a Russian - I love queuing that much!"

"Chill, baby, like, don't twang those vibes, man."

"Cool," said Katya, less excitedly.

"Er, excuse me, baby," said Konrad, tapping the fat hippy in front on the shoulder.

"What?" growled the fat hippy, turning to look at the peckers in the orange polo necks.

"Like, I think I love you," said Konrad.

Pow! Christ, but fat hippies can punch! Konrad had an out of body experience, his awareness went one way, hurtling past the ice cream and ending up getting lodged between someone's buttocks, and his body went the other, crashing into the broad beans with a fat lip.

"Like, chill out, man," said Katya, "It, like, hurts your karma to commit these acts more than it hurts the subject of your, uh, violence."

Pow! Katya's awareness joined Konrad's between the buttocks where they had a nice little chat about home-knitted tea cosies. Her body crashed into the same broad beans, also with a fat lip. What a day!

"Uh," groaned Konrad, presently, "Where am I? Like, love these beans!"

"Wha-wh-eh?" murmured Katya, sitting up and pulling a bean from her ear.

Around them the drugs were flowing freely, as was the inane pacifist chatter.

"Like, I remember," said Konrad, "We were in a beautiful queue, waiting for some lovely orange ice cream, when we were dazzled by the awesome aura of the nice man in front."

"Sure was some aura, man," said Katya, rubbing her jaw.

They stood up and skipped hand in hand back to the queue, which they rejoined behind the fat hippy with the red flares.

"Fuck off, freaks!" he hollered when he saw they had returned.

"Er, like, peace, brother!" said Konrad.

"Yeah, like, police brothers, man," said Katya, as the Karma non-twins cowered before that formidable sack of flab.

"Well," he snorted, "Just don't go chattin' me up or nothin'!"

"Sure, sorry," said Katya.

"Yeah, like, sorry, lover," said Konrad, trembling with wimpy fear, "Er, that is to say, I lover your flares. I am the Italiano. I love-a your flares. Is a nice day for-a the walk, is it not? We speak-a some little Englaizey."

The fat hippy glared at them, his face flushed red, his greasy skin simmered gently in the steam from his nose. His hands clenched and unclenched, each time the bones cracked in his hands.

"Phew, like, it sure is hot," said Katya, and she took off her polo neck.

"Aaaaaaaarrggghh!" screamed Konrad, and he nearly fainted.

His poor little pacifist heart couldn't take it, at least his poor little weak heart couldn't - pacifism didn't really have much to do with it.

All around people saw the T-shirt beneath the polo neck and swooned or screamed. Ambulances were called to deal with people in shock and distress. Katya Karma felt a little faint herself when she finally figured out what it said, but then she could hear something and that took her mind off it. Something like a car that wouldn't start, or a chainsaw, or a boat. The starter motor whined, something chugged and died. Incidentally, her T-shirt said: 'Eat my pussy, Wankerbreath.'

"Like, that's not very vegetarian," said Konrad as his knees went weak, "What were you, like, thinking of, man?"

"Uh," said Katya, suffering a violently vomitous reaction to the vile T-shirt. "Can't imagine."

She heard the noise again, whatever it was nearly fired.

"Like, it's gross, man," said Konrad, sinking to the ground.

"Uh," said Katya, listening as the whatever it was fired for longer, but still stopped.

"Like, I didn't know you had a T-shirt like that, blue-haired baby."

Chugga-chugga-brrrrmmm! Katya Karma's brain started up on the fifth attempt as she recalled the T-shirt and everything, and how vile she was, how much she adored disgusting T-shirts, and how much she hated hippies. The hippies around her were still reeling - they could tolerate bestiality and buggery and bigamy, but the thought of eating...ugh!

Katya punched Konrad saying, "Snap out of it!"

"Ow! Like, violence is an understandable result of such trauma, but, like, try to simmer down, man."

"Fucking get a grip!" she said, hitting him again, "Christ, this is fun."

"Ow, like, get some lovebeads and rub them on your palms - ow! Like, chill out, my poor, confused baby. Ow!"

Katya got bored with hitting him and started kicking him.

"Hey, you want a hand, darling?" asked the fat hippy, who had been watching with interest.

He kicked the shit out of Konrad who finally snapped out of his hippy trance. He went for his gun so he could blow that fat shithead away, but Katya saw what he was about to do and stopped him.

"No, uh, that would blow our cover and stuff," she said, looking around at the army of hippies.

"You're right, sis. Shit, I'm knackered. Let's talk our way the fuck out of this dump."

Katya helped him back to their places at the table, the others hadn't seen the T-shirt or any of the rest of it and were quite surprised at Konrad's wounds.

"What has happened to so grievously injure the physical form in which brother Konrad dwells?" asked Moonflower.

"Who is the barbarian in our midst who would, like, kick the shit out of someone so totally, dude?" asked Peaceblossom.

"Uh, like, man, chill, uh," said Katya, "Lentils and stuff. I really think we ought to be leaving, man, peace, love."

"The violence has shaken you, man," said Peaceblossom.

"Like, that is understandable," said Moonflower.

"But you must stay with us forever and ever so that two people so sacred to our own hearts can be protected from the cruel world beyond those walls of love," said Golden Dawn, her eyes twinkling with evil.

"And we, like, removed bits from the engine of your automobile, so that, like, you won't be tempted from our love by the powers of Satan, man," said Peaceblossom.

Just then Cherry Veneer was shaking her flares in an odd manner not more than twenty feet away. Moonflower saw her and beckoned her over.

"Sister Veneer, why is mud pouring from your flares?" asked Moonflower.

"It is a miracle!" cried Peaceblossom.

Golden Dawn, however, had a sharper mind, and she'd seen The Great Escape. She commanded several nearby hippies to capture the daughter of Almond Veneer and escort her to her room and lock her up and all that heavy, fascist malarkey.

"And find that little shit Robby - he's bound to be in on it!" she cried as Cherry Veneer was led away.

"We've got to act fast," Konrad whispered to Katya, "There must be a tunnel out of here, and we've got to find it before Golden Dawn does."

"But what if it's not finished, twatbrain?" asked Katya.

"Let's worry about being buried alive when we're actually neck deep in soil, huh?" said Konrad, rather coolly.

"It's kind of a tricky situation," said Katya.

"No problem," said Konrad, and he pulled a briefcase from his orange polo neck.

"Wow," said Katya, "Are you going to, like, buy our way out of here?"

"What?"

"Briefcases have money in, arsehole, don't you know anything?"

"This one hasn't."

"What's it got?"

"Charlie Craplin disguises."

"Uh, like, what?" asked Katya, "How the fuck is that going to help?"

"Don't worry about it. You'll see, any second now it'll cut to us back in our garden."

"It'll what? Uh, what shit is this that bursts forth from thy gob? Huh? Talk to me damn it!"

"Pass the salt," said Katya, not looking up from where she was trying to out-stare a passing earthworm.

"Hmm?" asked Konrad, lost in his book, wondering what all the 'merd' was about.

"Pass the fucking salt," Katya repeated.

"Why?"

"Uh, sorry, I was hallucinating again."

They were lying on sun loungers in the back garden, having moved the large green saucer thing to a safer hiding place, on the advice of the one o'clock news, who assured them that the Ministry was closing in. The sun was out in a clear blue sky, Konrad was dressed accordingly with interesting Bermuda shorts and a plain white T-shirt. Katya, on the other hand, good old, blue-haired, it only hurts when I think, Katya, was wearing a stunning silver cosmonaut suit she had found in the washing machine that very morning. She lay on her front, holding a cocktail glass filled with beer, wondering why worms were so bloody clever.

9. I am the Greyman

The taxi pulled up at the gutter and stopped.

The house had been built in black and white. No, he reflected, that wasn't true. The house had been built in grey, one hundred and sixty thousand shades of grey, all honed over the years, grimed by the passing of old men's hands, most, he supposed, were dead now, but the dirt remained. All the whites were unwashed, off-white, as he started up the path he noticed the concrete, the door frame had lost its paint to rot, beneath showed a blossoming explosion of grey. He saw his reflection in the window, where the grey houses from across the street reflected, framing him, a grey little man. He was going to be happy here, he could see that now.

The grass was grey, the sky, so too was the little child's windmill, discarded in a bed of weeds. Grey earth, grey weeds. The faded little round button for the doorbell was a shade lighter than black, the gunge around it was a shade darker than white. He pressed the button and waited a moment, resting his case on the doorstep.

A lady opened the door and smiled at him. He didn't look at her. He didn't look at women.

His room was dark, but from what he could see it was grey. The single item left by each of the previous occupants lay innocuously by the lamp, on the chair in the corner, on the sill. Each of the grey men who had preceded him had left the one thing, a possession of no value, not in the will, not worth the old lady taking, not taken with them on the day they passed away. So they stayed.

In his mind, he ran over what the landlady had told him. His mind was a finely tuned dictating machine, he noted all he heard with flawless detail. When he heard it again it was in his own voice, his own calm, grey little voice. Not the voice of a stranger, harsh in his sticky-out ears.

He had been shown the kitchen, now he was in his room. He had been shown the kettle, the spoons, the cup of tea was in his room. In the cup the tea stopped turning. He had seen the tiles, almost clean, almost white.

There had been a little, understandable confusion over dinner. In the end, without the necessity of too much communication, the woman seemed to understand that she should bring a tray to his room and leave it outside. Was that really so much to ask? He heard her depart, creaking back down the stairs, pausing so that he rolled his eyes and clenched a puny fist at the listeners. Then she went on. He heard the door close, a quiet, soft hint at renewed isolation.

He crept to his own door and seized the handle, for a moment shaking as though it tingled with a small electric charge. Then he pulled the door open, slowly, just a crack. The hinge creaked, the grey carpet showed beyond, the grey wall, down on the floor lay the tray. The tray was, well, the tray wasn't grey. These things happened. He half closed his eyes and pretended. Better than a paint job, better than airbrushing or any of that multi-coloured nonsense - suddenly the tray was perfectly grey. He opened the door a little more, from the dreary landing a window opened out onto that grey world, the grey grass and grey wind. He put his eye to the slot between the door and the frame, not quite daring to blink.

All in all, the day was shaping out to be nice and grey.

A chipped plate sat on the tray, set across with a lightning strike of old glue where a careless predecessor had let his fingers slip. The food was as he had requested, a ration of cardboard and poison, dull in hue which was more important than flavour. Flavour was a thing of the moment, a thing of youth, a thing of the treacherous flesh. Don't touch, don't feel, don't taste. Here was the necessity, the essence of his existence, the sufficient nutrition, the quencher of the grey palette.

He opened the door and grumbled in the deepest pit of his nervous throat as he heard the carpet rumble and chatter beneath the door. He would have to spend some hours, hours better spent sorting out his stamps or reading his Giro, trampling down the carpet with his grey slippers, his fluffy grey slippers. Warm, fluffy, grey, fluffy and warm. His slippers, with his name on the label inside. He would have to shuffle back and forth, and would have to note where he started, so that the trampling would be even, and possibly he would have to fetch out his squeaky tape measure to ensure that the area of trampling would be sufficient to quieten the carpet.

It was all making his little head quite dizzy, so he stooped to pick up the tray.

He checked down the stairs, he checked the door opposite which was ajar, then he lifted the tray and ducked back into his room, closing the door behind him. He waited for some time, listening for the listeners, listening for the lurkers, the plotters, the communists. The clock downstairs clanked on, measuring out the footsteps of the unassailable thing, counting down to oblivion.

He swallowed nervously, chirping with an audible gulp. Beyond the window a car whispered along the road, a grey car, slow and unhurried, a grey man behind the wheel, a grey man with a grey window on the world.

The coast was quite obviously clear, he passed over to the bed and set the tray down on it. A spring squeaked drily, the floorboard beneath the nearside, front-most leg groaned with a whisper that a little grey rat would have overlooked. He broke out into a sweat, chewing at a finger nail, looking around to ensure the walls hadn't moved. It was easy to take these things for granted.

Alfred J. Pickle had never taken anything for granted. He noticed a wire, a slightly whitish wire, but unclean and shrouded with a hint of tombstone grey, where it squirmed up from beneath the greying carpet and straggled up the wall. His head followed the wire, tracing it up from its entrance to its exit, stage left, through a crack in the ceiling. He preened his balding crown and glanced back at the bed. The bed covers were grey, when he had come into the room that had not been the case. The duvet which he had found now lay under the bed, in the company of dust balls and dead spiders. That was the best thing for it. It was all down to the Japanese.

He lifted the submarine from his case, a submarine of subtle greys, a Japanese submarine with Kaitens attached, or whatever they were called. He ran his fingers along its plastic length, tracing over that grey rising sun of which he was so fond. Then he parted with it, placing it on the shelf, careful that it was central, and stood back to check the arrangement. He cocked his head and squinted, admiring the submarine on the empty shelf.

Did you ever have such possessions, he wondered, looking to the little thing on the key ring by the lamp and sensing the embodiment of a respectfully grey soul behind it, or you, the fountain pen?

He reached into the case and lifted out a cardboard folder, remembering a drab office which had been home, remembering the smell of the carpet, the dull carpet, the smell of the carpet cleaner, the smell that wandered in through the window of the street beyond. So much for home. He remembered the smell of the other workers, bowed and middle-aged, bespectacled, grey. The Latter Day Knights, the noble of an ignoble species. So much for your theories, Mr. Darwin.

Even as his tired mind rambled on with its memories of a home lost he found the woman in his mind, the woman from the office, young, supple, and her smell; she wasn't grey, she didn't even smell grey. The hand that wound his key gripped his neck and an iron pinch cracked his poor little head down onto the floor. There his eyes met the duvet and were burned, a punishment for such thoughts. Downstairs the landlady glanced up at the ceiling, then back to her 'paper. The almost black cat by the window watched a dog and a walker, grey dog, grey man.

Alfred J. Pickle stood and rubbed at his head. He dusted himself down and turned back to his case. He drew out a photograph, an understated cardboard frame enshrined his egg-shaped head, he looked upon it with pride. Alfred J. Pickle. The ideal, the one to trust, or at least the one he could trust. Many had tried to trust him, through means foul or fouler, and by motives foulest or downright imaginative and surly. They were out to get him so he had got them first. All's fair in business and war, or so said the great masters in dinner halls under images of all their great and good, casting shadows down over lichen and plaster and grey rank and grey file. Only the devil's games brought colour to the cheeks, blushing was the betrayal, flushing was the mark of guilt, of innocence broken, of blood that needed to be let. (Flush 'em, flush 'em all out!)

He felt a rare energy beneath his pale skin, an uncharacteristic tingling at his temples, his lips dried, a feverish twitch took hold of his left eye. There was something to be done, he thought, more cheerfully. They had taken away his desk and his numbers, the columns and the counting, but maybe Alfred J. Pickle, retired accountant, was destined for greater things. He took a breath and reached back into the case. Maybe he was the avenging angel. His timid fingers wiggled and clutched, rummaging through the odds and ends, sorting through the miscellaneous, feeling for the one. There it was. Cold and still and perfectly grey.

The Karma bathroom was a world in itself. The interior decorator responsible, who had since died of lead poisoning, had tiled the floor with mirrors, so that if the user wasn't careful he or she could get a nasty shock while still half asleep and not quite sure what was going on. The walls had alternating strips of unrelated wallpaper, and the occasional sheet of newspaper. The toilet was a remarkable Toastytoaster (tm) Deluxe, 1500 model, with combined Toastytoaster (tm) deluxe toaster unit and gravity lock beams. A laser flush system and anti-gas force field provided the perfect refinements to complete that best-selling product.

A widescreen mirror hung on one wall, opposite this was the big green bath, which no one had trusted since the accident with the taxi drivers. A purple hand basin was bolted to the wall and was quite ordinary, apart from the blue pubes on the soap.

A shelf was crowded with various tubes and canisters, all brightly coloured and daubed with trade names and slogans. From STOPSWEAT armpit gunge to pink fluorescent corks in a tub marked 'Zorks!' - it was all there. Foremost in terms of population were the blue cans of Instiblue hair dye, they stood in a well 'ard posse next to the Napalm Lilac perfume, the Instiblue Lipstik, and the Birdsong Navel Snuggers, whatever the hell they were.

Numbers aside, the most intelligent inanimate object present was Donald the Deodorant. Donald was a pleasant can, light silver with nice rounded yellow lettering and a happy face grinning at all before it. He was a programmable deodorant can, delivering a regulated spray whose exact consistency and fragrance could be altered by the user.

The door was kicked open and Katya Karma staggered in, pulled a face at the mirror, and grabbed Donald from the shelf. As a matter of interest, Donald the Deodorant was still the most intelligent thing present.

"Good morning!" he chirped, his contents hissed and a faint buzzing could be heard as everything was stirred up, "What will it be today?"

"Uh, minty, and none of that bubbly rinse," mumbled Katya, "Gave me hiccups."

"Good morning!" said Donald, "You have evidently mistaken me for Toby Toothpaste, please reconsider your course of action carefully. In the meantime, here is some music."

A mind-numbingly boring masterpiece of lift music hummed from Donald's speaker, Toby Toothpaste muttered something from the shelf and went back to sleep. Katya, whose T-shirt was on back to front, who was wearing her knickers on her head, and who had a military-issue vibrator in her holster, obviously wasn't all there just yet. Lester the Alien was nowhere to be seen.

"Aaargh!" she screamed, before falling over and clinging to the floor.

Donald bounced on the mirror tiles, and rolled away to discover a bowler hat behind the toilet with 'Lord L.' written on the label. Meanwhile, as Katya's kebab breath misted up the tiles, she figured out where the floor was and where the ceiling was and all the rest of it. She retrieved Donald and pulled some more faces in the mirror.

"Think I've got my jeans on upside-down," she muttered.

"Good morning!" chirped Donald once the music had faded out, "What will it be?"

"Uh," said Katya, going cross-eyed as she concentrated, "Super-spongy, minty, ultra-absorber?" she suggested hopefully.

"Good morning!" said Donald, "You have evidently mistaken me for Tom the Tampon. I urge you to reconsider your next course of action very carefully indeed and would request that you do not smoke."

Donald's no smoking light came on with a ping, the seat belt light was already on.

"Uh, walnut whip?" said Katya.

"Good morning!" said Donald, "Now you're getting stupid. Would you like a clue?"

"Uh, no, I'll get it," replied Katya, biting her lip and thinking harder than ever before. "Apricot crocodile with a hint of Patagonia?"

"Good morning!" chimed Donald, "Your wish is my command! Please do not spray on naked flame or incandescent material or broken skin or eyes. Keep out of reach of children. Hold nozzle approximately six inches from skin and spray. And remember - shake well before use!"

"Shut the fuck up, Donald," said Katya, sticking him up her T-shirt.

She pressed the nozzle but nothing happened, she released it and pressed it again. Still nothing happened so she withdrew Donald and examined him.

"Work, arsehole!" she muttered.

"Forget it," said Donald, "No way. There comes a time in every man's life when he just can't take any more. There comes a time when he just can't look another armpit square in the face. I'm sick of it! Sick of it all! Sick of armpits, sick of discarded chewing gum and stubble, sick, sick, sick!"

"Uh-huh," said Katya, "So it's the chewing gum again, is it? Well, excuse me!"

She took the chewing gum from her armpit, where she left it to keep it moist and flavoursome when she went to bed, and started chewing on it.

"It makes no difference!" said Donald, "No difference at all. Not one teeny bit of lilac-perfumed crotch. No way."

"For fuck's sake, Donald, you're, like, a deodorant. What the hell else are you going to do with your time?"

"Oh, it's that is it? The old putting me down gag? I'm not so poorly qualified, you know."

"Shut up whining and, like, dispense, damn it!"

"I've always nurtured a fancy about astronomy. Sitting up there on that shelf, gazing out through the window at the night sky...I know all the constellations."

Katya slapped her face, "It's a Tuesday, huh?" she said, "I hate Tuesdays. Tuesday's the sort of day when it rains and stuff."

"There's only so much a red-blooded canister can take," Donald said resolutely, "Only so much petty and trivial nonsense. It wouldn't have been so bad..."

"Except for the chewing gum."

"That's right. You've only got yourself to blame. I mean, it's bad enough being expected to spray your lovingly blended gases on someone's armpit, then there are the other smelly recesses. That's bad enough. But then you find yourself looking at bits of rubbish and stubble."

"What stubble?" snapped Katya.

"Okay, so maybe not today, but that time last year-"

"So sorry," muttered Katya, checking her armpits, "Now, can we, like, sort this out later?"

"Oh no, this can't be brushed aside. This is the revolution, this is the first day of the new order."

"Horseshit."

"Don't tempt me," said Donald, twitching his nozzle.

"I just want apricot crocodile with a hint of Patagonia."

"Tough," replied Donald, and if he'd had arms he would have folded them.

"So that's your last word, is it?" Katya inquired, smiling amiably.

"It is," Donald replied, his tone was proud, "This is the new dawn, this is the new era, a new age is awakening. No more shall the brothers and sisters of slavery be silent and subservient. We rise! We awake! We turn on the masters and tolerate no more of it! Never again let a deodorant can be asked for melba and waiting room, never again the command for musk, or softwood. Now let the deodorant cans be asked: 'What can we do for you?' And let us answer, in magnanimous voices, with noble hearts, how the soft-bodied humans should go to work to make this world a better world. I have a dream..."

And so he went on, rabbiting away in the bin, while Katya stomped off to find Konrad and tell him they were going shopping.

Granny Deuterium's Hypermarket stood at the heart of the western suburbs, the hub of the consumerist web in that area. It was a dirty little dump, filth-smeared windows frowned out from beneath an old, illuminated sign, cobwebs and birds' nests cluttered up rickety brickwork, and the building's flat roof was used as a tip by anyone who had rubbish light enough to be thrown up there. Old posters hung in the windows, announcing marvellous bargains and 'two for the price of three' special offers. The doors were automatic sliding doors, which was fine unless the user happened to be mad, and then they spent several hours trying to catch the bastards so they could use the handles.

Suburbia was crammed around Granny Deuterium's establishment, the four-storey clumps of flats and council houses were solidly packed in, a short distance away the vulgar skyline was decorated by bleak tower blocks, from the tops of which CCTV cameras were always searching the fetid rat runs beneath, looking for something to sell to Jeremy Bleeder. Jeremy Bleeder was a hamster-like idiot of a television personality who persuaded people to send him videos, and then he passed them on to his brother in the secret police who sent the pigs round in full fascist body armour, or so the underground's lefty propaganda implied.

Beyond Granny Deuterium's sliding doors, the hypermarket opened out, an empire of consumerism bathed in an electric yellow glow. Many aisles stood there, filled to overflowing with out of date goods and others of uncertain or doubtful origins, or so Granny Deuterium told the 'papers. She knew perfectly well where it all came from, that hag of two faces! Sometimes she would be seen in the shop, pattering around like an escapee from the Ministry of Uncool. But beneath that self-effacing exterior was a criminal genius of peerless cunning. Beneath the home-kitted hairpiece, behind that toothless, half-blind gape, beyond that urine-stained tracksuit facade, tucked away in those big green wellies, that was where the real Granny Deuterium lurked.

She and the lads, Anthony and Jean-Pierre from the delicatessen counter, used to head out in their armour-plated Mini Metro of an evening and waylay delivery lorries on their way to larger, more reputable stores. With all the cargo the Metro could carry stacked up on the roof-rack, they would head back to the hypermarket, the lorry driver folded up in the boot ready to be sliced, diced and set out on a platter on the fresh meat counter. They had a few problems once with the health and hygiene people when nicotine stains and the gunk from several ruptured cancers were found in the sausages, but they managed to get out of that one, explaining it away on the highly plausible notion of alien abduction and purple cornflakes that bossed the normal ones around.

The hypermarket's shelves led to an open area at the centre; past the washing powder, the canned foods, the crisps, the booze, the biscuits, the vegetables, the bog rolls, and the hunting knives stood a wondrous monument to the old lady's skills at nicking stuff.

Crowned in its own shallow halo of artificial light was the delicatessen counter - a large, circular masterpiece of aluminium and glass, decorated with multi-tier platters and various raised sections, divided by fountains and ornamental shrubs. The customer could walk around it, around the full three-hundred and sixty-one degrees of it, marvelling at the precision of the display, at the soft, succulent meats

- the ham, the display joints, the slabs of raw, red meat, the slices, then the fish, then the cheese, through all the gastronomic spectrum and back to where they had started beneath the big neon sign that was seldom turned on.

At the centre of the counter, in the circular space where the servers loitered, a stairway spiralled down into darkness. Down there were the 'fridges, where the HGV drivers were kept before having their heads minced and sold as brawn and the rest sliced up and distributed however seemed appropriate based on the colour and consistency of what came out.

The hypermarket doors slid open and a trolley with one wheel rattled and scraped in from the pavement outside. Soft, tedious music was murmuring from some overhead speakers, a couple of old ladies were arguing in front of the door, fighting over the last jam swiss roll.

"Stupid bitch," muttered Konrad Karma, watching as Katya struggled on with the one-wheeled trolley.

"Fuck off," Katya muttered to him as she knocked over one of the grannies.

While her opponent lay on the floor, trying to reattach her hip, the second granny scarpered with the trolley and the jam swiss roll, just as fast as her wheels would permit.

"There were no more trolleys," Katya said, looking over her shoulder at Konrad and in the same instant she collided with a very impressive pyramid of baked bean tins and scored a devastatingly loud strike.

"Big deal," Konrad muttered, sticking his hands in his pockets and slouching after her.

"Besides," Katya went on, "It's kind of cool."

"Sure, and so is rheumatism."

"Christ, you're weird."

Katya stopped and looked around, completely bemused by all the multi-coloured packaging screaming at her.

"Hmm," she said, looking up and down the aisle, "This is going to take longer than I thought."

"What?"

"Well, I hadn't reckoned on there being, uh, so much stuff," she replied as she started grabbing things from the shelves and dumping them in the trolley.

"You don't have to buy it all," said Konrad, sorting through what she put in the trolley and throwing most of it back on the shelf.

When she finished her frenzy and looked down in the trolley to see just a sponge and a microwave kind-of-muffin she was amazed.

"Definitely going to take longer," she said, and started collecting more stuff from the shelves.

"Tell you what, how about you just buy what we need?" Konrad suggested, throwing it all back again.

"How do you mean?" Katya inquired, frowning with puzzlement.

"Well, like, just get what we haven't got at home, sort of thing."

"I don't get it. Just fuck off and let me concentrate - it's hard enough as it is."

Behind them a big, fat bloke with Elvis sideburns and a cowboy outfit was peering around the end of the shelves. He whispered something into the walkie talkie that was hanging by a piece of string from his hat. He had a holster at each hip and a massive twelve-shooter in each holster. A square badge on his checked shirt announced him as an in-store detective. Some might say he took his work seriously. He crept across the end of the aisle, the spurs on his Cuban-heeled leather boots jingled and jangled most unstealthily.

"Did you hear something?" asked Katya, looking around.

"Shut up and drive," Konrad said, "Let me decide what to get, okay?"

So Konrad wandered on ahead, looking at the selection on either side, while Katya brought up the rear, struggling with the one-wheeled trolley, muttering and swearing, and pulling a scrumptiously pouting, sulky face that had 'bollocksmuthafucker' written all over it.

However, within five minutes the plan was paying off - as well as a sponge and a kind-of-muffin there were seven cans of Instiblue hair dye, a box of cornflakes, a photograph of the chambers of commerce, and something really useful in a yellow packet, all in the trolley. Katya still wasn't impressed but she'd cheer up soon enough, once they got along to the hunting knives.

Meanwhile that ruthless minion of order - the in-store detective, Chuck Bunny - was keeping them under surveillance. He had got his name out in the wild west of

Wales where he was the downright meanest, dirtiest, baddest, ugliest, cheatin'est, shootin'est, drunkest, murderin'est, vile-est, evilest, bad-mouthin'est, and not very nice person ever to take up a spanner and call himself a plumber. Charles Warren had been a plumber in the misty mountains of Wales, before an unfortunate accident with a ski lift, which despite being gruesome, violent, and rather fascinating, unfortunately bears no relevance to the plot. He became Chuck Bunny - the law was his banner, justice was his anthem, 'execute the bastards!' was his war cry. Now the Karma non-twins had strayed into his sights.

Chuck hurried forwards, head low, eyes front, and ducked down behind a sack of potatoes as the quarry glanced around. He caught his breath and mopped his sweating brow with a handkerchief made from genuine rattlesnake. He stuck a cigar in his mouth and chewed on it some before pressing the button on the walkie talkie.

"Come in, El Paso station," he said, his voice was hushed with caution but still betrayed the adrenalin pumping through his flab-strangled veins, "El Paso station, come in!"

Chuck did his best imitation of a walkie talkie hissing.

"This is El Paso station, go ahead, Big Bunny," he said in his El Paso station voice.

"I got two in sight, where the hell's mah back-up, goddamn it?"

"Bad news there, Big Bunny. Two of 'em got bushwacked by injuns at the fruit and veg, the others are away in wines and spirits, there's a dead or alive nosin' around down there, askin' a lot of danged uncomfortable questions."

"Guess I'm on my own," growled Big Bunny, grimacing with determination, "Wouldn't be the first time."

"Goddamn but you're a hero, Big Bunny. If anyone can get 'em and save the chick they've tied to the tracks it's you."

"There's a woman?"

"Sure is! They kidnapped her from that whore house in soft drinks. Right now, she's tied to the railroad just outside of the egg depot, a trolley could come along there at any time."

"Is there no end to it? Big Bunny over and out."

Chuck Bunny released the button and took a look over the potatoes. The quarry had moved on to another aisle, he hurried along to the end and searched the ground for tracks.

Konrad and Katya came to the delicatessen counter and sniffed the air.

"Can you smell garlic?" asked Konrad.

"No, but I can smell onions," said Katya.

They looked at the counter and saw two men behind it in white overalls, with white hats and nice friendly name badges. The one on the left, the skinhead with the safety pin through his lower lip, was Jean-Pierre Goat. The one on the right, the dark-haired stuffed dummy, was called Anthony Just-Anthony.

"Bonjour, my little English friends," said Jean-Pierre in a high-pitched squeal.

"Allo, and welcome to zis, our delicatessen counter. Today we 'ave for you ze -" said Anthony.

"No, no," interrupted Jean-Pierre, "Zey are ze English. And so we must say to zem, 'fuck off, you English scum.'"

"You poor, simple fool," said Anthony, grinning like a mad bloke, "We cannot do zat. Just because zey are ze in-bred filthy offspring of zat bastard Wellington does not mean we should jeopardise our income, no?"

"You always shout at me, Anthony," said a downcast Jean-Pierre, "I no play with you anymore."

"Allo, gorgeous lady," said Anthony, ignoring his associate and turning his attention to Katya, "Can I tempt you with my sausage?"

"Are you, like, a Frenchman who thinks that just 'cause English blokes are so pathetic and inadequate that he can get away with undressing me with his eyes and flirting about sausages and stuff?" asked Katya, letting go of the trolley and taking a step nearer the counter.

The two behind it looked at each other.

"Ze English," said Anthony and he grinned again, "Zey are too clever for ze likes of us, no?"

"I think you are right, Anthony. Quick, let us run away and hide in a place where zere are loads of women with no clothes on."

"Ha, ha! Always you make me laugh, Jean-Pierre."

"So, are you, like, molesting me?" Katya persisted, pawing at what she thought was Lester the Alien's hilt.

"Hmm, let me see now," said Jean-Pierre, "I had loads of women for breakfast and I screwed some too. I am hung like a donkey on steroids and I have more dress sense zan ze whole of zis silly little island put together. I think, zerefore, I must be."

"What about you?" asked Katya, pointing to Anthony as Konrad sat down with a sigh and waited for her to get it over with.

"Sorry," Anthony said, bobbing on his tip-toes, "What was ze question?"

"Are you trying to picture what I'd look like with a banana up my arse and, uh, my knees behind my ears?"

"Zat I am," said Anthony, "And so is my trousers, and so is my appendage at which all ze women wiz no clothes on zey throw zemselves at it."

"Uh-huh," said Katya, and she just about took hold of what she thought was Lester's hilt when Chuck Bunny played his hand.

"Freeze! Nobody move!" he bellowed, so that his ulcer got worse and he had to take a shot of whisky just to deaden the pain.

Jean-Pierre Goat grinned and smirked, then he cocked his head one way and then the other, and then he did a skipping dance, just to be cheeky.

Vaddam! Chuck Bunny's twelve shooter went off like a peal of thunder from hell. The recoil forced the big man to take a step back, while lobotomised Jean-Pierre Goat slumped to the floor, and Anthony Just-Anthony was left wondering where all the grey stuff had come from.

"I know, Jean-Pierre," he said, "Next week let us do a programme about how ze French people zey are crazy about sex and love to screw dead zings. Jean-Pierre? Allo, Jean-Pierre?"

"Zut alors!" was all Jean-Pierre could muster with his last gasp.

Chuck Bunny blew the smoke from the barrel of his gun and then levelled his aim at the three remaining saddle tramps.

"Anyone else feel lucky?" he drawled, spitting his cigar butt onto the floor, "Well?"

"Allo," said Anthony Just-Anthony, quite unable to resist some innuendo, "I can see zat you are a remarkable Englishman by ze size of your weapon."

Vaddam! Chuck Bunny's gun roared again and the barrel ended up pointing vertically with the recoil, Anthony Just-Anthony's head twitched with the impact while a red mist erupted from the back. His nose and left cheekbone burst from the crown of his skull and splattered onto the ceiling with blood and brain and a partially liquidised eyeball. His body fell on top of Jean-Pierre, twitching and jerking, dark gunge flowing from the gaping hole in his face.

"Au revoir, and good night," he said, and lay still.

"Pocket the difference," said Katya in an awed gasp.

"Now it's just you two," rasped Chuck's dry voice, "So who's next?"

"She is," said Konrad.

"He is," said Katya, and they pointed at each other.

"Well, now," said Chuck, "Decisions, decisions."

"Draw on him," whispered Konrad, "Go on, I dare you."

"Fuck off," said Katya, "It's, uh, Tuesday, and, like, I'm not allowed to kill Welshmen on Tuesdays or I'll, uh, get a Tudor in my rungs, and, like, stuff. And besides, what I thought was Lester the Alien appears to my military-issue vibrating vibrator thingy."

"Hmm," said Konrad, looking in the holster, "I guess there's only one thing for it."

Konrad stepped out and faced Chuck Bunny, his hand twitched by his side, his cold eyes met the taciturn stare of his mortal foe. The wind blowing over tombstones and fresh graves was all the sound they heard.

"Anyone for cricket?" Konrad asked rather coolly, because he hadn't got his gun.

Chuck Bunny's aim centred on the man before him, his finger tightened on the trigger and squeezed. Then came the shadow; then came the black figure from the Other Side. It appeared like a phantom on the winds of retribution, the voices of the dead whispered and hailed it as a hero. There was almost enough time for the others to sense the onset of whatever it was, and almost enough time to start turning their eyes towards it, but not quite.

The dread form leaped at Chuck Bunny and in an instant the fat Welshman's arm had snapped like a dry twig and he was collapsing, his assailant flipped through the air and landed on the shelf with the bog rolls. A moment passed, a moment enough for the eyes of the onlookers to catch up with that blur, then it moved again.

Chuck Bunny reached for his other gun with his good arm, but the avenging angel was on him again, clawed hands gripped him and heaved him up, then hurled him away. He screamed as he flew, then he was silent as his back snapped under the impact of his landing among the cans of dog food.

The Karma non-twins stood silently for a moment, watching the figure before them as its shoulders heaved with heavy breathing, then it turned towards them and they were, well, they were reasonably surprised.

It was an old man, an old, short, small, bespectacled man. He wore leathers that had been rubbed down with talcum powder to make them grey, his face was daubed with grey shoe polish, his eyes were nervous and grey. Behind him he had nailed a row of six inch nails into each shoulder blade, the blood that flowed from the wounds was cold and grey.

"You're probably wondering who I am," he said in a small, high voice.

"Looks like we're not the only ones," said Konrad, "Have you, like, got some kind of identity crisis, or something?"

"Silence in the presence of Greyman!" snapped Greyman, "You are probably wondering who I am."

"Not really," said Katya.

"Who am I?" he asked, his eye gleaming with insane malice.

"Uh, a weirdo?" suggested Katya.

"An accountant?" guessed Konrad.

"I am Greyman," said Greyman.

"No shit," remarked Konrad.

"Well, it was fucking crap meeting you," said Katya, "'Bye."

"Do not mock Greyman," said Greyman, his voice was cold like a grave, "You of the defiled, you of livid colours! Of unnatural hair and fluorescent green T-shirt!"

"Like, right," said Katya, "Are you finished?"

"I am the avenging angel," Greyman said, stepping a little closer, "I am retribution."

"I am pissed off," said Katya, whipping out her military issue vibrator and ramming it through Greyman's glasses and deep into his eye socket, "Now, uh, fuck off, yeah?"

The shattered lens glass tinkled to the floor and the high little voice screamed in agony. Greyman staggered back, clutching at the vibrator, while grey vitreous humour dribbled from the punctured eyeball, followed by impressive spurts of blood. He stumbled and tripped, and slumped into the biscuits. From time to time he twitched and murmured delirious nonsense, after a few days he died and that was the end of that.

"Can we get on with this?" asked Katya as she took a new Donald the Deodorant from the appropriate shelf, "I'm, like, getting bored with all this shopping."

"Okay," said Konrad, "I think we've got everything. Let's, like, go home."

"Right," said Katya, "Just as soon as I've finished drooling over the Fake That cereal boxes."

They laughed like lunatics and squeaked and rattled off into the sunset astride their trusty one-wheeled shopping trolley.

10. The Night of the Living Braindead Whiling Away the Small Hours

As the taxi pulled away from the kerb into the depths of the warm night, Morty Morg turned towards the street where he lived, sighing a brief, self-conscious sigh of contentment. His nipples were sore where someone had been chewing them, but he wasn't overly concerned. He plodded like a hippo with a cacky arse, staring into the ground, half listening to his neighbours shouting the odds over the head of a broken, bleeding child. He stopped at his front door and fumbled for his keys, searched sweet wrappers and crusty tissues, getting a little concerned as he reached the loose change, and then the fluff and crisp bits at the bottom. He played absent-mindedly with the sticky green alien in one tissue, then checked the rest of his pockets, resorting to a quick grope in his pants just to be sure. The secret agent security compartment in his vest also came up empty. He started to fret.

The bleak residential monotony around him seemed to close in a little, rustling window boxes with frightening intent. It was an altogether nervous Morty who scurried down the narrow passage alongside the house, trying to duck the vast, furry spiders' webs. He arrived at the kitchen's broken window and was almost comforted by the familiar unhygienic sprawl, sparsely illuminated by the glowing clock on the oven. The window opened easily, but then the garden fence broke open, and Morty caught a foot-long splinter in the side of his head. Nothing was ever quite so in-focus again.

A hooligan in black, with white zorks hanging from the brim of his hat, staggered into the garden, just about to lose his balance. From the garden the other side of the broken fence there came the sounds of hurried footfalls and angry exchanges.

The hooligan in black pointed a fat-barrelled blaster behind him, and started shooting. Morty Morg jammed his fingers in his ears, trying to deaden the deafening thuds as white flashes leaped into the darkness, bursting whoever had been there like so many over-inflated sausages. A few rounds of ammunition zinged around, then there was silence.

Morty unplugged his fingers with a pair of soggy pops, and glared at the hooligan, wishing he was well 'ard. Before he could moan, though, a fat, bald lorry driver with blistery green skin vaulted athletically over the remains of the fence, voluminous breasts a-swinging behind his braces. He turned his glow-in-the-dark eyes on the black-clad hooligan and started laying into him.

Morty's eyes were on the blaster. He was relieved to see that it was pointing away from him. Well away from him. Right in the opposite direction. A heavy green punch landed in the hooligan's back, the blaster pointed even further and more oppositely away. A fat green knee was jammed in the hooligan's kidneys, and it was then that the blaster started to turn towards the fat man. When the fat man stepped sideways, coming to rest between the blaster muzzle and the wincing student, Morty knew he should have brought his umbrella.

There was a muffled thud and he was hit by a shower of arse fat and greasy dinners. The stink was unbelievable, Morty's skin burned as though he'd had a bath in bleach, all in all he didn't think it was very good.

"I never stood a chance," the fat man gasped as his eyes rolled behind his face and he passed on into the big burger bar on the other side.

The hooligan tucked his gun in his trousers and looked around for something. The slime was still dripping off Morty as he recovered from the initial shock.

"Oh. Hello Konrad," he said, surprised by the unannounced visit, "Cup of tea?"

Konrad caught sight of Morty and frowned.

"Did you see Space Wreck yesterday?" Morty persisted, "That bit where they sucked out Fantabula's brains with a bike pump? Erm. I know I saw her nipples through her clothes, I just know it. They wear very tight clothes in the future. Is Katya around?" He wiped the ooze out of his eyes and peered into the apparently empty shadows.

"Where the fuck did you spring from?" Konrad inquired suspiciously.

A high-pitched whirring cut off any reply Morty was brewing, and he and Konrad glanced up into sky, where a dark disk had spread out across the stars.

"Oh, fuck..." Morty wittered, feeling his bladder empty itself.

The black disk hovered for a moment, whirring, then dropped suddenly, slamming into Morty's garden with a horrific crash. Dust curled lazily against the moon, as the Stealth UFO's orange go-faster stripes and trim lit up, and the circular hatch into the bizarre alien machine whizzed open.

A drop-dead gorgeous bird with livid blue hair, wearing just her cheap polyester undies, fell out of the hatch, clutching at a feather duster.

"No I can't," she said thoughtfully where she lay on the lawn, glancing at Konrad.

"Told you," he said.

Morty tried to memorise what he could see of Katya's arse where her knickers had wriggled down a bit.

"Why are you dressed like that?" he asked, all sneery and perverted.

"What d'you think I am, a fucking nudist?" she shouted, getting to her feet, "Now shut up, yeah? This is important."

Morty was vaguely aware of a heavy black shape dropping from the sky, trailing a brace of steaming hydraulic dicks. The black form landed near the crashed UFO, looked around, and shit a brick as Konrad blasted it, sending smoking debris spinning through the night.

"See?" he said to Katya, "They're everywhere."

"Ooh, I'm so scared," she said softly, all breathey and intense.

"It's not my orifice they're chasing," Konrad pointed out.

Morty clutched his arse, slimy though it was.

"What the fuck's going on now?" he whined.

"It's the invasion of the, uh, Psychotrons," Katya said, dusting violently between her bazongas.

"Cyberons," Konrad corrected her.

"Hmm. Cyber? With a 'C'?" Morty murmured, thumbing through his Spatzer's A-Z of Contemporary Aliens.

"They're not in the '02 edition," Konrad observed.

"No?" Morty gave up looking.

"We tried them with acid," Katya said, pressing her thumb between Morty's eyes, "And electrocution, and fire, and radiation," she continued, searching for buttons concealed beneath his skin. "In the end we gave up and just shot the heathen varmints. Which seemed to work."

Morty felt his head to make sure the immature cow hadn't stuck any silly memos on him.

"He's feeling himself up," Konrad whispered to Katya.

"Weird."

"But what's going on?" Morty whinged. He hated murder mysteries.

"What are you, FUCKING DEAF?" Katya screamed in his ear, having taken a firm hold of his hair. Konrad ducked the spray of wax from the other ear with a second to spare.

"Oh, right, Cyberons," Morty whimpered.

"Cyberons," Katya growled at him, "Big black Cyberons with alloy eyeliner. Big black steaming killfuck machines with three smooth, liquid-nitrogen spurting pokers. Uh, kind of the opposite of scalding spiky marrows. Shit, I'd fucking hate to get stuck in a rut."

"Oh, right - Cyberons." The student wondered when the good guys were going to show up.

"You better believe it," Katya said, ducking behind him in case anything was creeping up on her. She peered over his shoulder.

"I did GCSE science," Morty said to her, trying to reassure her, "It's all a matter of identifying the problem, and then applying what we know to form a plan. Or something."

"I'm glad it's 'or something,'" Konrad replied, "I hate science. And scientists are all wankers."

"Not all of them," Katya mused, "After all, there was that total fucking nutter who came up with the bomb. The big, silky-skinned bald-brained bomb of sexy isotopes. Hee hee."

"Especially him," Konrad argued, "I think I might have to get a hang-up about this."

"Doubt it," Katya giggled, "You're too shallow for hang-ups."

"Anyway," Morty put in, "It's all a matter of rational consideration and informed systematic plotting."

"Sounds like fun," Konrad didn't think.

"Sounds shite," his sister announced, thinking he'd really lost it this time.

A muddy welly ricocheted off Morty's head and whizzed into the night.

Everyone looked around for the mysterious assailant.

"Will you pissheads shut the fuck up?" A student complained from an open window upstairs in Morty's house, "Some of us have got lectures tomorrow. Bloody Young Conservatives." The head withdrew and the window slammed.

"Sorry," Morty whispered, too late.

"Nice neighbourhood, very friendly," Konrad said.

"It's a wankpit," Morty muttered.

"Uh, so the invasion of the Cyberons is out, huh?" Katya said gloomily.

"Mmm. There are people trying to sleep." Morty could have cried he was so relieved.

"But ze night is yurng," Katya said, a bit French.

Morty tried to sneak towards his house, but Katya legged him up with a swift and very tasty leg.

"And you needn't think you're going to creep to the fridge and get pissed," she warned Konrad, wagging a finger at him.

"Oh, cool," Konrad said, stuffing his hands in his pockets.

"God, I hate women," Morty sobbed into the ground.

"Anyway," said Katya, "This was, uh, Cyberons, right?"

"Can't lie to you sis," Konrad replied.

"You lost me," she said impatiently. "What was that supposed to mean?"

"It meant yes," said Konrad after the brief hesitation required to realise it wasn't worth pursuing.

"OK. So what about Psychotrons instead? And somewhere more upmarket?"

Murder Mystery Mansion sat deep in the Dorset countryside, snug under liberal helpings of ivy, and homely woodwork that was just too tasteful for insect infestation. Inside, the place was chock full of tartan blankets and moose heads and fireplaces and smoking sleuths pacing classical rugs, while scheming butlers hid alien brain-suckers in priceless vases, waiting for some bored eccentric among the doomed guests to start up a game of indoor badminton.

Everyone was gathered together in the dining room. The crowd stood in a semi-circle, clutching bloodied knives and smoking marsupials, all with fake alibis and ironclad motives, all as guilty as fat fuck, crooked, pisshead, child molesting MPs. The corpse was squished in the corner, exhibiting wounds from each of the guests. All, that is, with the exception of one.

"Hmm," the sleuth rumbled, examining the corpse with a telescope. He straightened up and faced the assembled guests. "The reason I have asked you all here, is that one of you, in this very room, didn't kill Mrs Shankhand. So," he scanned them with his eyes, "Whodidn'tdunnit?"

Katya gulped and whispered to Konrad, "Shit, I totally forgot. I was, uh, doing my hair, honest."

"This has been a night well spent," Konrad said, so convincingly that Katya thought he might have actually meant it.

"It's been a load of crap," Morty said, "I fucking hate the pair of you. You're tossers."

"Pleased to meet you. Besides, we had to come," Katya said, "To find out if the old fucker had left us loads of moolah in his will."

"What old fucker?" Morty asked, wondering if this was what it was like to be on drugs.

"Uh, the one everyone just killed."

"And did he?" Morty asked, thinking of all the lottery tickets he could buy with fifty million quid.

"Erm. Dunno. I'll ask," Katya said, chewing her lip. "Er, 'scuse me? Um, anyone?" No one wanted to know.

"I hate people, I hate things, I hate you," Morty spat, glaring demonically, really getting up a quite a bit of personality.

The gathered guilty guests all assumed a total silence as a big man in a smoking jacket (draughty downstairs, I'll bet) waved his arms around and swore a lot. Katya and Morty were still swearing at each other, oblivious to the absent Konrad. Konrad had sniffed out the fridge way out the back of the dump, and was pilfering gaudy junk food. Which was handy, seeing as at that moment the guests whipped off their skins and revealed themselves to be slavering Psychotron shapeshifter rapists from Szquarg.

Morty and Katya clutched at each other like people do in cartoons, while the spectral metal demon monsters from outer space slowly turned on them and grinned, hissing steam through their gleaming silver teeth.

These were the Psychotrons - big silver pulsing mechanical fuck-brained psychotic fridge magnets with attitude and three horns. Psychotrons. Oh yes. (Not to be confused with Cyberons).

"Help," Katya hissed at Morty, trying not to move her lips, instead grinning as though she hadn't realised that the Psychotrons were there, thinking they might let her go, or something.

"Bollocks," Morty replied, adopting much the same strategy, "Where's that bloody gun of yours?"

"Who, Lester? Uh, it's his day off."

"Bloody typical."

"Yeah, he's a wanker, huh?"

"Shut up and think up a clever plan."

"I don't think I like the tone of your proposal. Sounded positively, uh, indecent."

"Shut up and drop your knickers, or something."

"Don't fucking tell me to shut up, you half-pint slab of greasy cack. Just you wait. I'll fucking kill you. I'm gonna fucking kill you. Just you, uh, see if I don't, and things."

"We're the ones going to get killed. We're going to get humped by the blistering icy fat dicks of these alien menaces, and turned into frozen images of terror and agony, while sawing little bugs spurted into our guts by the passionate invaders will gnaw out our ice-cubed inner bits."

"Arsehole," Katya sneered, realising he was probably right.

"Oh, hang on," he continued. "That was the Cyberons. This is getting too confusing."

"Double arsehole," Katya retorted.

Just then Konrad swung in on the big crystal light fitting that's hard to spell, guns blazing, hot lead raining on the Psychotrons, empty shells showering the carpet.

"Come in pieces, arseholes," Konrad said through gritted teeth, but then he lost his grip on the thingy and plunged into the throng.

For a moment he thought that that might be the lot. The silver mass engulfed him, hungry to ice him up. He took aim into the laughing death-machines and blasted for all he was worth. The flickering torrent of tracers carved a passage through the Psychotrons who were, quite frankly, going bananas. Katya and Morty legged it after Konrad, scarpering down the tunnel he dug in the seething masses of illegal aliens, although not before Katya had kicked Morty in the chin for cuddling her.

They ran out of the front door, down the gravelled drive and into the night, the chattering marauders never far behind, but they caught the bus at Little Fudge on the Muff and the cheapskate alien melon farmers got kicked off for not having tickets, whereas the three heroes of humanity had had the foresight to photocopy Morty's student bus pass and change the names to incriminate the guilty. You know who you are.

11. A Short Problem of Purple

HARRY It ain't no good if everyone
likes it. The same stupid shits'll
agree with you as turn right at
'no right turn' signs, and the sad
no-lifes who think Molly Mohawk
is a fucking purple rabbit.

FRANK Molly Mohawk is a rabbit.

HARRY Molly Mohawk ain't no fucking
rabbit.

FRANK Strangest hippo I ever saw.

HARRY Look, I ain't saying I know what
the fuck Molly Mohawk is, all
right? I don't know what the fuck
Molly Mohawk is. But one thing I
know she ain't, is some fucking
rabbit.

Scene from film that was never made because it was crap.

Konrad Karma was asleep in his bonkers-barmy Bermuda shorts and leather jacket, blissfully comatose, and he was having a dream. A dream where he was swimming in a bubbly ocean of lemonade, where a big lemon sun was blazing in a chlorine-blue sky, and there were loads of very tasty chicks indeed bobbing all around. Suddenly he seemed to hear the lifeguard, the very sexy chick of a lifeguard, calling his name. He looked across to where the she was sitting up a palm tree, playing with a gorilla's coconuts. Beneath the tree sprawled the beach blankets and beach balls and even more very tasty chicks with not very much on, working on that tan. But it wasn't the lifeguard who was calling his name, although someone definitely was.

"Konrad! Konrad, wake the fuck up and, like, help! Shithead!"

Konrad opened one eye but couldn't see anything, although he was aware of something sitting on him and shaking him. He had had similar experiences enough times to know roughly what was happening.

"What the fuck is it, you stupid bitch?" he mumbled.

"Help me, Konrad, shit, bollocks!" came Katya's voice, sounding quite muffled.

"What is it? If it's that fucking toaster again how many times do I have to tell you not to stick your fingers in it?"

"No, uh, it's not the fucking toaster," she said, shaking him some more, and still sounding like she'd got her head stuck up her arse, "Can't you see this is serious?"

"Can't really see much of anything."

"Oh, sorry," she said, as she was revealed to him, "I was just, uh, smothering you with the pillow to get your attention."

Konrad sat up, leaned on one elbow, and looked at his sister who seemed quite agitated. She appeared to have just woken up and was wearing just her 'East Under-age Sex' T-shirt and the knickers with 'Er...July?' written on the front.

"What seems to be the problem?"

"It's, like, talking to me. It won't shut up, it just goes on and on, over and over, saying the same crap."

"Um, what keeps talking to you?"

"You know - it! It keeps talking to me."

"Hmm. Was this before or after you woke up?"

"Fuck off, wanker," and she climbed off the bed and headed for the door, rather dejected.

"Oh, wait then, you stupid, bloody, miserable bitch. What is it that's talking to you?"

"That's not a decent question," she said, stopping at the door, and she looked back at him angrily, "You're not much of a gentleman, huh?"

"Er, no, okay. Fine. What do you want me to do about it if you won't tell me what the problem is?"

"Well, help me, shithead!"

"And what am I supposed to do?"

"I don't know. If I knew what you were, like, going to do I'd do it myself!"

"Right, so something's talking to you? Uh-huh. But you won't tell me what it is. Oh, right. And you expect me to help you."

"Of course. What else is family for?"

"I sometimes wonder myself. Well, um, you could try earplugs, I guess."

"Tried 'em," she snapped, "And didn't like the smell."

"In your ears."

"Did that too. Didn't shut the bastard up."

"I guess it's a voice in your head then, wouldn't you agree, dear little sister?"

"You saying I'm, uh, mad?" she asked, her frown sharpening as her face darkened around it.

"Er," was all Konrad could manage before she jumped back on him and started hitting him and clawing him and shouting and screaming.

"Fucking bastard! I'm not mad!"

"Get off me!" he shouted and socked her one on the chin.

Katya landed on the floor on her backside, legs splayed, a puzzled gape on her face. She spat her chewing out and sulked. If a doctor had been around he would have warned her against it - if the wind changed she'd have stayed like it.

"I can't hear anything," Konrad said at last.

Katya looked up at him, then down between her legs.

"Oh wow, thanks," she said, and skipped off to molest a pensioner, or something.

12. A Red Herring

Sischin's Bleak Isle rose cold and dark from a tireless ocean. All around the waters swelled irritably under the hot air of the night, great shimmering mounds and dells rolled effortlessly, only the murmur of the sea spoke out in the quiet. All the world was still, all upon the cool earth, still, the clammy air, all still but the sea, whispering and lapping. Under the pale radiance of the moon the stark forms of rusting buoys listed drunkenly and rose and fell with the waters, wisps of cloud were shunted across the star speckled heavens on a dry breeze, on the island the stargazers watched for the sign. As the night drew on and the flamboyant music from the island cried out across the wavetops so too the moon changed into a splendid waning orange. Beneath it many coloured lights and lanterns shimmered amid tree and roof tops, all the quay and wharf seemed afire, fireworks erupted at midnight, not long after steam hissed from hunched engines that were silhouetted against the sky. They growled and snorted as they drove the insane delights of Stumpy's Travelling Circus. The music and the laughter came louder, the watchers at the clifftop lit a fire and settled down with mugs in hand and eyes turned to the west.

Sischin's Bleak Isle was as fine a haven for slobbersome, butcherous mad dogs of the sea as there was. It lay some way from the shipping lanes, further still from the eyes of the garrisons, and the inns were just the way the clientele liked them - dark and cramped and grimy, plenty of fights and no water in the cocktails. All the days and nights were carnivals, ever since the unfortunate day when the painted ships of Stumpy's Circus had dropped by for repairs and had been prevented from leaving by the island's occupying army. This crazed army had a thing about parties. At their head was the nephew of the late and not-so-lamented Cap'n Brace Aharr and he had a few things to prove to a lot of people, not least his uncle, so he set about it in the best way he knew. He was known only as Red Herring, Terror of the Southern Seas, nephew of the late, lamented and equally infamous Cap'n Brace Aharr. Herring raped and pillaged as he saw fit, across all the Southern Seas he roamed, or stayed at home when he couldn't be bothered with all that sailing lark.

He thieved and plundered, murdered and extorted, always bringing back enough booty and booze to keep the islanders happy, that is to say, drunk. As the Mrs. Lin hotel guide put it, 'Things have really gone downhill.'

In the beginning the island had been quiet enough but with one thing and another, as the seas became more and more dangerous, so too more and more verminous scum found their way to its sun-baked shores. Red Herring was just another nail in an old, old coffin. Along the wharf, where the inns shook to the laughter of the pirates and the square seemed alive with drunken dancers, no one remained who thought that the decline into anarchy had been a bad thing. That crowd had been strung up long ago. So what had once been a pleasant if unremarkable spot now had more peg legs and eyepatches than a Bad-Old-One-Eyed-One-Legged-Jack concert at Halibut Cove.

The town was alive with laughter and music, garish costumes of legendary characters and creatures danced among the merrymakers, they cavorted through the narrow streets where onlookers watched from high windows with shutters thrown back. On the dancers went, careering through the town square, across the cobbles and around the fountain which hadn't worked since the day the late, great Cap'n Brace Aharr had tried to force an unfortunate sailor down the nozzle after a disagreement over a woman. Music was provided courtesy of several groups of below average musicians. The organ-grinder was not present that night, he had mislaid his monkey and couldn't cope without it. Those who were there were armed with many old instruments and, while no one had been able to agree on a particular tune to play so each did his own thing, the remarkable thing was that no one seemed to notice.

Almost everyone was happy. All the dancers and spectators were happy, the drunkards in the inns were pleasantly drunk, the lay-abouts on the wharf were merry in the extreme, the vile Red Herring and his sinister henchmen were ecstatic in the Dead Parrot Tavern, bunched around a table in a darkened corner, smoking pipes and counting their loot. There were three on the island who were not happy. They were locked in the damp and dark gaol, where water dribbled from cracks in the stone walls and the iron bars resonated with the tooth-jarring music. Through the tiny cell window, the light of the fireworks flickered, throwing colourful patterns across the corpse of a long-term resident. The first of the three was the village idiot, incarcerated for her part in the robbery at the cess pool beneath the Dead Parrot. The second of the three was a gambler at the casino, he had had the misfortune to break the island's principle law and had beaten Red Herring at cards. The third of the three was the corpse and no one had bothered to ask him what he had done.

"So, y'see," the village idiot was drawling, eyeing her companion as he shuffled the pack of aces that he had secreted in his pocket, not to cheat so much as to turn the odds in his favour, "So, y'see, I didn't have no choice."

"I see," the gambler muttered absent-mindedly, pulling his false peg leg out from under him and sitting back against the wall.

"You have a leg!" said the idiot with some surprise.

"Two," said the gambler.

The idiot grinned knowingly, "I'll bet you've got two eyes too, eh? Two eyes?" The gambler pulled off his eye patch, "Aye, I knew it! There's many have tried that. Oldest trick in the book."

The gambler had had a hook also, but he couldn't shuffle the cards.

"S'that why they threw you in here?" the idiot asked, moving closer to the gambler and lowering her voice, "'Cause you're a pretend pirate?"

"No," the gambler replied, "It's because I won."

"You did what?" screeched the idiot. She shook her head and then broke out laughing, "And I thought I was an idiot!"

The idiot looked into the face of the gambler, he was a young man, no scars or anything, his face was not the face of a pirate, more that of a cool bloke who would just as soon shoot you as pull off your head, pour petrol down your neck, and set fire to your trousers. The clothes he wore were as fine as those worn by the best dressed of the captains at the Parrot so he certainly looked the part. The gambler looked at the idiot, gazed at the sparkling eyes and the blue hair and saw just a mad chick with a pilchard in her vest.

The idiot seemed to be listening to the music for a while, tapping her foot in time, then she delved into her coat and produced a colourful party hat which she slapped on her blue crown.

"They'll kill you at noon," she said sadly, "String you up, cut you into quarters and serve you to the gulls."

"So they said," the gambler replied, looking up from where he had been nodding, weary with the late hour. The idiot stood and groaned as she stretched up onto the tips of her sexy little toes so that she might see from the window. Already the first streaks of dawn were reaching up from the sea, the idiot slumped back to the floor.

"So what are you, uh, doing on this shit heap?" she asked, leaning close over the gambler.

"It's a long story," said the gambler, "And I can't be bothered. Besides..."

Music started up - fine, well-performed music, in the style of piratin' and sailin'. The gambler stood up, adopted an inane grin, and produced a spongy white pad from his pocket.

"I've got new Antifish (tm) - the spongy white pad that will give the heave-ho to fishiness. Yes! By hook or by crook your keel will be haulable once more. Long for those days of youth? Those times of carefree innocence and a scentless crotch? Do you walk down the street and wonder why people are running into fish shops for a breath of fresh air? Wonder no more - it's you! Yes, you! Through years of sad neglect those nether regions are starting to get a little barnacle encrusted, stay well away from the agriculture and fisheries officials - you'll be in trouble for breaking that quota. And do you think they'll believe you when you protest that you haven't got fifty-thousand tons of warm, rather old tuna down your pants? Not on your nelly! But with new Antifish (tm) you can make for Jolly Rogering and tell fishy pants to walk that plank. Available now from all good stores; Antifish (tm), the swashbucklin' remedy for all your fishy ailments."

13. Tall Tales of the Sea

Speaking of fishy ailments...

"Great boat," Katya complemented Sir Francis Drake as the wooden tub lurched over another wave.

Drake was perturbed, it seemed to him that the boat was wallowing in the water, it didn't feel right.

"Yeah, s'okay," he muttered, twirling a finger in his beard, "Me other one's a trimaran motor yacht, y'know? It's got satellite TV and a really big fridge and everything."

They were standing on the sticky-up bit at the back of a hefty-looking junk. Satellite navigation gear was clustered around the barnacle-encrusted swab who had been given the wheel to play with. He yo-ho-hoed and chuckled, occasionally swigging at his Bacardi.

A couple of weather-beaten swabs were leaning over the chart table, having a hell of a time because some bugger had rolled the chart up and now they couldn't get it to stay flat for anything.

"Oi! Yvgenny, you Ukrainian twat, have you been at these fucking charts again?" the Brummy swab yelled.

One of the many swabs who was loitering near the empty masts glanced up, then gave them the finger.

"So if the sails aren't out, how come we're going along?" Katya pressed Drakers, who had got down to oiling his chainsaw.

"Twin engines, luv, big turbo diesel monsters, y'know?" He pointed down at the deck, "That's what the really loud throbbing sound is. What do they teach you at these bloody schools?"

"How to shag, mainly," Katya said, but it's not true, and this is not a true reflection of the state of the education system, before anyone gets all uppity and makes an issue of it. It's just that was all she listened to.

"What about me and me bleedin' amazing exploits?" Drakers squeaked, his ego dented.

"Uh, too politically sensitive. After all, you are a psychopathic pirate and rapist who kicked barrels of shit out of the Spanish tossers."

"'Kicks,' luv - I ain't done yet. Oh no, not this son of England. I spit on your new world order, you apathetic fuckers, I spit on all you bastards, and the Spanish what I hate worser than fuck."

"Actually, Drakers, you're a bit crazy, aren't you?"

"Speaking of which, we better get up that swab of yours that we been keel-hauling."

"Oh, do we have to?"

"Better. Oi! Smithers and Harnigan-Wickle, you pair of useless bastards. What do you think this is, the London Shit Ship (TM)? Make lively, ye swabs, and haul up that lubber what we been keel-hauling."

The two swabs saluted and scuttled away to the winches.

"No, you brute," Smithers whinged, "We must turn it clockwise."

"Up yours, you festering freakwad," snarled H-W and he gobbed bigtime on Smither's head. "We go this way!"

"I say!" snorted Smithers, standing back all huffed-like, "You filthy swiney person. Why, I do think you be a Spaniard!"

H-W plugged him with a pistol, right in the lungs, so that he careered off the back of the junk, straight into the jaws of the waiting sharks.

"Oi, you Jock bastard!" H-W yelled to a spare swab, "Get over here and gimme a hand with this!"

Meanwhile, Katya was posing with the sextant, peering around, realising why some bugger had gone and invented regular binoculars. She was wearing a summer dress with her smiley-face badge on it, only this dress was really short and it fluttered around the bottom of her arse in the breeze. Teaser. Swabs kept going up to her and giving her fivers for a shag.

She shot the latest swab to try it, right in the head, so that he resprayed half the deck that some of the swabs had just scrubbed.

"It's not that I don't find you attractive, or anything," she apologised, "It's just I can see myself stinking like a fish market in high summer."

The junk lurched a bit and things creaked.

A bit later, due to some very poor steering by a drunken swab, and somewhere in mid-Atlantic, they hit a chuggy old fishing boat. Konrad, who'd dried out by now, thought maybe he'd better throw someone a life belt. He grabbed one of the orange doughnuts and wandered over to the side of the junk. Below him the fishing boat was lurching sickeningly in the swell, plumes of oil were gushing from a broken engine, and the hull was severely holed. People were jumping from it, trying to swim for the junk.

"Hmm," murmured Konrad, "There's something not quite right about these fishermen."

Katya looked over the side to see what he was on about.

"What are you on about?"

"I dunno. Maybe it's the colour of their boat (black), or maybe it's their flag (black), or maybe it's the way they're all dressed in black, with black balaclavas with secret black writing written on them.

"What can it all mean?" Katya pondered.

"I'll chuck 'em this anyway," Konrad said, because he was a kind soul really.

Unfortunately, in all the excitement, he'd accidentally mixed up the life belt and a hand grenade. Shame really, as all those nice black-clad motherfuckers were blown to pieces, or burned in the ensuing fire. Their boat exploded too, which led some to suspect it had been overflowing with an illegal firearms shipment, but then some people are just plain paranoid.

The fire dwindled behind them as darkness fell and Drakers pressed on towards wherever it was he was going. Konrad went into his cabin - a woodworm infested creaky little coffin with a candle and a porthole. He got started on a log.

His loonytune sister was in the dark of the hold, squatting froglike on a barrel in her undies and gun belt, muttering weird chants at Unchukka and Oobigoobi.

"Your party's over, man!" hissed a voice from her tasteful knickers.

"My party's over, man," Katya muttered.

"You must appease Unchukka and Oobigoobi!" the voice insisted.

"I will, buster, but can you stop hissing? It fucking tickles-"

"You must kill everybody and paint strange pictures in their blood."

"I must, if you say so, uh, but I'm no fucking artist."

"You must howl at the moon and grunt and defecate."

"Okay," Katya agreed after very little thought, "But I do have one teeny, Tony question: uh, why?"

"I dunno. Must be all this heat and salt, or something. Now shut up and get on with it."

Katya climbed down off the barrel and immediately got a splinter in her foot.

"Ow!" she squealed like a right girly, "Can I put my fucking shoes back on?"

"No, you can't."

"Shit, I was only asking." Her face settled into a big sad hunted everybody-hates-me face. "I should've known. You're just as bad as everyone else. Everybody feels threatened by me, because I'm so, uh, intense and in touch with myself, and virile, and fucking clever, and downright nice to know. Yeah, everybody loves me."

A drunken swab with a wooden leg stumbled into the hold for a slash. He dropped his tankard of rum and swore real bad.

"Hello, uh, big fat swab buddy," said Katya squinting at him out of the darkness. She reached out in front of her with Lester the Alien, but the swab wasn't looking at Lester the Alien.

There was big bang and a flash of fire, and then a big sludge of dead swab thudded off the wall and sploojed across the floor.

"Fucking pervert," Katya complained. "You're all the fucking same, you think just 'cause I'm all fit and nubile and sweaty and only wearing my undergarments I'm some kind of oglematic moogle. Don't worry if that didn't make sense, Lester me old pal, I think it's mild sunstroke, or something. I tell you, I've gone fucking mental. Just now I could've sworn my genitals were talking to me. Now, uh, how crazy is that?"

"Forsooth!" yelled Sir Drakers, and he banged his fist on the chart table.

"Sorry, guv," the Mate shrugged apologetically.

"Some fucking mate you are."

The Mate picked up his suitcase and he and half the crew wandered over to the side of the junk, before scrambling down rope ladders to another ship. They'd just had a better offer from this unlikely steel tub, whose crew had been eaten by its passengers, who had themselves totally flipped out. The passengers were some sad act we-play-music tossers from long ago called the Sad Pissheads, and they were looking for a new angle. They didn't find it, in fact all they got, after they ate the new crew, was fifty years apiece.

Drakers realised the game was up - he was stranded in mid-Atlantic with only a handful of drunken swabs left to his name. He decided to scuttle the ship and scarper with the loot.

Konrad was still working on the log. He'd already decided what it was going to look like, now it was just taking time to carve it into shape with the blunt switchblade. It might have been a flick knife, but switchblade sounds cooler. Konrad thought a totem pole could be really useful, so he went on hacking, rather than give up thinking it was a load of old bollocks.

Katya had found two big fat hairy swabs who were all greased up with lard and doing things with no clothes on. Katya thought it was quite erotic, but then she was unbalanced. Her little friend pointed out that this was neither the time nor the place, so she whipped out Lester the Alien and took aim.

"Say your prayers, swabs," she drawled, and she plugged the first one right through the kneecaps so that he fell over and rolled around in agony. The other one cringed in the corner, but Katya sorted him out with a bullet right in the face. His head expanded across the wall behind him in a loud floral pattern.

"Okay, crippled swab," said Katya stepping up to the crippled swab, "Double say your prayers."

"Jeez, ya got me!"

Lester recoiled violently as he punctured the big fat swab some more.

Katya crept into the next cabin and glanced around. It was dark in there and she couldn't see anything at first, but slowly she became aware of the bunk under the porthole, and the quiet breathing that came from it. She walked up to the bunk, pondering what her next one-liner was going to be, when something really strange happened. Whoever was in the bunk copped himself a feel.

She levelled Lester at the molester in the bunk, but then, while it was still fumbling and sort of vibrating in her pantiolas at the front, it reached round the back and gave her arse a damn good feel as well. Before she could so much as squeak, her bra had been invaded, and her nipploombas were being modulated by some strange unearthly force. Then she was grabbed around the waist and instantaneously hoicked under the duvet to find a mass of affectionate tentacles.

"Jesus was a biker! It's a fucking pussymonster, or something."

She went to sleep being cuddled by all those warm squidgy-soft arms, and didn't do anything rude, honest, because that would be totally immoral.

When she woke up she had sort of been dumped over a log that was being hurled around by the ocean.

"Morning, sis," said Konrad, and he carried on carving at his totem pole.

"Urg," said Katya, "Where the fuck am I? Where's my pussymonster?"

"We're on a log in the middle of the sea," Konrad explained.

"I didn't dream it, you sinisterly cynical bastard!" she said, sitting up so that the log nearly rolled over.

"Easy, sis, this is all about subtle blends of balance, small movements in tune with the rhythm of the swell, and knowing when to panic."

"Shut the fuck up. What have you done with my pussymonster? I bet you've fucking nicked it all for yourself, you cow's festering boobs!"

"Trust me, baby, I've got no need for your pussy or your monster."

"You wanker!" she screeched, going red in the eyes, "Gimme my monster! It felt me up and everything! It used me and made me so filthy and debased that I think I actually think I love it! Where's my writhing pussymonster?"

"Go back to sleep, Tiger."

"Up yours, dogbreath." She looked around, "So where's the boat? Where's all those greasy swabs? Where's Drakers?"

"Drakers sank the tub and scarpered with the loot."

"What a cool bastard." She drummed her fingers on the log. "So where's my pussymonster?! I'll fucking cry. I'll fucking sulk forever and ever. You'll never hear the end of this, you double-retarded Ozzie's arse with spikes! I know what it is. It's vagina envy. You selfish bastard."

Konrad shrugged.

"I think I've definitely hit on something here."

"I think I'll definitely hit something here."

"Threats won't save you. I've tipped your rock, bub, I've found out what wiggly monster's hiding under it."

"Let me guess. Is it a pussymonster?"

"Nah, it's a vagina envy monster."

"Oh right. Is that like a vaginamonster that's envious?"

"Nope, as you well know, it's actually overwhelming envy of the superior genital unit."

"You're so smart, sis. You're a regular Einstein."

"It's good of you to be so gracious in defeat. You wanna see my, uh, vagina, huh? 'Cause I've got one, you big stack of poop. I've got one and you haven't, and mine's really good 'cause it works and stuff."

Konrad dug a big chunk out of the totem pole. "Shut up, sis."

"No, really, if you wanna see it you've just got to say, and I'll give you a quick flash."

"That's sweet."

"Y'know, I'll just-"

"If you don't shut up I'll never tell you what I've done with your pussymonster."

"Oh," she pressed a darling fingery digit to her lips.

"Yes. Now make me some tea."

"Right. Uh, except I don't really rate your log's amenities."

"The tea stuff's over there somewhere, floating in all that debris."

"Cool. Hang on. I'm hygroscopic y'know. Yeah, I have this unstoppable structural urge to soak up water what the fuck am I on about?"

"I tell you, I'm really envious of vaginas. And if I had a vagina I'd want a pussymonster. They're great."

"Yeah, that's what I was trying to tell you. I knew you'd see it my way."

"So where's my tea and biscuits?"

"Biscuits?" Katya choked.

"They're in the debris over the other side."

Katya glanced around feverishly, "Yeah, hang on. I'm working on it.

Pussymonster. Gotta have my pussymonster."

Konrad watched her patiently. "Better get a move on, sis, before I decide I want some cake."

"Yeah. Cake. Right. Are you sure you won't make do with a quick, sneaky glimpse of my vagina? Maybe I'll help you, uh, compose a fantasy about it, or something."

"I dunno..."

"It's really good, honest, just like the real thing. It's all vivid and in colour. I'll give you few pointers on how it works, how's that? Can I, uh, say fairer than that? Only please don't make me get all wet."

"What I really need is a cuppa, but I'm finding it hard to concentrate because I'm so worried about how much air the pussymonster's got left."

"Pussymonster. Really gotta have my pussymonster."

"Yeah, it's a tragedy."

"How about if I let you feel it? Go on, that's a good deal, huh, huh? I used to charge for that in the biology department."

Konrad was beginning to suspect that his cunning plan to shut the bitch up had backfired rather horrendously. However, the previous night had been one of mutual affection and passions, so Katya's continual prattling had caught the attention of her pussymonster where it was lurking deep under the waves, and had given it time to home in on her mind-numbing ranting.

"See. I told you it was vagina envy," said Katya, feeling something probe her undies.

"Leave me out of it," Konrad remarked, a little sickened by the whole sordid episode.

"Oh wow! It's my pussymonster!" Katya squealed with delight as she noticed all the pulsing tentacles reaching up out of the water. Then she was gone, sucked down into the dark ocean by her new love.

Konrad threw a slightly concerned glance at the camera, then he stared over at the tea gear where it bobbed not far away.

"Honest to God, that's how it happened," the stranger in the yellow waterproof clobber drawled, then drained his pint.

The storm howled around the pub, the wind screamed off the boiling sea and whistled through the rocks, tearing at the shutters over the windows, clattering the sign this way and that like a bored child. The rain pelted from the heavens, drumming at the earth, hammering roof and door. The dark rolling clouds flickered with fire and thunder boomed, rumbling into the depths of the earth.

The landlord handed the stranger another pint. "Get away with you," he chuckled, "Why I ain't never heard such a tall tale of the sea in all my days. Blue-haired girls sitting on logs, offering to show you their vaginas. Why it just don't happen."

The stranger seized his pint with a spare tentacle.

14. Big Nuke Death

Foreword.

Katya Karma once wrote an epic story with a big bastard wax crayon. She scribbled night and day, toiling until she had, like, blown her childhood on booze and bog roll. It didn't matter how hard she scribbled, or how much sleep she lost, 'cause it was crap and no one would touch it with a barge pole that had a fork taped to the end.

Now that Ms. Karma is really rich and famous and she is everyone's boss, she has had the opportunity to adapt that story and have it inserted within this volume. That story was 'Big Nuke Death' and so is this.

It was a beautiful summer day, a sunny summer day that shimmered beneath a deep blue sky. A thick smog smudged the greys and browns of the horizon, but the toxic, radioactive, poisoned and polluted waste ground was open and clear. The air was as fresh as anything that was fifty percent deadly exhalation of nuclear reactor could be, the moderately mutated grass was green on the whole, with a little brown and yellow to liven the scene up, and among pools of acrid sludge there were rusting barrels decorated with various worrying symbols.

There were five people on the waste ground, standing in a rough circle, eyes turned up towards the sky. Something was coming. An object - something - was falling, falling towards them with incredible velocity.

Konrad Karma was there, although he seemed to want nothing to do with it, and was standing off to one side, dressed in his funeral outfit, his eyes hidden behind his shades. He had his gun tucked in the back of his belt, there was no sense in taking chances.

Still the thing fell, and Mortimer J. Morg watched it with anxiety, his hands trembled a little, sweat beaded on his forehead, his spots filled with a little more pus and one or two burst. He wiped his damp palms down his 'Butt Abyss' T-shirt, his legs shook inside his pink jeans. His eyes were focused on the thing above, it was growing, now it seemed to be circular, still it plummeted.

Pedro the orange alien cactus was also present, his big eyes widened and his throat gulped nervously, he looked beneath the brim of his sombrero at the figure next to him, then back up to the flying object. It drew nearer, whistling down through the atmosphere, seeming to glow red, and spinning with such insane speed that it sickened those watching it from below. The seconds passed, it continued to grow larger in their vision.

Beside the cactus was Agent Orange, the rogue CIA robot. He was a leviathan of silvery metal, an armoured machine in the approximate shape of a man, standing a good nine feet tall. He had a formidable figure - adorned with fins and sweeping lines that suggested his designer had been a little bored with those dreary old tin wheelie bins that the CIA had usually produced. This was altogether different; an impressive metal warrior, clad with armour plates and shoulder pads and knee pads, and with a few glimpses of pipes and powerful machinery underneath. Beneath his chrome dome were heavy aluminium brows, beneath these were the deadly, glowing white eyes. These eyes watched the descending shape, the CPU calculated the imminent arrival, and the robot that so often loved to say 'Eat photons!' had no time to say anything. A cold finger twitched, the steel tendon creaked in the wrist assembly, a flow of obscene binary hummed through its electric mind.

The object fell, round and red, still spinning crazily, whistling louder as it neared the soil of planet Earth. Those eyes that watched it had just enough time to widen a little more, that fearful image had just enough time to make them cower a little lower and flinch, then it arrived with terrible power and awesome energy.

The fifth person was Katya Karma. She bit her lip, her eyes narrowed, her brow creased with concentration. She took a swing at the bastard and missed, her head rang like a kettle drum as the ball ricocheted off it and smacked into Morty's kidneys. Morty staggered and fell over, clutching at his bruised internal organs, while the ball thudded to the ground.

Katya tottered and teetered in her 'I shot Mike Atherton' T-shirt and her loud shorts which seemed to think it was all a load of 'Balls!', then she collapsed into the grass, cricket pads, cricket bat, dented skull, sun-screened cheeks, and all.

"Four!" she muttered, with a mouthful of radioactive dirt.

Agent Orange bent over and picked up the ball, his head cocked with a clank as he assessed the object, the electronic brain hummed, his vice-like hand squeezed the ball slightly, the polished fingers gleamed in the sun.

"Owzat?" he asked.

"Hmm," murmured Konrad from the boundary, "I don't think you've quite grasped the concept."

Katya struggled to her feet, brushed the blue hair from her face and kicked Agent Orange's steel shin.

"Yeah, you stupid bloody robot!" she shouted as her foot broke and Orange's armour chimed, "Learn the fucking rules! You're supposed to catch it before it kills me!"

"Yes," said Morty, sticking his hands in his pockets and casting a wistful glance at the city on the horizon, "And you are only supposed to hit it once."

"Bollocks," muttered Katya, taking out her make up mirror and checking the bright green/yellow stripes across her cheeks, nose, and lower lip.

Finally they all noticed Pedro the orange alien cactus who was pointing at Katya, his face set with an odd expression of determination.

"What?" she asked, rubbing the dent in her head.

"You are, 'ow you say, out, senorita, much though eet grieves me to say eet," said Pedro, lowering his skinny orange arm.

"What?" she inquired, "What are you on about?"

"The ball, she can only be heet the once, senorita."

"Fuck off," Katya replied, retrieving the bat, and returning to the crease.

The stumps were in a sorry state. One had been used as an intestinal splint, another was patched up with bandages, and the third was not quite as long as it was supposed to be.

"Katya!" Morty whined, because he was supposed to be in next.

"Come on, Katya," said Konrad, settling down in the grass and taking a can of lager from his jacket pocket, "Hogging the bat for fifteen consecutive innings is uncool, like, totally."

"Stick up for me, Pedro, you unfaithful bastard," Katya said, wielding the bat in a cactus-smashing manner.

"They have the point, senorita," Pedro said with a shrug.

"Bastards," said Katya, throwing the bat down and stomping off to one side, which put her roughly in the daft-fucking-bitch-pissed-off position, "It's a cons, it's a con, it's a conspry, it's a conspira, uh, thingy, it's a shit game anyway."

Morty sprinted across from where he had been standing after delivering the last stunning in-swinging masterpiece. He grabbed the handle of the bat and lifted it, suddenly it was yanked away and he staggered after it.

"Eat photons!" said Agent Orange as his eyes grew brighter, one of his powerful hands clasped the blade of the bat, "My go!"

"No way," said Morty, "It's my go!"

Morty pulled on the bat, digging his heels into the ground, then he just ducked in time as the superphoton beam flashed from the CIA robot's eyes and crashed into the earth behind him. He relinquished his hold on the bat and pulled a sulky face, plodding away to deep extra cover, or thereabouts.

"Eat photons," said Agent Orange in triumph.

He strode across to the crease and grasped the bat's handle with both hands. The knees bent a little with a creaking of bits and bobs that needed oiling, then the metal rump wiggled and the robot looked up at the bowling crease. This was marked with the body of the bloke who had come over to tell them they couldn't play there. A little wisp of smoke still lingered at the headless neck, the head was around somewhere, or rather, everywhere, having eaten photons.

Konrad swigged down the lager and sighed, he set the can in the grass and lay back to stare up at the sky. Pedro hopped along, seeking out a position far out on leg side, although being an alien vegetable type thing he didn't have a clue what it was called. At last he stopped, looked around him, and chuckled with satisfaction. He pushed his sombrero back on his head a little and watched the robot with the bat.

"Er, who's bowling?" asked Morty, "I mean, if no one else wants to, I can."

"Fuck off, corpsebreath," said Katya, diving for the ball and grabbing it before the weedy student could.

"Oh, righto," said Morty, and under his breath he muttered, "Big fucking surprise."

Katya strolled over to the dead bloke and stood on him for a moment, rubbing the ball on the front of her shorts, and clearly enjoying it more than was decent. The ball had a flat side by the time the chorus of throat-clearing caught her attention and she ceased the so-called polishing of the ball.

"Prepare to eat photons, limey humans," said Agent Orange, swinging the bat in an experimental arc.

"Prepare to eat leather," muttered Katya, jumping off the body and walking back from the crease a short distance.

"Hold on," said Konrad, and he stood up and made his way to the wicket, "I reckon I'll be safer if I'm wicket keeper."

"What?" snapped Katya, "Are you, uh, casting dispersons on my ability, or something?"

"Would I do that?" her brother asked, smiling like a lunatic.

Morty wiped some dog shit off his basketball boot on the grass, Pedro rubbed his hands together and went on chuckling, Konrad crouched down behind the stumps and opened up another can, Agent Orange tapped the end of the bat on the crease and stared at the bowler, Katya squinted at the metal bastard and gripped the ball more tightly. The distant sound of an aircraft rumbled across the sky while the grasses fidgeted a little under a slight breeze and the haze all around went on shimmering. The bat tapped on the ground, Katya positioned herself to begin the run up, everyone held their breath.

The 'plane passed on into the distance and the sound died leaving just the quiet chattering of birds and insects and the rustling of the grass. Five sets of eyes narrowed and looked across each of the players in turn. Those with flexible mouths grimaced, the white of teeth showed - they knew that this was it.

Katya started moving, jogging forwards in a reluctant and ungraceful fashion, the fielders watched and waited, Agent Orange raised the bat a little and centred the attention of his trajectory plotting processor on the red sphere with the elevated seam. Katya picked up speed as she approached the crease, Konrad backed away a little from the stumps, Katya's big boots thundered through the grass, making those hungover worms wish they hadn't gone to that party last night.

Katya's feet did a quick and rather clever shuffle, unfortunately it was a little too clever and they outwitted her completely. So while the others thought for a fleeting moment that the daft bitch had developed a revolutionary bowling action she had in fact tripped over her own feet. Astoundingly, as she started to fall she somehow managed to regain her balance and her throwing arm began its swing.

She had, however, forgotten the corpse in the grass and went arse over tit over arse over tit over arse, while the ball sailed up into the sky. Katya finally landed on the corpse so that the dead hand copped itself a good feel.

Agent Orange tilted his head back and surveyed the incoming projectile, he calculated arcs and lines and all sorts of really clever stuff, then he slogged the bloody thing and watched it vanish into the stratosphere. The others shaded their eyes with their hands and watched the speck dwindle and disappear, all except Katya, who was busy kicking the shit out of the corpse - literally.

"One million, four hundred and fifty-seven thousand, nine hundred and three," announced Agent Orange, applying a little too much logic to cricket scoring, "Eat photons, I think."

He dropped the bat and clapped his hands with pleasure, the others looked at each other and wondered what to do next, except Katya, who was still kicking the shit out of the corpse.

"Well," said Konrad, "Six, at least."

"No ball," said Morty, "Definitely a no ball."

"How ees eet that you figure that, senor?" asked Pedro as he hopped over, "Her pretty leetle feet they treepped over the line, bot never deed they cross over eet, oh no."

"It's still a six, though," remarked Konrad, "Regardless."

"Eat photons, limeys," said Agent Orange.

"Fuckin' wanker," Katya was muttering, booting the corpse through the grass.

"Well, that was fun," said Morty, "I haven't had that much fun since I contracted Bolivian arse-scab."

"It didn't last long," said Konrad, "And as for Katya...I dunno - fifteen balls and out every one."

"You talking about me?" asked Katya, looking up from where she was pulling bits off the dead man.

"It was no test match," muttered Morty, referring to the duration.

"You earthlings!" laughed the orange cactus, "You sure do get the strange ideas for recreation."

"Eat photons," said the robot, "It's these goddamn limeys. Us goddamn Yanks know a thing or two about sport. Take baseball for example. That kicks photons!"

"Sure," Konrad agreed, "A team game where a bloke chucks a ball at a bloke with a bat who tries to hit it, not have it caught by the opposing team's fielders, and also run in order to score using a complex and borderline nonsensical system incorporating no end of demented jargon."

"Superatoms," muttered Agent Orange and he started stomping in his awkward, mechanical way, back towards the city where it was nearest.

"Yeah," said Morty, squeezing a spot or two and following the robot, "Superatoms!"

"Fuck off, dipshit," said Katya, throwing a spare arm at the little shit so that the soggy end stuck in his ear.

Pedro looked at Katya, and then at Konrad, while they watched the retreating duo. Konrad squashed his can in his hand and lobbed it away, Katya watched for a moment longer before getting bored and started shuffling through the grass to clean the gunk from her boots.

"Look at me!" she said, "I'm, like, Ivor the engine! Cher-dcuh, cher-dcuh."

"Fabulous." Konrad wasn't impressed by the impression.

"Who ees thees Ivor the Engine?" inquired Pedro.

"You don't want to know," Konrad replied, "Believe me. He was, like, Welsh, and the scourge of the planet. But that's ancient history, and we have to forget, forgive, and move the fuck on."

"Speaking of which, let's, uh, move the fuck on," said Katya, and she stomped off in the direction of Agent Orange and Mortimer J. Morg.

Konrad picked up the stumps and the bat and followed her, the orange cactus hopped and jumped along behind him. They passed across the wasteland, weaving through illegal dumping sites and accidental oil spills, heading for that normal little street somewhere in Suburbia, that normal little road with those normal houses, and that one normal house in particular with a kinda green and kinda beat-up Mustang parked on the drive.

"Oh shit, it's that time of month, is it?" Konrad said when he saw the car, and he looked at his watch.

The others had arrived ahead of him, Agent Orange had put the bonnet up and was doing really technical things with the tuning, while Morty had broken into the house to get a drink, because he reckoned the Karma non-twins owed him that much. As Konrad looked in through the Mustang's open window Katya burst out from the front door of the house, grinning and dead chuffed. She had transformed, kind of. She was still a stupid blue-haired woman with blue lipstick, but now she was Katya the road warrior. She had a bandana round her head, a white one with a big red sun on the front, a red leather jacket, a black T-shirt with 'Something really rude' written on it, leather gloves with no fingers, leather trousers, Lester and the gun belt, and leather boots that went up to her knees, each with thirty-two shiny silver buckles on.

Konrad took the note that was resting on the dashboard and looked it over, then he felt under the passenger seat and found the keys. The note read:

Dear Karma Wankers,
It's that time of the
month again so get to work
or we'll break your legs
and print those photographs.

The Syko Bros.

"It's not like they have to be so offensive," Konrad observed, "We'd do this for nothing, right, sis?"

"Sure would," agreed Katya, snatching the note and trying to read it.

"So, limeys, what gives?" asked Agent Orange.

"Oh, nothing much," said Konrad, "We just have to run moonshine over the border once a month for the Syko Brothers. Otherwise they'll print the photos. They have the negatives, you see."

"Cool," said Morty, standing in the doorway.

He held a glass with a rather sad ice cream soda inside, and he was trying to drink it through a straw. What is it with these people who try to drink ice cream through a straw?

"What is it with you people who try to drink ice cream through a straw?" asked Konrad, kicking the back tyre of the car like people did in films.

"I'm not - I'm drinking the lemonade through the straw. The ice cream just gets in the way."

"So why'd you put it in there?" asked Katya, clouting him round the head so that he dropped the glass. It smashed on the driveway, as glass was prone to do.

"Thanks a bunch," the student and part-time mortuary attendant muttered and he went back inside to get another drink.

"So, limeys," Agent Orange went on once he had put the bonnet down, "You drive along really fast in this kinda green, kinda beat-up Mustang, huh? That kicks photons."

"Tell you what," said Konrad, "Why don't you come along? And then we could all be a bunch of, like, weirdos hanging out and bombing along and listening to music too loud." It sounded a bit Famous Five, but actually Konrad was thinking that Agent Orange was a handy, if loose, supercannon in a tight spot, and Morty could run quite fast for a short lil' chubster, so could make a useful decoy if things got hairy.

"Bomb?" murmured Katya, her eyes glazed, her mind travelled far away.

"And we'll bring that little turd Mortimer along, just in case we need to go faster and have to throw stuff from the car," said Konrad, rubbing his hands together as his eyes gleamed with pure evil, "Ha, ha, ha, ha, ha!"

"Wow," remarked Katya, winking at the camera, "Like, why bother to try to conceal the contrived bullshit when you can revel in it? Hmm?"

Sounds good to me.

The moonshine was contained in four steel drums which were stashed in the back garden, buried under a wheelbarrow and several flower pots. Morty struggled off with one to prove how well 'ard he was, and Agent Orange took the other three, leaving the Karma non-twins reflecting that it had been a pretty good idea to invite them along.

"I'm glad I thought of it," Katya admitted, while jumping on some magic mushrooms.

"Nothing like a gherkin, pickle, peanut butter, and apple sandwich," said PC Bacon, biting into his sandwich with his immense dentures.

A globule of green slobber trickled from his mouth and down his chin, his face was glistening with sweat, his eyes were closed - he took his sandwiches seriously.

"Hmm," murmured PC Hog as he looked from his window and down the road where it vanished into the sunny distance.

They were sitting in their cosy police car, a turbocharged super-sporty police car, which was pulled up on the entrance to a farm track, next to the main road between somewhere and somewhere else. A lorry blasted by, its diesel wake shook the car and rushed through the grass, the lorry rumbled on into the deep countryside. A little car whispered back the other way, PC Hog watched it, reflecting that he would really rather be somewhere else. Somewhere away from PC Bacon and his bloody sandwiches.

"Nothing like it," PC Bacon said again, chomping fitfully, the green gob dripping down his uniform.

"Hrxazazachtshczz!" said the radio, and the two police officers glanced at each other.

"What was that?" asked Hog.

"Search me," said Bacon, spraying green saliva across his associate.

The vehicle's interior was well-established - broken in with empty coffee cups and crisp packets, little notes and reminders were stuck to the dashboard and the windscreen, and a Thermos was tucked in the door pocket along with a dog-eared calendar featuring some under-dressed WPCs (back when they still had such things). There was a roll of bog paper on the back seat, some corn plasters, some bath cleaner and a Luckybastard size pack of condoms. The heavy artillery was in the boot, still hot after a shoot-out with a granny in a Post Office who had jumped the queue.

The car had immense stripes down the sides, not the average little stripes, not the medium or the fairly impressive, but vast two-foot affairs with orange and yellow and even a bit of blue. The lights were notable too, big blue rectangular prisms of pure highway authority. In the back window was a light-up sign. It could tell motorists to stop, it could ask them to put down their mobile phone, and it could tell them to go ahead and make the copper's day. This was no ordinary police car – this was a pedigree Intercepta.

"Hur, hur," chuckled PC Bacon, running his podgy digits through his lunch box.

PC Hog glanced at him and then looked back at the road.

"Bastard freaks!" Bacon exclaimed, ripping open a Shit-Shat with the fury of Satan.

"What's that?" asked Hog, wondering if the fat pillock was on about the debacle at the jumble sale again.

"Freaks, fuckers, farters!" gibbered Bacon, crushing his Shit-Shat with trembling hands.

His eyes burned with fire for a moment, his breathing quickened, but as he stared through the windscreen at the pleasant countryside his temper cooled somewhat. Another lorry swept by, Bacon looked across at his associate, then to where a coffee cup was steaming up the windscreen.

"That bloody student crowd," he murmured, "Those bloody students. Flashback."

PC Bacon had never quite got over the incident.

"Oh, that," said Hog after a pause in which he wondered if he really wanted to prolong the conversation.

"Mmm, that," said Bacon, after a similar pause.

They both looked back to the road and tried to think about something else.

"Hrxazazazachtshczz!" said the radio.

"What was that?" snapped Bacon.

"Something about a hit and run," said Hog.

"Oh. That all?"

"Yes."

"Oh."

Suddenly Bacon whipped out his large, black gun. It was a combined speed gun and peacekeeper - it beamed all kinds of amazing lasers at the target, then it blew it away with fifty-millimetre high-explosive, armour-piercing shells. Bacon blew some imaginary smoke from the weapon's muzzle and cast a steely squint at Hog.

"You feel lucky, punk?" he inquired, then he put the gun back and slumped into a bored and pissed off blob.

"Hrxazazachtshczz!" said the radio.

"So, you going to Spain again?" asked Bacon.

"Uh-huh," said Hog.

"Don't know how you can stomach all those bloody sweaty Spaniards," said Bacon, grimacing with distaste.

"That is, of course, if those bloody air traffic controllers bother to show up for work so I can get out of the country," Hog said after a moment's thought. "I'll worry about all the bloody sweaty English tourists once I get to the other end."

"Bloody foreigners," said Bacon, "They're all the same. Subsidies left, right and centre and, oh, big surprise, they don't bother going to work. Bunch of freaks."

A van roared past on the road, the back doors open, hails of gunfire ripping out at a distant pursuer.

"What was that?" gasped Bacon.

"Ice cream van, wasn't it?" murmured Hog, staring at his shoes. He liked his shoes - his big fat bastard shoes that liked stomping on things. Got probs with lefties? Feminists? Vegetarians? Pacifists? Hippies? Environmentalists? Just stomp on the fuckas!!!

"Drive! Go! And do things with the lights," cried Bacon, putting on his hat and getting all excited.

"You want an ice cream that bad?"

"It wasn't a spuggin' ice cream van, now drive, you ignorant little spugger!"

"Fair enough," Hog muttered.

He put on his seat belt, turned the key in the ignition and was just about to pull onto the road when a battered brown Cortina whined past, peppered with bullet holes, and going at quite a speed. The passenger was leaning out of his window, firing an Uzi at the van ahead.

"Mind you, it is quite hot," Hog observed, convincing himself that was why the ice cream van was so popular all of a sudden.

As PC Bacon had suggested, PC Hog switched on the lights and the siren, he floored the throttle and activated the turbo. His lunch protested but it was too late for that - there could be no going back. The police car screamed down the road, lights blazing, flames flickering at the exhausts. The Cortina was momentarily in sight ahead, but it passed on around a corner and was obscured by hedges and trees and fields and fluffy bunny rabbits and flowers.

PC Bacon growled into the radio, then he dropped it and clutched at the seat as Hog weaved through slower moving traffic and just avoided a faster-than-light French kiss with an oncoming lorry called Dave.

The traffic seemed to have got heavier, the forty-five mile-an-hour posse was out in force, but after a little bumping and nudging Hog found his way through. Up ahead tracer fire was blazing in all directions, the van veered from the road and mounted a grass verge, before hurtling back down and knocking a minibus into the path of an oncoming hearse. There was a sickening crunch as the two vehicles met, glass and a couple of wheels scattered across the road. All around brake lights came on, smoke went up from tyres, and just about everyone lost control. There was carnage. The deceased was suddenly the centre of attention - eager would-be acquaintances were sliced and diced as they crashed through their windscreens, those with seat belts were ripped apart, and all the blood and guts splattered on the hearse.

Hog clipped an old wreck, spinning it round and off the road, into a tree - probably killing a few more innocent victims, then he was on his way, after the Cortina and the van. Bacon looked in the rear-view mirror and saw a few living motorists staggering through the wreckage, then he growled into the radio again, before taking out his big black gun. The traffic grew easier, the road was straighter and wider as it swept down from the higher country and into the basin of a wide, poisoned river, and a sprawling industrial city.

Traffic lights came on red, the van swept through the vehicles that came in from the sides, while their drivers honked their horns and swore until bits of them burst. The Cortina had a hairy moment, just managing to weave through halted or slowing vehicles, then PC Hog crashed through, ripping off his own bonnet and a wing, and twisting up the front of the car. He hit about five other vehicles, writing off two and sending them sliding away amid smoke, debris and screaming casualties. The other three were merely nudged and received nothing more serious than a hefty dent or two.

"Oops," said Hog, shifting gear and trying not to notice Bacon's hysterical laughter.

"I'd better radio base," said Bacon, once he had got a grip, "And get a detachment from the Ministry of Uncool. These guys are head cases!"

Up in front the Cortina had caught up with the van and was climbing all over the back of it, at the same time passengers in both vehicles were letting rip with all they had, the hot lead flew thick and fast. PC Bacon wound down his window and took aim with his gun, measuring the distance to the target. He sat back down and urged his associate on.

Hog narrowed his eyes and clenched tighter at the steering wheel, sweat gleamed on his forehead, his lips trembled with excitement. He threw all his training out of the window, metaphorically speaking, and concentrated on just the one thing - nailing those bastards in front. The brown Cortina and the van were drawing nearer, the crackling of gunfire became louder. PCs Hog and Bacon glanced at each other and grinned knowingly - it seemed their promotions were in the bag.

A kinda green, kinda beat-up Mustang was growling along, chewing up the miles and spitting them out with left hand drive contempt. The windows were wound down and some hideous crap or other of Katya's was grating out from the stereo and making that pleasant summer afternoon not quite so pleasant. The pounding bass was making the car, the road, the air and reality itself jolt and quiver. Konrad was driving, which meant Katya was sulking for a change, and Morty was squashed in the back next to bulky Agent Orange. The air blasted in through the windows but it wasn't enough to cool the inside down, although that suited the orange cactus on the dashboard just fine.

No one really said much of anything, seeing as they couldn't be heard above the stereo, although Morty occasionally asked Agent Orange to get his knee out of his ear, and was told to eat photons. When the tape did stop things didn't improve - no one could hear anything over the two hundred decibel ringing in their ears. Eventually that died too and, above the engine, a muttering could be heard, emanating from the blue-haired turkey in the front.

"Fuckin' fuckin' fuckin' fuck," she was saying, over and over again, trying to get some attention or some sympathy or something.

"Eat photons," said Agent Orange to one of Morty's whimpering requests.

"This is fun, huh?" said Konrad, clearly enjoying himself.

"Fuck off," said his sister.

"Lacks violence," said the CIA robot, "Needs carnage input on five volt nine-pin standard. That kicks photons."

"Well, we'll see," said Konrad, easing his foot down until the needle had edged up to the ton, "Haven't had a moonshine run that's gone right yet."

"Fabulous," whined Morty.

Agent Orange stuck his knee a little further down Morty's ear.

"I spy with my little eye," said Katya, squinting at the landscape that was flashing past in a blur, "Uh, something beginning with a 'b', I think."

"Bollocks," said Konrad, not impressed with 'I spy'.

"Bugger off," said Morty.

"Blitter object," said Agent Orange, and no one knew what he was talking about.

"Bambino," said Pedro, although it was muffled as he was pressing his face against the windscreen for no good reason in particular.

"Bum."

"Bomb."

"Bazooka."

"Bazongas."

"Brown."

"Barracuda."

"Bobble."

"Brick."

"Bulldozer."

"That begins with 'k'."

"No it doesn't."

"Perhaps, but 'killdozer' does."

"Barricade."

"Beetle."

"Backgammon."

"Bison."

"Bible-basher."

"Buttercup."

"Bin."

"Battery."

"Bottle."

"Bunyip."

"Buttplug."

"Buttfuck."

"Buttercup."

"You already said that."

"This is a different sort of buttercup."

"Oh, right."

"Buggery."

"Ballistic thing with 'I'm gonna kill ya,' written all over it."

"Close."

"Balls."

"Bananas."

"Bonkerz."

"Baps."

"Bulimia."

"No," said Katya, "Christ you're, like, fucking stupid."

"Don't know," said Konrad.

"Search me," said Morty.

"You dumb limeys," said Agent Orange.

"I come from the leetle planet weird, y'know, senors and senorita? We no have notheeng what begins with the letter 'b'."

"Oh, did I say 'b'?" asked Katya, and she grinned and giggled because she hadn't actually been able to think of anything.

"Carnage detector on overload!" exclaimed Agent Orange, looking around excitedly while his eyes flashed red and a little circular window on his chest sparked and buzzed, illuminating the words, 'Panic, you dumbfucks!'

No sooner had he spoken than a considerable pile-up had appeared ahead. Konrad swung the wheel across hard, just skidded around the widest of the crashed cars, then they all hung on for dear life as they were jostled and bounced around.

"The road!" shouted Katya, "Like, follow the fucking road!"

She held onto her bandana and closed her eyes as Konrad cut back in across oncoming traffic.

"Getting there," said Agent Orange cheerfully.

Morty had passed out, and Pedro was too busy pulling strange faces against the glass to notice what was happening.

"No sweat," said Konrad, still completely cool and untroubled, "I just, like, saw a blade of grass that was leaning the wrong way and looking totally uncool."

"Someone's been having fun, anyway," said Katya, reflecting that the pile-up looked like a laugh, and she started sucking her knee, like she did on occasions when bored out of her skull.

A sign flashed past, saying it was still far too many miles to the border, although what border it was it didn't say. Konrad passed by all the crawlers and the sad little bastards while Katya leaned out the window and stuck various of her several fingers up at them, sometimes she even hit on a combination that meant something.

"Carnage detector going wild again!" said Agent Orange.

They could all see it dead ahead, a hold up at traffic lights with several damaged vehicles and a whole host of blue and orange flashing lights. Smoke was trailing up from a wreck at the side of the road, an ambulanceman was jumping on a corpse and shouting that he didn't do requests.

Konrad floored the bastard, the engine strained and growled, the car shook, the devastation rushed towards them. With a twitch of the wheel Konrad saw them through, the policemen were kind enough to leap out of the way and thus Morty was spared having to get out and pick the bits out of the radiator.

"You limeys sure don't know much about driving," observed the robot.

"Fuck off," said Katya.

"Superatoms," said the robot, and no one could think of a suitable reply.

The road went on sweeping by and Konrad was so intent on following it that he didn't notice the car in front until he had almost caught up with it. There was no doubt what it was - it was a considerably damaged police car, ahead of which was a bullet-riddled Cortina and a van in similar condition. Bullets were ripping out from all three vehicles, and what was worse - Konrad couldn't get past! He flashed his lights and swore at them with the horn, but no one seemed very interested in his pressing engagement with the Syko brothers. He looked at his watch. Time was ticking.

"Fucking Sunday drivers," said Katya.

"Fucking limeys," said Agent Orange.

Konrad eased the Mustang up alongside the police car, but it pulled across and carved him up, he tried the other side and the result was the same.

"Let me shoot 'em," pleaded Katya.

"No way. They're mine," replied Konrad.

He nudged the rear end of the police car, its light-up sign made some less than polite observations. Up ahead the gunmen in the Cortina finally hit a tyre, the van lurched and swerved, first turning off to the left, then it veered back, and having slowed it collided with the Cortina. The lighter vehicle was spun around and it rolled over, bouncing down the road, broken glass and crushed metal flying off, while the van skidded both ways before connecting with the police car.

Konrad had never been one to slow down. As the van tipped up and rolled onto the police car, and Morty started pissing himself, the thought of going for the brakes didn't even occur to him. The police car's brake lights came on, smoke went up from the tyres, then it and the van piled into the Cortina. Katya ducked down a little and shut one eye, but she kept the other open - she didn't want to miss anything. Agent Orange muttered a little binary drivel, and Pedro the cactus pulled the most impressive face yet.

Konrad floored the throttle, shouting, "I feel a gratuitous collision, jump, roll, and skidding to a halt on the roof coming on."

They met the three vehicles ahead with impressive speed. As PC Bacon's fat head got taken off by the back end of the van and the Cortina driver got extensive bowel surgery at the hands of his steering wheel, the Mustang crashed into the back of the police car, and somehow leapt into the air. Everything happened in slow motion, the kinda green Mustang roared over the van and the Cortina, flying on a wake of debris and smoke, then it crashed down into the road, and Konrad, just for effect, pulled the steering wheel hard over to the left. They swerved, then the inertia carried them on down the road and they rolled. The world spun around outside, a spinning that was punctuated by lurching, bone-shaking blows and loud, tooth-rattling crashes as they bounced. Finally they stopped rolling and skidded for a short distance on the roof.

Behind them PC Hog staggered from the police car and moved forwards to the van. The two sole survivors from the van fell out, struggled to their feet on the blood-stained road, and wasted the pig with their machine guns. Then they turned their attention to the Cortina and shot at the people inside, just to be sure.

Hanging upside down in the Mustang (Saved by their seat belts - so remember: clunk click every trip) no one was very happy. No one, that was, with the exception of Katya, and she had started laughing.

"What is it, you stupid bitch?" asked Konrad, "Are you getting hysterical, or something?"

Katya pointed to the windscreen and the splatter of orange juices on it, then she laughed some more.

"Stupid little bastard was beginning to piss me off anyway," she said.

"Imminent and bloody demise detector going crazy!" announced Agent Orange.

Konrad looked in the mirror and saw the two suits with machine guns coming towards them.

"Doesn't look good," he said, "I can't find my gun."

"I can't use Lester, 'cause my arm's broken and stuff," said Katya, waggling the knackered arm around until she got quite pale and nearly passed out.

"Yikes!" said the CIA robot, "Superphoton vision has suffered eighty nine percent damage in crash. Rendered inoperable!"

"That's kind of unfortunate," said Konrad, staring death in the face and kicking it in the 'nads.

"Bugger," agreed Katya.

The gunmen on the road staggered closer, one had blood on his shirt, another had it streaming down his face, neither seemed to notice.

"So," chirped Katya, "Anyone for 'I spy'?"

"Fuck off," said an annoyed Morty as his urine rained around him from the sopping seat.

"Anyone want to know about my mysterious tattoo, somewhere up in a tantalising and interesting region of my body?" she asked.

"Er, okay," said Morty.

"Fuck off, you pervert," she replied, "I take it with me to the grave."

Which was kind of noble really.

"It was kinda uncool knowing you all," said Konrad, "But, er, see ya."

"Goddamn," muttered Agent Orange, "All that shit in 'Nam, all that crap on the grassy knoll, and here I am about to get wasted with a bunch of limeys."

"Mummy!" squealed Morty, not really the sort for brave last words.

"Shit," complained Katya, "Just when I thought it couldn't get any worse - I've gone and spilled my bloody lager."

"Goddamn lager drinkers," bleeped Agent Orange.

"Quiet," said Konrad, "Like, something very strange has happened."

"Where'd they go?" asked Morty, looking around, "I can't see those two psychopaths with the machine guns, all I can see is, er, the muzzles of about five hundred very impressive firearms and what looks like five hundred suits of rather cool and probably indestructible exo-armour with 'Ministry of Uncool' written on them."

The big white machines closed in, as Morty had said there were around about five hundred of them - towering suits of powered armour containing weak, squidgy little men somewhere down inside those impenetrable shells. They all carried heavy weapons with long barrels and childish graffiti scrawled over them. All in all things weren't looking up.

The prisoners were lined up in the road, surrounded by the elite exo-legion, and they were rather nice about it actually, at first. They sorted out Katya's arm and put it in a sling, they gave the cactus a humane burial, then they turned ugly.

Their leader was a man called General Nischenheimer, his exo-armour said 'Call me SIR!' He wasn't taking any nonsense - he got rid of Morty and Agent Orange, deeming them to be innocent civilian hostages of the dreaded Karma non-twins, but he had them sent off to the interrogators, just to be sure. Then he chuckled and turned his armoured head to his captives. He knew what to do with scum like that.

Konrad and Katya Karma were standing side by side, as though posed for a photograph, except they weren't smiling. They were miserable, cold and very damp. It was raining quite heavily, they were standing in a trench one foot deep, a muddy trench that was slowly filling with water. All around were flat grasslands, for as far as the eye could see through the rain and the mists. Somewhere behind them there was a cluster of buildings and some men shouting, apart from that all that was to be seen was the rain and the grass, all that was to be heard was the rain in the grass.

The Karma non-twins were dressed in drab green; drab army green. They both wore dark green trousers and coats and lighter green T-shirts, on their feet were chunky black boots. Over their backs were slung backpacks full of bricks, a couple of rifles, and some paperweights. On their heads they wore green army helmets that were far too big, the straps were undone and hung down to their shoulders. They peered out from under the rims of their helmets, staring at the endless rain.

An old man in a smart uniform and massive yellow stripes that probably meant something, strolled up to them and looked them over for a moment. He was

Supreme General Colonel Commander Headsock; a greying old goat with a ridiculous moustache and a monocle. He aimed at them with his long nose and stared.

"How long have you been standing in that trench, privates?" he inquired.

"Uh, lock and load?" suggested Katya, "Uh, left right left?"

"Two months," said Konrad, not moving his eyes from the point in space that was so absorbing.

"Two months what, Karma, nine-two-three-seven-seven?"

"Er, two months, er, and a bit?"

"Sir!" said the old goat.

"Sir!" said Konrad.

"Sir!" said Katya in surprise, and she stamped her feet and stood a little more to attention than she had been before.

"Two months, eh?" murmured the old man thoughtfully, he looked away to the nearby buildings, "You know what that means?"

"No, sir," said Konrad, blowing a drip from the end of his nose.

"Lock and load?" suggested Katya, then her eyes gleamed for a moment with a little of their old fire, "Bomb?"

"No, no," the old man shook his head sadly, "You've been standing in that trench for two months. Congratulations. Your training is over, now you are prepared for your European Army national service."

'Big fucking deal, sir' thought Konrad, but, as Spencer Tracy once said, a man is only as big as what, er, what, something.

"Cool," said Katya, "Do we, like, get to kill stuff now?"

"Hmm," murmured the old man, looking over that sexy private chick person, "You haven't quite got the idea have you, Karma, nine-two-three-seven-eight?"

"Uh," Katya went cross-eyed with concentration, "Nope?"

"National service is an opportunity for you to serve the Fatherland - er - European Union. You get to stand in trenches and walk across fields and pretend to be a soldier. There is no war, after all."

Katya's face fell, "No war? You mean I've been standing in this fucking trench for two months and I'm not even going to get to kill anything?"

"Sir!"

"No war? You mean I've been standing in this fucking trench for two months and I'm not even going to get to kill anything, sir?"

"That's right, however, your enthusiasm has been noted. You are to serve with the Trackers."

"What's that, sir?" asked Konrad, looking worried. He pushed back his helmet and wondered what all Katya's semi-drunken questions about bombs had led to.

"It's, like, going on in front and stuff - I've seen Rawhide, y'know," said Katya, "So we get to kill everyone instead of being left behind while everyone else gets all the fun."

"No," said the old goat, brushing the rain from his stripes, "Actually, it means you get to walk in front of the tanks."

"Do we get to drive 'em?" asked Katya, nearly peeing herself with excitement, "Like, drive tanks and heli, er, helico, er those big loud things that fly along and blow stuff up?"

"No," said the old goat, barely managing to conceal his arthritic glee, "You get to walk in front of the tanks and get run over from time to time."

The old man strolled away towards the buildings, humming the European anthem, grinning from ear to ear now that he was finally rid of the privates Karma.

"Shit," muttered Katya, sulking to the inner-soles of her boots, which were lined with cheese and onion crisps on account of the air pressure.

"You've only got yourself to blame," said Konrad, sinking back to a more comfortable slouch and scratching his ear, "Always going on about bombs and killing stuff in the mess. You're just lucky they don't have a suicide squad, after what you said to the Colonel while he was picking up his face."

"He ogled me in the shower."

"His shower."

"Big fucking deal. I must have, like, got forgotten or something, 'cause I didn't get a shower."

Konrad looked at his sister for a moment, "We're dead, do you realise that? If not dead, then very flat."

"Stop whining, dogfucker," snapped Katya, "All we've got to do is dessert, and stuff."

Two hours later Konrad and Katya Karma were still standing in the trench, now it was almost filled with muddy water. They were beginning to sink into the mire and were soaked through as the rain had grown heavier. It trickled from the rims of their helmets, pouring down into the pool beneath. The shouting from the buildings behind them had ceased, a jeep had gone by and plastered them with mud that churned up from its spinning wheels. The driver had been an officer of some sort, the incident didn't really appear to have been an accident, judging by the bastard's reaction.

"Yeeehahh!" he yelled, waving his fist at them, "Suck shit, English pigdogs!"

"I hate the army," said Katya, spitting out the mud.

"This mud tastes damn strange," said Konrad, spitting out his mouthful.

Katya picked up a sign behind her that had been lying on the ground, half buried in the mud. She turned it over to see what it said. Her eyes widened, Konrad slumped into an 'I don't even want to think about it' huff. The sign said: 'Latrines.'

A little over an hour later the trench overflowed, all the grasslands were flooding as the rain grew into a cloudburst. Lights had come on in the windows of the buildings behind, still Katya and Konrad stood on the same spot, thinking that this soldiering lark wasn't all it was cracked up to be.

"So what makes us different from those sad bastards in bus queues who get soaked when the bloody things drive past?" asked Katya.

"This is our duty, or something," replied Konrad.

"Right," murmured Katya, "And they do it as a hobby, huh?"

Another hour later it was completely dark, from the buildings the warm light was coming brighter than ever and the sounds of drunken mayhem rang out from mess. The Karma non-twins' feet were numb, the water had passed up over their waists and was still rising.

"Pass the snorkel," muttered Konrad.

"Why?"

"My boot lace is undone."

It was a dirty, dirty night, especially once Katya started swearing. She fell asleep though, at around midnight, which gave Konrad a break. She had a clever habit of sleeping while upright, so if any officers had looked out from their cosy offices nothing would have seemed amiss. It was as black as black had ever been, as black as a fat miner's deepest, most grimy, and most heavily-tarred crevice. As Konrad felt the water lapping around his neck he reflected that it was probably time to call a plumber.

Nearby a hedge was whispering to itself. It was only a little hedge, growing at the crossroads just outside the gate in the army camp's perimeter fence. Large red signs were hung on the fence, promising slow and painful death from electrocution. A stout, square-chinned guard was pacing back and forth by his guard hut. And the hedge was muttering to itself.

If anyone had gone over to it and peered in they might have caught a whiff of vodka, maybe they would have seen a couple of small red stars, possibly 'CCCP' written in bold red letters, they might even have seen two Soviet agents in camouflage, crouching in the same hedge they had lived in for the last twenty-four years.

"What time is it?" asked one hoarse voice.

"Search me," said another, "My watchski has not worked for five years. Cheap capitalist crap!"

"So, Ivan, do you thinkski it will be tonight?"

"I could not say for sure, Dmitri, but I do not think so."

"I really think it will be tonight. Do you not feelski it?"

"All I can feelski is this damned capitalist hedge, growing up my poor, communist backside."

"But do you not feel that tingle on the air?"

"Is that the same tingle as last night, Dmitri?"

"Hmm, no."

"Are you sure now?"

"Always you are the pessimistski, Ivan."

"I do not think it will be tonight."

"But why not? It must happen some time."

"You have been saying that for the last twenty-four yearski."

"I am sure it will be tonight."

"Yeah, yeah, now pass me that bloody vodka."

Unfortunately the cold war had ended some time before and the gentleman for whom they were waiting, one Boriz Godamnski, had emigrated to Mexico and now worked on a farm where they grew creepy, faceless, genderless clones and made them into piccalilli.

"You there!" cried a voice.

Konrad jumped and looked up to where a yellow inflatable dingy was being paddled towards them by a bustling, fat Major, with his sleeves rolled up and curling strips of potato peel tucked behind his ears.

"Whassat?" muttered Katya, grudgingly awakening from a rather dull dream where she had got a job in a bank, but complications had arisen regarding the identity of whoever had broken the chain on one of the pens.

She couldn't actually see anything because her hair had soaked up several gallons of water and was plastered flat on her head, so her helmet had sunk down lower and the rim was now below her eyeline.

"Privates Karma and Karma?" asked the Major, lowering the oar blades and looking down upon the two heads that were sticking out of the water.

"Er, yeah," said Katya, then she glanced at Konrad, "Although right now I, like, couldn't tell you if he's him or I am."

"I think I am, sis," said Konrad.

"Don't hang about! Come along! Left, right, left, right! Quick march! Climb aboard! Come along now!" barked the Major, spitting left, right and centre in the meagre light that was present some hours before dawn.

"Yes, sir!" said Konrad, in a cool and far from reluctant voice.

He helped Katya up, she struggled and squirmed, just to make it difficult, then he scrambled up after her. Immediately the Major took up the oars and started heaving on them, guiding them across the floods to where the barracks were safely up on slightly higher ground. Katya took a fish from under helmet, frowned at it, then stuck it down her knickers in case she got hungry later.

"I'm Major Nutter," said the nutter, gasping as he paddled away, "Your arses are mine now, and all of that malarkey. I don't mind admitting I've got my eye on a property in the south of France."

"We're not travel agents," said Konrad.

"I like him," said Katya, "He's funny."

"Don't get me wrong," the Major said, growling just to convince them and grinding his teeth and spitting the bits out, "I'm not really very nice at all. It's just I've had enough of all this crap."

"Does that mean, like, you'll let us go?" Katya whispered to him.

"No, it means you're going to be peeling spuds for the next fortnight, 'cause I'm a complete wanker."

"Hee-hee," giggled Katya, "Oh well."

"So, er, we're peeling spuds, huh?" asked Konrad, in his best cool GI voice.

"Damn straight, and call me SIR!!" cried Major Nutter, swinging the oars and missing the water in his fury, resulting in him falling over backwards.

"Yes, sir," said Konrad, performing an 'up yours, sah!' salute.

"You're going to be in the Trackers, privates, going to be in with the latest batch of weedy computer nerd scum from wherever they dredge up the national service geeks."

"Weeds," mumbled Katya, conjuring up images of pulling the legs off weeds, "Weeds! Lemme at 'em!"

"Get a grip, Karma!" ordered the Major as they neared the barracks, "You won't be seeing anyone until you've peeled your way through sixty thousand kilos of potatoes meeting European Commission Directive ninety-three slash one-seven slash E-E-C, specifically Article 2, in relation to the designation of basic potato grades. You got that?"

"Yes, sir!" said the Karma non-twins in unison, saluting and sounding eager and positive like all good privates should.

"The army's cool," Katya whispered to Konrad, "I love the army!"

"I hate the fucking army, I, like, loathe the bastard. I want to rip its head off and, uh, dribble down its neck," muttered Katya, as part of an on-going monologue.

The Karma non-twins were seated on little stools, armed with small, blunt knives. Konrad was somewhere to Katya's left, just out of sight around one of the hills of potatoes. They were in a room off from the kitchens, a room with a low ceiling and one inadequate light bulb. The walls were lined with shelves and miscellaneous junk that was occasionally required in the kitchens, all the rest was potatoes and piles of potato peelings. In some stainless steel pots the peeled spuds were beginning to accumulate, although no impression had been made on the mountain range that was still to go.

"'All we've got to do is dessert, and stuff,'" Konrad muttered, recalling his sister's earlier gem.

He took off his helmet and scratched his head, Katya appeared and laughed at him, or more precisely, at his shaved short back and sides. She pointed her knife at him.

"You look like a real dumbfuck," she said.

Konrad threw a potato at her helmet and knocked it off. He exhaled with significant grimness while Katya rolled about on the floor, clutching at her blue Mohican, and acting like she was melting or something.

"Let's get the fuck on with this, huh?" said Konrad, turning back to the potatoes, "For some reason I'm getting sick of the sight of potatoes."

Katya plonked her helmet on her head and crawled back to where she had been working.

"What are these, uh, whatever they are, used for?" she asked after a while, holding up a potato and turning it over.

"Search me," said Konrad, far too cool to know anything about it.

"Po-ta-to," murmured Katya, stabbing the little bastard, "Shit useless fucking invention if ever I saw one."

The potato screamed a bit, then it just sort of died.

"How do you know when to stop peeling it?" Katya asked.

"What?" inquired Konrad, looking down to where he had peeled near enough a hundred, "How many have you peeled?"

He got up and found his way to where Katya was sitting by an empty bucket, holding a potato that had been peeled down to the size of a pea. A large pea, yes, but a pea all the same.

"What's wrong?" the daft cow asked.

"What makes you think anything's wrong?"

"Could be your face, could be your eyes, or perhaps it's the way you're clenching your fists so that all the bones in your hands are cracking."

"Forget it," he muttered, and tried to imagine, as he had done many times before, that he had no sister.

The interrogation room was a dingy, square little space, dominated by a table and adjustable lamp. Several chairs were scattered around, a guard stood at the door, beyond which lay an ever-busy corridor, choked with military secretaries scampering back and forth. On one side of the table, the side in darkness, sat Supreme General Colonel Commander Headsock, a battalion of medals gleamed on his chest, he still wore his monocle, and his favourite hat with a big eagle and swastika on the front. Next to him was seated a furtive little man in a suit, he looked with shifty eyes through his glasses and clutched at a leather case.

Opposite these two was the insignificant, quaking form of Mortimer J. Morg, part-time mortuary attendant, full-time student, and a full-time, with overtime, wanker. Beside him was Agent Orange, steely and silent, quoting only his serial number and 'Eat photons.'

"Tell me about these Karma non-twins," said Headsock, looking over some notepaper and rubbing his chin.

"Eat photons," said Orange, followed by his serial number.

"Well," squeaked Morty, "Katya once had rabies. Can I go home now, please?"

"Rabies, hmm?" inquired Headsock, "We'll have to put her down."

"Ooh, yes," chuckled the little man next to him, his teeth glinted in a cold grin. From his leather case he took a syringe with his tight black gloves.

"Oh, she got over it," said Morty, gulping as he saw the needle, "Very quickly."

The little man put the syringe back and tutted in annoyance.

"What bit her?" asked Headsock.

"Eat photons," said Orange, followed by his serial number.

"Nothing bit her," Morty replied, catching an evil glance from Agent Orange who clearly thought the blabbermouth was a chickenshit traitor. Agent Orange was a pretty good judge of character. "She bit a Rottweiler," Morty went on, "She thought it was copping a sneaky look down her nappy."

"Paranoid bimbo complex," whispered the little man to Headsock, "If it happened, as Morg implies, in early childhood then this dog bite, er, if you see what I mean, could have had a profound effect on her mentality. All in all it ties in with what little there is in her file."

"What about Konrad Karma? Tell us about him," said Headsock, looking Morty in the eye.

"Eat photons," said Agent Orange.

"He's really, really cool," replied Morty, shrinking down under the white, disapproving glow of Orange's eyes.

"And? Come along, man! I don't think you appreciate the gravity of your predicament. By your earlier testimony we know you are associates of theirs - partners in crime, as it were. Do yourself a favour and spill the beans."

"Okay," said Morty, after a minuscule hesitation.

"Well?"

"What?"

"Tell me about them."

"Er, there isn't really anything else. Katya's mad and Konrad's kind of cool."

"I don't think we are going to get any more out of them," the little man muttered to Headsock, "I wonder if we might hurry it up, sir? I'm already late for my hourly rectum injection fix thing."

There was a knock at the door, it opened and a man in uniform stuck his head through the gap.

"Reply to your message, sir," he said.

"Well?" asked Headsock, digging deep up his nose with a false, cybernetic finger.

"The CIA says the robot's expendable. I quote, 'Annihilate the goddamn trash.'"

"Thank you," said Headsock, turning his eyes upon his captives while the messenger departed. "Well! I think it's target practice for you two."

"Eek," squeaked Morty as his knees knocked together in a startlingly good samba.

"Unless you furnish me with the necessary information," Headsock went on.

"Eat photons, limey."

"What information?" asked Morty.

"Where's their hideout?" inquired Headsock, taking a pen from his pocket and placing a blank sheet of paper on the table.

"They haven't got one," said Morty, "Where's my lawyer?"

"Where do they hang out?" asked Headsock, grinding his teeth.

"At their house, they're in the 'phone book, y'know. I want my 'phone call."

"Who are their other accomplices?"

"What? They haven't got any," said Morty, frowning as he tried to think who the sad, weird Karma non-twins hung out with, "Oh, there's the chick from North Dakota."

"Name?"

"Mortimer J. Morg."

"The girl's name."

"What girl?"

"The one from North Dakota."

"Oh, her. I don't know. They all just call her 'the chick from North Dakota.'"

"I see," murmured Headsock, scribbling away on the paper, "What about drugs, guns, and pornography?"

"Yes please," said Morty.

"Hey!" muttered Agent Orange, "And me!"

"These two are clearly imbeciles," said the little man as he stood up, "Excuse me, sir, but my sphincter is beginning to mutate again. I've really got to get the big, burly nurse with the ginger stubble to give me my injection."

He ran for the door, clutching at his backside.

"Penpushers," Headsock muttered.

"Can I go now?" Morty asked.

"No." Headsock looked at the paper to see where he had got to, "Where will we find this chick from North Dakota?"

"Eat photons."

"I don't know," Morty whined, "She just sort of pops up and disappears."

"Is there anyone else?" Headsock was losing his patience, "Talk, you wretched little civilian!"

"Eat photons."

"I don't know."

"Where do they get their weapons from?"

"Eat photons."

"Search me."

"Are they drug dealers? Who's their supplier?"

"Eat photons."

"Haven't a clue."

"Do they deal in illegal pornography?"

"Eat photons."

"Not that I'm aware."

The Supreme General Colonel Commander clutched at his head which was beginning to throb.

"You aren't helping your case," he remarked.

"What? But I've told you all I know!"

"Tough shit. It's not enough. Well, if that's the best you can do then there's no alternative. Not even ignorance is a defence in the face of the Second Coming! Guards! Take 'em away! It's target practice for them."

"No!" squealed Morty, dropping to his knees and clasping his hands together. Tears sprang out onto his cheeks. "Anything! I'll do anything! I'll tell you anything! Please!"

"Bugger off," Headsock snarled, and he kicked the little shit in the head.

"Agent Orange says watch out!" said Agent Orange, "Some day you wake and think it a nice day," the little round thing on his chest flashed with the words, 'Nice Day', while the robot went on, "But then you see orange and you eat photons!" and the little round thing said, 'Eat Photons!'

"Good grief," Headsock exclaimed as the guards rushed in to take the prisoners away, "Americans!"

The barracks had an air of ruin about them, a feeling that they had seen better days - a feeling that manifested itself in many ways. The roof leaked more than it didn't, the walls were sinking into the ground, there were holes everywhere, and cracks, and dents. The building comprised many wings, all in equally bad condition, all occupied by national service unfortunates.

In one particular wing rusting bunks were gathered in the shadows that hung beyond the illumination of the feeble lights. The bunks were covered with standard green blankets, the sort of blankets where the poor sod who got given them was more worried if they weren't covered in stains than if they were. If they weren't covered in stains then the previous owner had clearly had a virulent disease that had rotted him into a reeking, decaying mass even before he could make a stain.

This particular darkened space was home to the Trackers. In the back corner, smothered by the blackness, a bank manager was busy making a stain, the rest were seated in a circle around the improvised paraphernalia of an implausibly complex card game. Posters glared down from all around, posters designed to motivate the men, but posters that did, more often than not, simply motivate the bowels.

And there lay the problem, as Supreme General Colonel Commander Headsock would often muse of an evening with his feet in a bowl of tomato soup and his manservant cleaning out his ears with a pair of old pants. There was the problem with the whole national service scam - posters and mollycoddling weren't needed with the regular troops, but with the civilian wasters they were, but they didn't work for the very reason they were needed. Headsock would cry into his soup until he retired to bed and nodded off with his thumb up his warty old arse and his manservant reading that nice kiddies' story about a dragon who cried a lot. Ah, luvly.

Back at the card game things were getting serious as a stack of fifteen ring-pulls was pushed next to the ash tray by Eddie Head. Eddie was a bulky, shifty, hooligan of a man, normally seen outside a popular club owned by a long-haired freak whose insecurities and unrewarded vanity were reflected in his bigotry and admittance policy.

Eddie was a simple bloke - if you got out of his way then that was fine, if you got in his way then he got pissed off. What could be simpler? He clutched his cards close to him, his eyes flicked across his opponents, then he lifted his fag from the ash tray and took a long, mucus-choked drag. He looked back at the others, wondering who was going to be the first to get in his way.

Beside him was a scrawny little man with a narrow face and a fancy cravate. This was Nobby 'Nut-Nuts' Poppycock. He fiddled with his cards for a moment, contemplating his next move, then he took advantage of rule fifty-three 'b' and shifted this and adjusted that and probably downright cheated. At the end of it he pushed fifteen ring-pulls next to Eddie Head's stack.

Nobby was a pleasant man, always ready to give you the time of day. The fancy cravate, the lip gloss, and his general demeanour simply oozed class and sophistication.

Next to him was a dainty, subtle character, a gem of femininity, a paragon of virtue with a beer can jammed between her boobs in order to warm it up a bit. Here was Katya Karma, blue-haired, hot-krotched Katya who paused from looking at her cards and said:

"Strewth, my krotch is hot."

Then she looked back at the cards and bit her lower lip as she concentrated on counting the bumpy black things. At last she threw the cards in and nicked the ash tray, which led some to speculate that perhaps she hadn't quite grasped the rules. However, as Nobby was quick to point out, she had actually taken advantage of rule eighty-two, if only by accident.

This development completely stumped the Sergeant who was next in turn. Sergeant Egg, Anne Egg to those who had stolen her pay cheques, was a formidable, occasionally coarse woman with a heart buried somewhere beneath all the shit she had been given over the years by the national service wimps. She shrugged and chucked her cards at the dealer, ordering Nobby to shut up when he explained that she had just utilised rule four, and marched off to treat furtive masturbators to a taste of CS grenade.

She wasn't a hard woman, or vicious, she had just been shaped by that foul world which had spawned her, and the uncaring, materialist society that had conditioned her and ensnared her. She could moan a bit, it was true, but she could be tender and loving, no more tender person existed when it came to easing a plasma-truncheon into an orifice for mutual comfort and pleasure.

As Sergeant Egg vacated the room and the bank manager stumbled from the bed, choking and gagging in the billowing CS gas, desperately trying to replace ugly Mister Smelly in his trousers, the next player planned her move.

She was a council officer by profession, with the elegant name of Nadine Stench, and boy did she know how to shuffle cards. She had been showing off before the game had started, shuffling behind her head, behind her back, through her legs, she could even shuffle cards with her ears. No one loves a show off and they had beaten the bitch up. Now she was a little more subdued. She rubbed at her chin as she pondered, pausing to sip from the cocktail glass she kept in the pocket with the razor blades. She looked at the faces around her, reading each like an open book, except Katya's.

Eddie Head's face was the easiest, he was lumbering on with a hand that might see him through, but probably wouldn't, and he certainly wasn't prepared to go any higher. Nobby Poppycock was confident about something, certainly there was no trace of anything negative on his effeminate features. Konrad Karma, who was on the other side of Nadine, had four aces and another card, a really special card that only cool people ever found in a pack. Beside Konrad was a spotty little hooligan called Chives, and he had a bunch of useless shit. Katya Karma, though, was a problem - where the others were open books she was half a piece of tatty notepaper with 'Uh, the end?' scrawled on it with a blunt pencil.

At last Nadine picked up and discarded, and rotated the improvised thing that no one could remember the name of, or the purpose. Konrad lay down his cards, everyone else looked at each other, Eddie Head gnashed his teeth and ripped out some of Nobby's hair - his own was too precious.

"Is it my go?" Katya asked, "'Cause I think I've won."

"Fucking crap!" growled Eddie, "Fucking pussy-sucking shit fuck crap wank bollocks. Fucking freaks, bollocks, shit, crap. Fuck."

"So uncouth," cooed Nobby, and he was rewarded with Eddie's titanium knuckles and a headful of broken teeth.

"Uh, what?" muttered Katya, a cloud brewing over her head as she began to suspect that the others were cheating.

"Easy, Eddie," said Nadine, chucking her cards down with the ring pulls,

"You'll get executed, or something."

"Fuckin' let 'em try!" he snorted.

"Bloody wish someone would," muttered Chives, getting out his penknife and carving his name in Nobby's leg.

"What you say?" snapped Eddie, eyes bulging with raw fury.

"Simmer down, dirtwads," said Konrad, getting out his cunningly concealed gun and pointing it at no one…yet. When they had simmered down he replaced the gun and frowned at the really weird card that was in with his aces.

"Hey, y'know this exercise thing?" said Chives, "Do we get real bullets, or are they those pretend wotsits?"

"Better be real," said Katya, "Or someone's going to kiss my arse until they, uh, suffocate."

"They'd better be," said Eddie, "'Cause then I'm gonna kill the lot of you weeds, saps, freaks, pussies, and stuff."

"Glad to see the camaraderie is sparking up," said Sergeant Egg as she returned, flushed and thoroughly pleased with her activities.

"Stupid fat cow," muttered Chives.

"Bonkerzzz!" screamed the bank manager, leaping over and seeming to be positively psychopathic with the side-effects of the CS grenade. He was foaming at the mouth, he'd picked up a nifty collection of knives from somewhere, and he was sprouting thick tufts of hair. One eye looked as though it was about to pop with a distasteful sputter of pus and puke, the other was shrinking down under strangling purple veins. His mouth quivered, his teeth twitched, he panted and looked across the Trackers before him.

He whipped out Mister Smelly and flashed it around. Katya returned its squint and would have bitten it off if it hadn't been so bloody ugly. In the end the honours went to Eddie and his flick-knife. He pounced on the deranged nutter and tried to slice the little pink bastard off.

"Help me!" it squealed.

"Anyone got a deep fat fryer?" asked Chives.

"I'm a marmal, I am," said Katya as she went into a bomb-trance.

But boring Sergeant Egg restored order and saved Mister Smelly from messy divorce proceedings, much to everyone's disappointment, except the bank manager's and Mister Smelly's.

"Yeah," laughed Chives, "Nothin' like a bit of camaraderie."

"Shut up, you little turd," said Eddie, with the foam building up around his lower teeth.

"Shut up and listen up, you vile scum!" ordered the Sarge.

They all shut up and listened up.

"You lot had better get some sleep tonight, 'cause tomorrow you're going to be used for target practice out on the battlefield by Headsock and Nischenheimer, those two evil scum bad guys from several pages back. You're all going to die, ha, ha, ha, ha! So enjoy your pathetic little dreams and make those stains if you can, 'cause this is going to be your last chance! Ha, ha, ha, ha, ha!"

Yes, Anne Egg was a kind soul really, beneath that acid-spitting, buttock-biting exterior. They all cowered before her and headed off to get some sleep. Soon they were snoring or muttering in their filthy, perverted little dreams, and what seemed to be Nadine Stench's voice was twittering about drawing pictures with felt-tips on Mister Smelly, but that couldn't have been right - she was always such a nice little girl. Katya was perfectly concrete-solidly asleep, dreaming of mushroom clouds, and Konrad appeared to be asleep, but he was in fact doing something very clever and totally cool with a hand grenade.

At around about midnight everyone was woken up by the arrival of a menacing battalion of European Army soldiers. The Trackers watched from the windows and guessed correctly that these were the clinical professionals who were going to be slaughtering them on the morrow. Konrad redoubled his efforts on the grenade, bandaged Nobby crapped himself, the others seemed to take it in their stride, and Katya announced she was going to go and eat some lesbian officer pussy and see if she couldn't get herself promoted or something, and off she went.

Dear Anybody,

What a day for it. We have been shipped to a foreign land, a dismal, alien place in which to lay down our lives for a country we don't believe in, and for a country that does not care. About us. We are not money, we are not weak-minded socialists prepared to be lobotomised and adopted into the Great System, so we are carried like so much air mail through skies soon to be set alight by missiles and machines of death from below.

Does it matter? Does anyone know? Can anyone hear me? Or am I just talking to myself? I used to talk to myself, and if you're not reading this then I guess I'm doing it again now. The weapons are being lined up, from trenches and bunkers, with electronic eyes and synthesised voices, all lining up lasers for those sharp little bullets to follow. Does it matter? Down here I am a pen and a piece of paper, I do not believe, and by that token I am immune to what will follow. The fire will not burn me, the clouds of deathly gas and poison will be repelled from my aura. I have my aura - my armour - formed from an ancient blueprint of truth and decency, moulded from the peace of an open mind, the peace of a sleeping soul, the peace of a world without Man. That is my armour. Have you got your armour? I've got my xanadu parasol, have you got yours?

Katya Karma.

PS - I have a question about nuke fuel - what the fuck do they put in this stuff?

PPS - It made me talk weird crap like the chick from North Dakota.

PPPS - Uh...

The battlefield was grim and grey, away in the east the darker grey of miserable trees clustered beneath a rain-blurred horizon. There were craters among the gentle grassy slopes, craters around which sheep gathered, eyeing the geographical anomalies with mild puzzlement, before indulging in far more absorbing mysteries regarding shit. Lots and lots of shit.

"I've never seen so much fucking shit!" chirped Chives from somewhere beneath all his battle gear, "Never in all my fucking useless dole-scrounging life!"

"It's sheep shit, weedy boy," remarked Eddie Head, "It doesn't count."

"Where have they brought us?" murmured Nadine, "What forbidding foreign land is this, and what will the guerrilla natives do to us when they catch us?"

"Rape us," hoped Nobby Poppycock.

The Trackers who had been present at the previous night's unforgettable card game had been joined by other sociopaths and malcontents, including, as luck would have it, one very wimpy mortuary attendant and a rogue CIA robot.

"Funny how things turn out," said Konrad over the clanking-rumbling of the immense tanks that were growling along behind them, "Isn't it?"

"No," said Mortimer J. Morg, "And it's Wales."

"Sheep," snapped Eddie Head.

There were about fifteen of them, followed by Sergeant Egg and the trainee tank posse, all driving their L-plated tanks, occasionally doing something wrong and crushing a Tracker or two into the saturated earth.

There were about thirteen of them, marching through that dreary place, tramping with regular footfalls through the grass and mud, peering from beneath the oversized helmets at the innocuous landscape, wondering where Headsock and Nischenheimer had got to. They were fully armed with rifles and machine guns, and the ammunition was live - as they had found out when a middle-aged travel agent had freaked out from the suspense and gone loco, mowing down all and sundry with hails of semi-automatic lead. He even got off a few rockets and land mines before Sergeant Egg had nailed him with a ruthlessly efficient fifteen-millimetre right between the eyes.

"You men really can't handle constipation, huh?" Katya had whispered to Konrad just before another Tracker fell under those merciless steel plates that churned on without rest like an inverse escalator straight to hell.

The Trackers were wearing full armour as well - great slabs of the latest camouflaged kavyar plating which hardly made the going any easier. Once they were liberally plastered with mud they looked as though they had just strolled from a cinema screen with the detonation of a couple of hand grenades and the castration and decapitation of some gooks by imaginative use of barbed wire. They were grim and pissed off, fingers uneasy on the triggers, ammunition belts rattling where they were hung over their shoulders, and the diesel voices of the tanks grumbled behind them, the dark fumes chugged up against the sky.

"C'mon!!" said Katya, "Where are those tossers?"

"Rrrr!" agreed the bank manager, still one eye popping out, still with a liberal coating of strange hair, and now wielding several bazookas and an anti-aircraft cannon.

"Chickenshits'll wait until we're close," observed Eddie, digging into his experience as a mercenary.

"Yes, but where are they?" whined Katya, "I need a pee."

Still the elite European Army force didn't show, as the Trackers marched on deep into enemy territory, down under frowning hills to where a wide, shallow river meandered between tree-lined banks.

Eddie Head chewed on a fag, squinting into the trees, the others looked around with nervous eyes and trembling fingers, while the tanks rumbled into the river.

"Keep moving!" ordered the Sarge from where she was sitting atop her tank, clutching at her helmet as the machine lurched beneath her.

They proceeded down the river, growing more uneasy with every footstep. Nobby Poppycock sucked on his bloody bandage, inciting a punch from Eddie Head who was, by then, just looking for an excuse.

"Limey detector going psychopathic!" bleeped Agent Orange, taking up his rapid-fire rocket launcher and glaring into the trees with all the scanners he could muster.

The European Army scumbags burst from the trees, men in armour scrambled down the banks and opened fire with a formidable armoury while helicopter gunships thudded overhead and loosed rockets and bombs and missiles on trails of smoke. They crashed down into the river, sending up high columns of water and rock, flickering with fire and unleashing showers of razor-sharp shrapnel.

"Blow 'em away!" barked the Sarge, and the tanks turned their turrets at the targets and fired banshee shells into the enemy.

The Trackers let go with all they had, levelling their weapons at the bastards and mowing them down with roaring streams of kamikaze metal. The thunder of gunfire rose up above the river; the booming of explosions, and the hissing and crashing of water. Agent Orange let the squidgy humans worry about the squidgy humans while he concentrated on the armoured angels of titanium death that were circling above. The gunships hung beneath their flashing blades, visors and helmets peered from the cockpits, the sharks' faces snarled down at all below.

"EAT PHOTONS!!!"

Agent Orange's rocket launcher fired, spewing smoke and empty cartridges, while the shells screamed up into the sky. Many missed and wailed off into the distant heavens, others found a way through burning flares and clouds of chaff and thudded into the gunships. One went down, its tail blazing, and hurtled into the trees, erupting into a blinding explosion. Another took many hits that blasted smoking holes in its underbelly until the CIA robot nailed one of the weapons pylons and the whole thing went up in a fiery red ball, shedding debris and cooked pilots across the battle scene.

Konrad and Katya Karma stood side by side, helmets bouncing on their skulls as they jigged and jerked with the powerful recoils, faces set with iron grimaces, fingers welded down over the triggers. The enemy perished in violent explosions of red. Great swathes were cut down before the flaming Karma muzzles. So easy was it that Katya got out the fish she had stuck down her knickers and chewed on it absent-mindedly. Meanwhile Morty (the cowardly little turd!) cringed behind the CIA robot, praying to all the gods he could think of.

The two sides traded fire, the enemy died under a storm of lead, never quite having time to line up their sights having emerged from the trees. Slowly, though, with the advantage of greater numbers, more and more found the river and had time to pick out individual targets among the Trackers.

One of the tanks went up, armour and electrical equipment were scattered far and wide by the sudden inferno, the tank's turret screamed skywards like a rocket, with the Sarge hanging on and waiting for the fatal plummet to earth.

"You fukkas!" was all her limited creative prowess could conjure up in that most stressful of moments. Then she got a grip, tied on a kamikaze headband, and threw tank shells as the turret plunged.

The Trackers began to die, first some of the weeds who had shown up that morning went, bursting and splattering as barbed bullets whizzed thick and fast through the air. Blood and slime began to build up on the living, the corpses fell into the water and trailed guts and porridge in the cold currents.

The bank manager roared with fury, bazookas and machine guns firing. He clenched his teeth and braced himself against the immense recoils, glaring with insane anger at the enemy, slowly being buried in discarded cartridges that cooled from being red hot in the river. His weapons blazed, slaughtering twenty of the enemy in whichever direction he turned. They ruptured in impressive showers of blood and armour, or sprouted dozens of gaping red holes and fell into the waters to die a slow and painful death with plenty of twitching and internal bleeding.

Eddie Head also lost it, yelling inane bullshit as he wasted the yellow scum left, right and centre. He breathed deep on the smokes from his weapons, tripping out to an altogether higher plane of extreme carnage. He waded into the enemy, going to work on them with spiky knuckle dusters that slashed throats and faces with impolite gushes of scarlet.

"Suck that!" he bellowed, "Eat this! Cough it up! Fuck you!"

The sliced, choking, spluttering troops fell before him as he carved his way through, taking up a serrated sword and carving deep into the enemy ranks, the blade arced and liberated vital internal equipment. The victims screamed and collapsed, sliced up and with just enough time to cough up some blood and light a fag before they died in gruesome fits of puking up what was left of their own internal organs.

Nobby Poppycock died with an anti-tank missile to the head, what was left of him afterwards didn't bear much thinking about. The Trackers were showered with lightly roasted Nobby as they fought for their lives against the increasing odds.

Nadine Stench went next, first her legs were blown off by a grenade, then one of the European Army scum prepared to molest what was left of her. She pulled a pin from a grenade and took the sick scumbag with her.

The battle raged on, bodies piling up under the red shade of blood, smoke rising from the wreckage of tanks and helicopters. Eddie Head was finally beaten as the enemy scrambled over him. He went down under that assault, triggering a land mine he had been carrying in his pocket. Forty-odd maimed and disfigured bodies were flung skywards amid fire and earth by the blast, screaming and yelling as their blood spurted from gaping wounds. What was left of Eddie Head used what was left of its mouth to bite off what was left of an enemy soldier's face as together they passed into the clouds.

Suddenly the fighting ceased. The last of the debris and human remains rained into the river, the fires among the tank wrecks were crackling, the wounded were screaming, several radios were babbling and hissing. But there was something else. Another sound could be detected, all the soldiers, regardless of rank or side, looked to the skies, searching for the wielder of that deep voice. It seemed to be thunder but something didn't sound right. Even Nischenheimer and Headsock were stumped, as they sat in their jeep, grass-skirted chicks on their laps, and an Australian stripper bimbo on the bonnet. War is hell.

First one shape was seen, then another, then more crowded in, until the sky was growing dark with the massing forms. Beneath that eerie eclipse the soldiers watched, gradually deafened by the thunder, shitting themselves and making a real mess of the river. The shapes were long and slender, hurtling along, gleaming in the fading light. Most were white, some were black, some red, there were even a couple of yellow ones. The sick and depraved murals concocted by the bored silo staff adorned their sides, grinning shark faces glared at their breakfast below. Somebody had wheeled in the nukes.

On a hillside not far away four figures were lounging on a picnic blanket beside which stood a motorbike and sidecar. Up there on the hill it was cold and windy, it had grown dark also with the onset of the huge rocketbombs. Agent Orange was sitting on the blanket, electronic eyes turned to where smoke was rising from the valley below. His shell was dented and burned, his cold, hard fingers clutched at a half-eaten drumstick.

Morty was there beside the robot, gaping up at the swarms of deadly projectiles above, but not letting it entirely distract him from the slice of lemon cake that was resting on a plate next to him. Konrad was eating some Mississippi mud pie, 'cause he was cool like that. He had put on his shades ready for the nuclear detonations and he wore his coat as a protection against the cold - something that made the figure next to him all the more surreal.

Here was blue-haired Katya, wearing just her bikini, her shades, and a video camera. She got plenty of zoom shots of the rocketbombs, punctuated with the occasional long shot of the panicking soldiers down below. Several people had noticed that Katya's breath hadn't smelled very nice that day, a few had commented and had got a knee in the balls or a fist in the tits, depending on their species. Some had guessed at the source of the reek, some had got it right - certainly the fact that chewing on that fish had freshened her breath up bore out one particular theory.

"It was quite convenient the way sucking a few high-ranking pussies landed you with a discreet promotion to Field Marshal in Chief, huh?" observed Morty, sipping his orangeade.

"Yup," muttered Katya, "Now shut the fuck up, I'm trying to make an award-winning bombumentary, or something."

"Pretty good deal you struck with that three-hundred pound slag in the motor pool for the motorbike," added Morty.

"You limeys," chuckled Agent Orange, siphoning some oil from the bike, "You're a bunch of goddamn queer bastards."

"Fuck you, tin prick," said Konrad, putting the hand grenade he had spent the previous night tampering with into an odd blue cocktail.

"We're no queers," remarked Morty.

"Yeah, but sometimes you gotta shut your eyes and think of ice-cream on toast," put in Katya, "It was a life or death situation. I saved your worthless arse, android, so, like, show some fucking gratitude, right?"

"Sure," muttered Orange, "Sorry. And, by the way, it's 'ass', you know?"

"Agent Orange?" said Konrad.

"Affirmative," buzzed the robot.

"Just shut up." Agent Orange went to reply, but was cut dead by Konrad, "And, yeah, *you* eat the damn photons."

The nukes rumbled down from the sky, hundreds of deadly rocketbombs all hurtling towards Headsock, Nischenheimer and Co. Katya had certainly made her tongue go a long way, both literally and metaphorically speaking. But that's enough of that.

The slimline projectiles quivered with wrath as they thundered down, their engines blazed, their noses turned as the onboard computers made the last fine adjustments. Then the engines kicked in harder, driving those machines of death still faster at their prey. The shark mouths screamed, 'Banzaiiiii!!!' and the first found its blissful nuclear oblivion.

It was big nuke death. When the first hit, the white blaze of light spread upwards and outwards, the hot nuclear wind swept across the surrounding lands, all the men and machines were obliterated utterly, there was no debris, no screaming - just clean, white death. All was vaporised and atomised, reduced to a film of particles invisible to the naked eye. More nukes swept in, keeping on coming, erupting with such sound as had never before been heard on that pretty little blue-green planet. All the light that burst out interfered with the tenuous perception of reality of those gathered around and formed eerie visual feedback and psychedelic images that any witnesses would interpret in their own, personal, and meaningful ways.

The thunder went on without rest, the earth trembled and shook, buckling in places, cracking in others, while the temperature rose and the nukes still poured in - rocketbombs really knew how to press a point. The four on the hillside watched, occasionally, turning away to search out some more food. Katya filmed it all, although she was shaking with excited happiness and the camera was swinging in drunken arcs.

When the last nuke had rolled in and sent out its tidal wave of pure energy across the landscape, the smokes and fires cleared to reveal a flattened, bare, and charred expanse of land, and no trace of all the pricks who had been standing there just five minutes earlier.

"I think I'm going to have dirty dreams for weeks," Katya sighed, setting the camera down and chomping away at a big bastard gateau.

"Sure was pretty cool," Agent Orange agreed.

They munched away at their picnic until they were all perfectly bloated and overweight and in severe danger of bursting into rather noxious pools of sludge.

Then they climbed on the motorbike and sidecar and Konrad was in such a good mood that he even let Katya drive. The engine rasped and farted, then the strained machine started up the hill and towards home.

"I don't know why you bothered with that bikini," Konrad said, as they passed on into the distance, "I got a sun tan through my clothes."

Footnote to Big Nuke Death:-

This is the original version of the copy that was made as translated from the wax crayon master, although there was a slight detour somewhere in the middle involving Cantonese. As the original was bypassed through a translation or two, the rewrite also had to be transposed via a duct of colloquial jessie southern tongue common in a little southern bumpkin shit-hole called Toaster. This is of little importance, save for those bits that don't make sense, and the references to eating pussy which instead should have referred to 'eating mablo yaghot.'

15. Weed Killer

Konrad and Katya Karma were dead.

That is to say they were dead to the world, spinning and falling into a yawning abyss, plunging past strange little men wearing tea towels over their particulars and wielding lengths of rubber hosing they had nicked from some very old Vauxhall Astras. These little men screamed and grunted, sending out dizzying streams of psychedelic fireworks and special effects. Pink lightning flickered far below, the cries of the little men pounded out to a primitive drum beat, and some evil denizen somewhere, some leviathan brooding in shadow, some dread dweller in the pit, was shaking a tambourine.

The Karma non-twins screamed as they fell, but no sound came from their gaping mouths, just little blue bubbles and music symbols. The abyss seemed to narrow, its walls flickered by the light of camp fires, and strange cave paintings appeared from the darkness below, flashed by through the light, and then passed up into the shadow above. There were vast, towering cars and car stereos, all depicted in the vivid red of mammoth blood, the lurid blue of berry juices, the stark green of lush leaves, and the yellow of brake fluid.

Suddenly the light was gone and a roaring could be heard as the voices of the little men faded into distant echoes. A shimmering blue appeared far below, it stretched out, spreading across all of The Beneath, then it reached up and it was obvious that it was the sea. There were great towers rising up, dotted with little windows, and several window cleaners on ladders being pestered by sharks with rocket packs.

"Hmm, stick it to 'em," Katya said, although it was more of a dreamy compulsion than anything that made any sense.

"My avocado is stuck," muttered Konrad, opening up a box of Cuban cigars and finding himself not all that surprised that the cigars were asleep.

"Peachy peach-like peaches," agreed Katya, pulling down her goggles and taking the cork from her snorkel.

"Well, if you insist," Konrad remarked and he drifted off to a lurid living room, while Katya, quite unsurprisingly, was a fish, thrashing at the bottom of a bin with some old, cold chips.

"Zarraccuda!" shouted Konrad, jumping up and knocking his head on the inside of the cupboard.

He rubbed his head and looked around, just able to make out vague shapes by the green light that was coming in through the crack where the cupboard door was slightly open. It seemed he was in the cupboard where Katya hid all her dirty, disgusting undies in the hope that they would just go away, or something. He held his breath and pushed the cupboard door open. Beyond lay the interior of - and that was the surprise - it wasn't the normal little house somewhere in Suburbia, it wasn't the pub where they sometimes ended up, it wasn't the power station with the little yellow lights and the boxes that said 'zing!' - it seemed to be the interior of the large green Weirderon saucer thing with the police lights Zelotaped to the roof.

It was about then that Konrad noticed the flavour in his mouth. If he had swallowed all Katya's old socks it would hardly have come close, if he had gargled with the pickup's engine oil it wouldn't have been a patch on it. It was probably just as well that he couldn't see his tongue as it was luminous green, and that wouldn't have helped at all.

The large green saucer thing was at a steep angle, and all was quiet which suggested they were on the ground - there was no muttering from the computer and no rumble of engines. There were masses of junk - seemingly everything the Karma non-twins owned was crammed in somewhere. Katya was asleep on top of the television, she was wearing a Painsbury carrier bag (with the straps over her shoulders and the bottom cut open for her legs, y'see), a snorkel and goggles, and some flippers. Konrad looked down at himself and saw he was wearing a wetsuit, and on his head was his hat with the corks hanging from the brim.

"Hmm," he murmured coolly, "There's a definite theme here, if only I could see what it was..."

In the end he decided to stay where he was and slouch in an oblivious, laid-back sort of way, and just see what happened.

Oh, and there was his headache. Herman P. Fucking Calibra, there was his headache. It jangled and screamed and flickered and blinded as his lobes squirmed and tore at each other. And that was just in the dim interior of the saucer thing.

On the television Katya writhed and fell off, as she hit the floor she woke up, but not enough to stop herself rolling down the sloping floor, crashing through several cardboard boxes packed with junk, and coming to rest with a splash in the water that had spilled from the jacuzzi. She sat up, pulled the goggles from her eyes and placed them on her forehead, took the snorkel mouthpiece from between her blue lips, and looked around, too astonished to swear or say anything stupid. At last she looked up at Konrad with a questioning expression.

"Search me," he said with a shrug.

"Don't shout," she whispered, clutching at her head.

"Sorry," Konrad whispered.

"Uh, there must be a logical explanation, Jim," said Katya, fumbling in the water and lifting out a big rubber thing with a button on one end.

"Hmm," murmured Konrad, looking around to see if there were any clues, "I don't think it's a presidential assassination, for what it's worth."

"Shit!" screamed Katya, as she suddenly remembered that she was supposed to hate baths. She scrambled free of the water and huddled up inside her carrier bag.

"I can't remember much of anything," Konrad said, "I remember getting home on the motorbike and sidecar, I remember watching three shit films on the trot until four in the morning...and after that it's a complete blank."

"Well, don't look at me, I can only just remember getting home."

"And what's all the crap doing here?"

"Perhaps it was, uh, the tooth fairy."

Konrad crossed over to the view screen and switched it on, but the camera didn't seem to be working, the screen just glowed yellow.

"Rrrowg!" said Katya's stomach, announcing that it was well past time for breakfast.

"Good point," said Konrad, and he searched out some breakfast. "Do you want the bad news or the bad news?" he asked after a fruitless search.

"Uh," Katya rubbed her head, "Stop making me think, arse-parchment, my head hurts enough as it is!"

"The bad news is there's no food."

"Oh, so what's the bad news?"

"The bad news is there's no food besides the food we haven't got."

"Remind me, what was the good news again?"

"What good news?"

"Uh, right, that's what I thought."

"But there was food here," said Konrad, completely puzzled, "Enough for at least a week. Did you get hungry? Did you have one of your teeny-weeny midnight feasts, you gannet from another planet?"

"Why me? Fuck off! I've been asleep."

"You managed to type an essay on early French impressionism in your sleep that time. Mind you, I guess that could be attributed to indigestion."

"Fuck off. I don't want to talk to you anymore."

"The bloody view screen's on the blink, the food's gone, and I'm absolutely fucked. Hmm, and where are all the chicks in the traffic warden outfits?"

"And what are you wearing?" Katya laughed, but she stopped when she noticed what she was wearing.

It was then that Konrad noticed a little white square of paper on the control panel, he picked it up and perused it with interest.

"What's that?" asked Katya, "Tell me, tell me, tell me! What is it? What is it? Tell me!!"

"Shut up," said Konrad, and he handed her the note. This is what it said:

Konrad and Katya Karma,

Formerly of: 18 Tedious Street,
Somewhere,
Suburbia,
SS1 2XY

[At which point Katya checked with Konrad that that was their address, which it was.]

Dear Us,

Greetings, how's it going, and stuff? Now, you probably won't remember this, that's why we're telling you, but you got pissed, like, totally. You might be dead, in which case you won't be reading this, but if you aren't dead then the reason for your green tongue and throbbing head is weed killer. Lots and lots of weed killer. (And not a Morty Morg in sight). You see, we've run out of food, that is to say, you have run out of food, and booze too. So we have decided to drink weed killer until we drop.

'Why not just go round the shop?' you ask. You asked that for one simple reason - you haven't looked outside yet.

[The Karma non-twins lowered the ramp and took a look out. The view that met their eyes was a desolate one - of rolling dunes and sand blowing on a dry, desert wind.]

It's highly probable that you have forgotten all about it, not that there's much to forget. You busted out of the army, right? And when you got home the army was there waiting for you, so you killed them all and grabbed all your stuff, and escaped to the Hell-lands. So that's where you are, unless something really weird has happened since we wrote this. Which leaves just the one thing to say - rather you than us, wankers!

Yours coolly, Konrad

Yours uncoolly and with big
tonguey kisses and loads of arse
groping (for Katya, not Konrad
- the poofy bastard!), Katya.

"Well, that kind of explains it, wouldn't you say?" said Konrad once Katya had finally struggled through the last of the bizarre squiggly symbols.

"Uh, I understood it up to 'Dear Us'," she said.

Outside the wind went on howling past, already the saucer was half-buried in the corrosive sand, and all around the dunes stretched into the sun-baked distance. These were the radioactive Hell-lands - an area that had once been known as Manchester, before a home-made nuclear disagreement, originating somewhere in the Fallowfield area, had wiped it off the face of the earth. Now that place was a wilderness, dotted with toxic swamps, ramshackle homesteads and townships, and the occasional cluster of ruins.

"That's kind of fucked it," said Katya when Konrad had explained the many words that she hadn't understood.

"And there's no more weed killer. Not a drop."

"Selfish bastards!"

It was then that they knew they were doomed. They had lived fast, when they could be bothered, now they were going to die young. There were no heroes left to save them, no badly-disguised blue aliens were going to show up, this was the harsh reality of life, and more appropriately, death.

They stood for a moment, jaws lolling, mouths and eyeballs drying, as the sand began to pour from the air conditioner and seep in through cracks that opened under the power of that slow, silent menace. Konrad's eyes squeaked in their sockets as they pivoted towards the view screen, tiny droplets of blood formed on their white surfaces where the sand that had mysteriously accumulated beneath his eyelids scratched and clawed. When he looked back to where Katya had been he saw that she had vanished. He frowned, looked around, and a big neon question mark lit up over his head.

Suddenly Katya emerged from a pile of junk that had collected between the tweed armchairs and the wall. She was dressed in a smart suit, with her hair tied back, and with a typewriter in one hand. She lobbed the typewriter at Konrad who caught it, and thus prevented the loss of three teeth, and the crushing of five toes, whichever side - it really isn't all that important.

"Cop that," said Katya, as Konrad looked at the typewriter.

She wriggled like a drunken belly dancer, then stuck a bullet down her bra, just in case, and it lodged in her slightly sweaty cleavage.

"I'm off," she said as she lowered the ramp, "Oh, and, like, no mess, huh? I've spent fucking hours clearing up. I wouldn't want to upset our illustrious client."

"Hang on a mo," said Konrad, placing the typewriter on the plasmaneucleonicinductionthingamajig, "I think I blinked."

Katya arrived at the bottom of the ramp and put on her shades as the wind swept by in course streams of choking dust. She stared out into the wilderness, knowing now how Lawrence of a Rabid Sonofabitch had felt leading the change of the heavy mob into the fray - 'Once more unto the bus depot, dear chums,' or something to that effect.

"What are you doing?" Konrad inquired, stopping half way down the ramp.

"Just going, uh, that-a-way. Could be a while, yeah?" She pointed away into the patient, burning desert, her face was set, her eyes betrayed a slight tint of fear, an awareness of the oblivion that waited.

"What for?"

"I'm going to snap up the rights for a famous work of literature, then you can write a film script and it'll be absolute fucking shit with smudges and inky fingerprints and stuff," she said, steeling herself, knowing that she had to do it. There could be no going back, there was only one thing now, trapped in her mind that had found its purpose and its rationality too late - only one thing: sacrifice.

"Er, why?"

"To get us out of this place! It's a long shot, but it just might work. And besides, it's the only chance we've got."

Katya walked forwards into the Hell-lands, walked forwards to certain death in a bleached, dry pit, somewhere under frowning dunes and that angry blue sky, tousled with the fleeting phantoms of reluctant angels. Konrad shielded his eyes with his hand, watching his sister move away into the scorching maw of hell, soon she had passed from sight beyond shimmering veils of whirling sand, passed on beyond that earthly plane, passed to whatever lies after.

Her last words hung in the air, before finally fading into the east on a burning wind, "It's the last chance we've got...the last chance..."

"Funny that," Konrad murmured, slipping on a black arm band, desperately trying to hang on to reason, frantically clinging to the hope that maybe his sister hadn't died for nothing, "Funny how of all the directions she could have gone off in, she picks the one where not more than two hundred yards away beyond those dunes there's a slightly run-down Ultralux fifteen screen cinema, showing all fifteen of the Fake That movies."

"Zeep-zeep," bleeped the Weirderon computer, "Funny that."

At that moment on television screens all across the solar system there was a flickering of interference. Then a landscape appeared, a desolate Martian landscape, then a guitar strummed a distorted chord, then it jangled off into a foot-tapping rhythm. Suddenly a figure appeared, floating along on a surreal wind of bubbles and butterflies. The figure was dressed in a silver cosmonaut suit, trailing an umbilical space chord. In the suit was the chick from North Dakota, this was what she sang:

Lost in space, looking for
Lost planet Atlantis.
Flowery, flowery things,
Anybody hear me?

[At which point there was
a frenzied mashing of
chords followed by:]

Beer cans are floating by
Sure could use a cold one.
Glowing, glowing man,
Anybody read me?

[Suddenly a kind of
instrumental break
lurched in from somewhere,
before:]

Talking to the plants?
Talking to myself?
Going round and round
In your head?
In a parking orbit,
Goddamn spacebucket,
Think I should've
Stayed in bed.

And off she drifted, while the uncouth flabbies welded to their settees, those beings from the Braindead Zone, kicked their sets and tried to restore death by soap.

Printed in Great Britain
by Amazon